GOOD TIMES, INC.

GOOD TIMES, INC.

A NOVEL

PHILIPPE PASCAL

authorHOUSE®

AuthorHouse™ UK Ltd.
1663 Liberty Drive
Bloomington, IN 47403 USA
www.authorhouse.co.uk
Phone: 0800.197.4150

Published by AuthorHouse 7/10/2013

ISBN: 978-1-4817-9766-5 (sc)
ISBN: 978-1-4817-9765-8 (hc)
ISBN: 978-1-4817-6845-0 (e)

I want to dedicate this to Juerg in memory of a wonderful life together
and to Rose who stood by my side during the entire process

CHAPTER 1

C hewing on a pencil, watching the hand on the clock in the front of the classroom moving slowly toward the end of the lesson, Phil asked himself once more, *Why the hell am I sitting here?*

Phil grew up the youngest member of a family of accountants in Westchester County, only a few miles north of Manhattan. It seemed, even from his first breath, that he was committed to becoming another member in the dynasty of Sherwin & Sons Accounting, Inc. His grandfather founded the business, and his father followed suit, as did the two older brothers, with no questions asked. Several years later, Phil came as a late addition to the family, but at a very early stage in life, he had already found pleasure in the diversity of life and knew that numbers were not really his thing. He loved going to museums and daydreaming on long walks while consciously planning an escape from the routine.

Phil's childhood and youth were sheltered, and although he enjoyed tremendous freedom, his parents were sure that once he reached college age, business school was his destiny. In order to avoid all discussions, he left them their hopes, but whenever the subject of his future came up, the monologues his father conducted left him rather indifferent. He could never comprehend how anyone could get so excited over somebody else's tax return or anything else involved in the daily routine at the office. The brothers never seemed to question their destiny and were funneled right into the company.

As a young man, he never really had a girlfriend, but could get excited instead just looking at a painting by Rothko or traveling into the city on his saved pocket money to visit a matinee at the

1

Metropolitan Opera. His mother always suspected he was different, but she never voiced her opinion on the subject. She was happy that everything was smooth at home, and with the exception of her three-week vacation in summer, all her time was devoted to the care of her four men.

At the age of fifteen, Phil finally found the courage to tell the parents he was gay. At first, they thought—like most parents—that this was a passing phase, and if the right girl came along, he would reconsider. He always got goose bumps when his brothers brought their boring girlfriends home, and escaped these gatherings as much as possible. He lived by the motto "better alone than in bad company."

In high school, he spent time with his very good friend Carl, with whom he ventured into the first sexual activities. They enjoyed their sleepovers with multiple orgasms every night. They experimented through the Internet and were inspired to copy all the acts they demonstrated on the gay porn sites. At school, they had to keep their private lives a secret, but when alone, they went at it like rabbits. Some of their schoolmates were anxious to find out more and teased them about their very close relationship, but Carl and Phil decided not to reveal any of the secrets until prom night, the last they would spend together with their classmates. Carl was going to UCLA to study performing arts, while Phil had his father's dream date with Columbia University's business school, where he did get permission to take a second major more to his liking: art history.

Before school started, he was permitted a summer off, so Carl and Phil packed up and traveled Europe. They had a wonderful time, spending more than three months visiting all the sights in Italy, France, and Spain. It was *magnifique!* The days were filled with culture, the nights with sexual rumpus. He took each day and night as if they would be his last, knowing that a slow death spent compiling numbers would be his fate in the years to come. Phil envied Carl very much, and in his head, he created various scenarios of how he could escape his destiny at this point.

Back home, they said good-bye, and Carl left for sunny California, as Phil settled into his dorm on Amsterdam Avenue, close to the Columbia campus. At the time, he didn't care why he was there; just the thought of having his own space and living in the Big Apple was exhilarating! He needed very little at first: a few objects to decorate the new place—a studio with a small kitchenette and an even smaller bathroom. But at least it was his. He knew this was temporary. His goal was to have a real apartment soon.

Phil loved New York. He loved the street noise, the hectic shuffle, and above all, the possibilities of the lifestyle he had been dreaming of for so long, away from all parental control! To have all of this, he even accepted the curriculum his father imposed on him. After introduction and registration, he soon started classes and tried to make the best of it. The art history courses were much more to his taste and obviously brought him great grades, whereas the business and administration part of his education were a drag. Having little experience at a big university, he just followed instructions—nothing more.

At first, he regularly commuted home to Westchester for weekends, but with more work—and especially more fun in the city—these trips were reduced to only the major holidays. He became a true city boy, with a tremendous knowledge of the numerous gay hangouts, Phil had many friends, in school and out, but most of them were meaningless one-night stands.

After two years, he still lived in the same dorm room. Things did not develop as initially planned, and the idea of a glamorous lifestyle was on the back burner for a bit. Still, Phil was okay with this arrangement and had accumulated city experience, which was more important to him than luxury. By now, Phil had actually found comfort in the shabby apartment; at least it was his own. He had a strong urge to learn all he could about the aspects of gay life, and New York certainly offered the best. On a cold Friday night, Phil decided to go bar hopping; given the unpleasant temperature, he wore both a sport jacket and a coat.

By 10:00 p.m., he was leaning against the bar at Taurus, chatting with one of the bartenders as the place started filling up with the after-dinner crowd. The music was loud, and in a little while, as the first round of drinks settled into their bloodstream, the guests began to shed the chill of the night. His eyes wandered; a few contacts reacted favorably as they flashed him an affirmative grin. The door opened again, and a group of five well-dressed businessmen made their entrance. At first, he thought they might be lost, as they didn't seem to fit the scene. They settled at a corner table and ordered drinks, Phil became curious. He was attracted to mature men, especially those who were well-dressed and in good shape. Such was the case with all five.

Phil decided to make an inconspicuous move toward their table, to find out more about them. With a nonchalant look on his face, he wandered closer and took a position, just standing there by himself, looking bored. One of the gentlemen got up and headed for the men's room; he was tall with salt-and-pepper hair, well-groomed and very sexy. When he passed Phil, he threw a shy grin in his direction and continued on his way.

Phil was trying to come up with a plan quickly to get his attention, when by chance, he was bumped, and his drink spilled all over. He looked up and met two beautiful, deep-blue eyes with an apologetic look in them. "I am so sorry. Can I order you another drink?" he asked.

He nearly automatically said no but then explored this opportunity, saying shyly, "That would be nice. Scotch on the rocks, please."

The gentleman waved the waiter over, ordered the drink, and then introduced himself as Daniel. They exchanged a few pleasantries, and then he asked if Phil would like to join his party. Now with feigned hesitance, all the while thinking, *Eureka!,* he followed Daniel to the table.

Phil was introduced by Daniel to his friends, who were extremely cordial. They crowded into the booth, making space for all to sit down. The waiter brought the drink, and they started with small talk. Chris, the youngest in the group, was very talkative; his way of expressing himself made Phil suspect that he was somehow new at this. During the next thirty minutes, he learned they were from the West Coast, visiting New York to participate in a tourism convention. Being in this bar, it was obvious they all had a secret in common, one certainly hidden from their wives back home. Daniel explained they were hotel owners who meet regularly at conventions and such. There might have been some play among them, but in principle, they were all interested in younger guys.

The evening was great fun. After many more drinks were consumed, Chris suggested, "Let's go to Stage and watch a few hot dudes take their clothes off!" They asked Phil to join them, as he had not been before, he thought it could be fun. One of the guys closed the tab, and they bundled up and left the bar. The club was not too far, and a short walk in the brisk air would do them all good.

The entrance was a small door, leading past a guy who sold admission tickets. A steep, narrow staircase led up to the second floor; the lack of ambiance suggested the place was a real dump. Phil didn't mind; he was in good, fun company—probably the only way to visit such a joint at his age. When they reached the upper floor, seductive music greeted them. A heavy curtain separated the coatroom from a large room with a round center stage. There were only a few guests in attendance, and Phil was clearly the youngest by far. The waiter greeted and led them to a table near the stage. Through an outdated sound system, a manly voice announced, "Directly from Las Vegas, gracing our stage for three nights only, this is Chuck!" Timid applause welcomed the dude on stage. He had a perfect body, hidden in a sailor's uniform, but his face was rather plain and oozed very little sex appeal.

He moved rhythmically to the loud music, hypnotizing the men with his suggestive moves, and when he ripped his white shirt off his perfect chest, big smiles blossomed all around the room. Observing the guys in the party, Phil could clearly see that Chuck would have been the dream solution for their night. The waiter took drink orders, after which all eyes again concentrated on the stage. A flicker of light, and the sailor pants flew through the air. Chuck now stood in a sequined G-string, luring all eyes toward him. Daniel took out some cash, and Chuck swiftly moved closer to their table, lowering himself enough that Daniel could stick a dollar bill into the elastic. This immediately encouraged the others to follow suit. Chuck showed more willingness to free himself from the last piece of clothing, quickly realizing their table was the most charitable.

The music got faster; he jumped up and disappeared behind a curtain, but only for a second. When he showed up again—his take now stashed—only Chuck and the G-string remained. He moved seductively, suggesting that the small garment would come off soon.

Chuck knelt before them, effortlessly slipped the latch, and showed off his full nakedness. He had a very nice piece, half-erect and more than willing to be touched by his good sponsors—if there would be a little more green coming his way, that is. The table mates caught on fast and proceeded to honor his manhood with five-dollar bills. Phil was amazed that these men would so frivolously throw money at such a performance!

This ritual continued through the performances of Jack and Simon, who showed their best moves after Chuck. In Phil's businessman's mind, he calculated that each of the guys must have spent fifty dollars or more, simply on a possible touch. They were nearly plastered, but before leaving Stage, they exchanged cards and agreed to meet the following day for brunch.

Downstairs, they wished each other a good night. Daniel proposed Phil could spend the night with him, but he was too drunk, and needed a few hours of sleep before brunch. So he took his leave in a cab, heading back uptown.

Brunch the next day was great fun. All the guys told Phil stories about their conquests of the past. It was an introduction to a new aspect of mature gay life.

CHAPTER 2

Monday was another school day, and with the holidays approaching, the published exam dates drew near. In Phil's least-enjoyable course, the professor scribbled an assignment on the blackboard as the students entered the classroom. Once they were all seated, he explained. The task was to create a business plan for a fictitious company, legal aspects as well as investments and possible profit. Phil was afraid this would come sooner than later; He remembered the same assignment from his brothers' time in college. Excitement bubbled among the other students as they finally felt ready to create something of use.

Phil couldn't think of a line of work that would give him a thrill; he just wanted to avoid the grown-up business life. The professor explained some outlines how to approach the problem, instructing the students to be as realistic as possible. This, to Phil's baroque mind, was already the first difficult hurdle to clear; the subject was dry enough. He was hoping for assistance from his family, who were familiar with this. All reports were due by January 20, and the paper would count as 50 percent of the final grade. *Oh shit, I have to do well on this; otherwise, I won't pass the course!* was all that went through his mind.

Back at his place, he dropped into the only comfortable armchair he owned and felt sorry for himself. He hated this class, but it was important to do well if he wanted to stay in the city, so he took a piece of paper and started to make notes on businesses he would enjoy heading. The first thought was either a company to represent musicians and singers or something in the art world, a gallery or auction house. While he was mulling over more possibilities, his eyes fell on the small pile of business cards from the weekend.

Like a strike of lightning, he came up with the idea of a male escort service. It would have to be very luxurious, catering to a wealthy and distinguished clientele, like the gentlemen he met at the bar. The excitement welled up; he was now sure he had found a way of making this a fun project.

The first move was to research. Phil turned on his computer and Googled "male escort." Thousands of results appeared on screen. He clicked on the more intriguing ones but soon found out that even though they offered escort services, it was mainly a nicer way to say *hustler.* He wasn't opposed to this at all, but in his imagination, he was thinking of the full package. He pictured an apartment in a great location. He needed to recruit good-looking men of all ages with above-average intelligence, cultured guys, able to move in any situation and company. He had to find a discreet way of advertising the services.

It didn't come easy, as he found no indication on the Internet of where he could find a similar business, only individuals who were marketing themselves. There were plenty of escort sites, but none came close to a real establishment of his dreams. Next he looked into other service-oriented businesses and soon found that most of them worked on a commission basis. Apparently, he had to go the same way if he wanted to succeed; and the "material" he had to offer would be of the highest quality.

For the project, there was starting capital, and with it, they had to create a compatible and realistic enterprise. Phil called a number of magazines and asked for their advertising rates—the glossier ones to sell the service and the less-expensive ones to recruit good men. He had no idea how much money men were ready to spend on such services, but he knew who to ask. After two rings, Daniel picked up in a businesslike tone, but when he heard Phil's voice, he immediately softened. He was still in New York, so they arranged to meet for dinner. He would be returning to L.A. the following day, and as the last of the group still in New York, he was happy to have company for later.

Phil inquired, "If I wanted to ask a few personal questions, would you be willing to answer them?"

He laughed and responded, "All you want and more." He proposed they meet at 7:30 at The Four Seasons on Park Avenue. Phil had heard of the place and knew it was quite formal. He dressed in a dark suit and tie, as if meeting a client of his imaginary company. He became very excited about the project, and knew he could make an impact with the idea. Dressed and ready to meet Daniel, he told himself, "This is going to be a good time." He started laughing, went back to the papers, and scribbled on top of page one: "Good Times, Inc." Now he had a name for the joint!

Daniel was already waiting at the bar when Phil walked in, with a big smile on his face as he waved him over. "So good to see you!" he beamed. "I was afraid to be all by myself tonight. This is going to be much more fun."

Phil ordered a drink and took a sip as the maître d' informed them their table was ready. They followed him to the remotest cozy corner of the restaurant. Immediately after sitting down, Phil excitedly told Daniel about the project. He smiled. "A bold move, but why not?" He agreed this would be something new, and certainly, there could be quite a demand. Phil wanted to know if he'd ever hired an escort; his slight blush gave him the answer in the affirmative. Once the initial shyness passed, he started opening up.

The waiter mentioned a few daily specials not found on the menu. They both decided on the rack of lamb, with a salad to start. Daniel picked a bottle of red wine he thought would go well with the meal. A brief questioning glance by the waiter in Phil's direction made him aware he was contemplating whether he should ask for an ID, but he turned on his heel instead and soon returned with two large wine glasses. Daniel continued where he left off and, now more at ease, he told Phil about his experiences with hired services, some good but mostly bad; he generalized it as sex for money. There was no understanding, and in most cases, he was relieved when the hotel door closed behind the escort, and he was again alone in his sanctuary.

"There was one exception, a graduate student," he said as they attacked the main course, "from Columbia University, a sweet guy, probably not the best physique, not worked out like most, even shy at times. He was in desperate need of money and tried it this way. We agreed on a price, and he came to the hotel, on time, and when I suggested having a drink first and get to know each other, he seemed pleased. He was not rushed for a later appointment. He was funny, intelligent, and the complete opposite of former experiences. We talked for over two hours, and at this point, it became rather awkward how we begin the physical part. He asked to use the bathroom; I simply got up while he was out and laid on the bed. When he returned, he sat next to me, and everything took its course as if we'd done this many times before. It felt great. His name was Alfred, and he made me believe whatever we did was genuine. Not once did I have the feeling he was watching the clock or even flexing his muscles to impress. Sex with him was great, and he had a way of making it the most natural experience one can hope for."

"Why haven't you called him again?" Phil asked.

"Well, I did, but he couldn't meet me; he was on a study trip in Canada. I was thinking of calling him tonight, if you hadn't called me before."

Daniel said Phil should try to contact Alfred, that he might have some answers and suggestions. When asked how he found or contacted the guys, he told Phil it was mainly over the Internet, but also sometimes in a bar downtown. In regard to the rates, he was very vague. "That depends on the evening and the person. Alfred, for instance, asked 150 dollars, even if he stayed the entire night. When I gave him five hundred the next morning, he seemed more than overwhelmed by the gesture. Others might ask two fifty and are out after forty-five minutes. You see, it's very different, but I personally discovered that expensive does not always equal great."

Phil took in very carefully all that Daniel shared and made mental notes. He brought out his address book, wrote Alfred's phone number on the back of one of his business cards, and handed it to Phil. The waiter came and relieved them of the empty plates. They finished the wine and Daniel said, "It's too bad you didn't ask Hank these questions." Hank was one of the group from the other night, probably the least attractive. According to Daniel, he's keeping a guy in San Diego, apartment and all. Hank is paying this guy a monthly wage and letting him live in one of his places, and they see each other once or twice a week. He's somewhat unhappy with the situation but doesn't know how to terminate it without creating too much of an uproar.

They ordered coffee and spoke about this and that, and Daniel suggested having a drink at his hotel. Phil was good with this and even hoped he would make a pass at him. After he paid the bill, they left the restaurant and went to the Waldorf close by, his home away from home, a beautiful tower suite. Phil sat down on the sofa, and Daniel poured two scotches on the rocks and joined him. They each took a sip, and it wasn't long before Daniel started to caress Phil's thighs. He got excited and leaned over for a deep kiss, still holding his glass, trying not to spill its contents. When they came up for air, Phil took another quick sip, put the drink on the table, and was ready for the next go. Daniel ran his fingers through Phil's hair, and soon their lips met again.

Both aware that this was going further, they clumsily started to loosen each other's ties and unbutton each other's shirts. It was fun, and Phil loved the hairy chest he discovered. They undid their pants and let them drop to the floor; soon they were both naked and lip-locked, moving toward the king-size bed. Daniel was a passionate lover, and his maturity showed vast experience. He knew how to please, but at the same time welcomed whatever Phil brought.

After lubing him thoroughly with his tongue and mouth, he swiftly covered himself with a condom and slowly started to poke into him. It was wonderful as he moved in and out; Phil just gave himself to him. It all felt so natural, and when his muscles began to quiver, his breathing heavy, the young lover knew this wonderful act was rapidly coming to a climax. Phil started to work on himself, as he wanted this to have the full effect with simultaneous orgasms. When he saw Daniel's tortured expression and heard his pleasure cries, he started squirting juice all over his chest. Daniel fell on Phil in exhaustion, covering him with his body until their breathing normalized a little. Then he raised his head, looked him in the eyes, and with a wide smile, kissed him again.

Both a mess, they were in dire need of a shower. Phil decided to go first, and while he was washing his belly, Daniel joined him in the oversized stall. He lathered his back, and with his finger probing deeply, gave him a good internal cleaning as well. Phil searched for his lips, which were more than ready to respond. He turned around, and under the pouring water, they continued kissing for a long time. When they left the shower, Daniel handed Phil a towel and a thick, fluffy robe. All dry and snuggled into the soft robe, Phil returned to the sofa and to his drink.

Daniel came and joined him, topped off their glasses, and remarked, "If you can find guys like you, Good Times, Inc. is certainly geared for success."

When Phil went home to Westchester over the weekend, his father, anxious to know how he was doing, asked if he needed some assistance with the project. Phil told him he was establishing a service-oriented business and would do some preliminary research before putting things in writing. He seemed impressed with the enthusiasm and happy his son had finally come around.

Phil tried several times to call Alfred. When he finally got him on the phone, he told him briefly about the assignment, and they agreed to meet for lunch on Monday.

In a coffee shop on Broadway, Phil waited. Alfred told him only that he was over six feet tall, with rather long, straight hair. He kept the entrance under surveillance, and finally he walked through the door. Phil waved him over, and with a bright smile, he sat across from him in the booth. Phil thought he was cute in an intellectual way, but he agreed with Daniel: he was not the standard escort.

Phil told him briefly about the plan. He thought this was hilarious and said, "If you want to have my insight, I want a copy of the report in return." Phil agreed, and Alfred started his story. He told he was doing escort work only when he was in need of money, but so far, he'd had quite a lot of good experiences too. There were some jerks, but in principle, he had been lucky. He fondly remembered Daniel, said he was probably one of his favorites, but unfortunately, they met only once. Alfred presumed that his looks attracted a different kind of client than the average hustler.

He went on to explain, "There is a client for everybody out there. Some like it fat, some small, some smelly, and some like the intellectual type." He said Phil's concept sounded very appealing to him, and if he ever makes this a reality, he should really look him up. They had a good time and agreed to meet on Friday at a bar in Chelsea where many guys work, just to have a beer and a few laughs. He gave Phil a lot of information: how to find the guys, what to look for, and what not to overvalue. He made some notes, not really knowing how to include them into the report yet, but he was convinced they would come in handy later.

CHAPTER 3

Phil went back to the dorm and started searching for a good location in an affluent and secure section of town. He found many apartments listed, but most of the rents exceeded the budget. He needed to be in a residential area, a place where he could live and host possible clients, with an office and a lounge where customers could relax. A three—to four-bedroom apartment was what he imagined. The *New York Times* offered little to his needs, but he continued searching, hoping to find something suitable before the weekend.

The young entrepreneur browsed through the *Observer,* where his eye caught a small ad for a sublet. *Large pre-war apartment with spacious rooms, wood-burning fireplace for sublet in prime location.* He called immediately, and a very talkative, elderly man answered the phone. Phil asked only a few questions, and what he heard sounded absolutely perfect. The gentleman gave him the address, and they agreed to meet in a couple of hours.

With the M4 bus down Fifth Avenue and a short walk over to the given address. The majestic lobby included a very friendly doorman, who rang Phil up. There were only two apartments per floor. He pushed the bell, and the older gentleman, Jeremy, opened the door. He was smartly dressed, and when he saw Phil, the young man thought he detected a lustful smirk on his face. He motioned him inside his place, which was rather somber but very cozy. The furniture was tasteful, and the overall décor very smart. Phil was ready to move in, the rest sight unseen. Jeremy asked if he would first like to see the apartment. Phil nodded in excitement, and received the grand tour. There were two large bedrooms, both with comfortable bath en suite; a den, which was used as an office; a large living room, perfect for the lounge; a smaller maid's room with a shower bath; and a dining room next to a butler's pantry off the kitchen. It was perfect, but most likely out of reach financially.

After the tour, he asked if Phil would like something to drink. He sensed that Jeremy was lonely, and some company would do him good, so he accepted, the host poured two glasses of sickly-sweet sherry. Phil sipped politely on the glass, nearly choked, but managed to keep a straight face. Jeremy seemed to enjoy it very much. Phil sat on the large sofa, and the older man placed himself close by in the armchair, staying in reach of Phil's knees, which he "accidentally" touched several times. A vibe was felt, but Phil thought by letting him enjoy the company this might be favorable to the outcome of the plan.

Jeremy told he had a niece in Florida who wanted him to move down, and he was planning to sublet the apartment. The place was rent-controlled, and therefore he would not ask too much. Phil told him he planned to run his business from here, but it would be quiet. He also mentioned that it was service-oriented and catered to a high-class clientele. Jeremy was intrigued and discreetly continued questioning further. The young businessman was still not sure how far he could spill the beans, but thought Jeremy would probably understand. This place would be perfect for the project, and in Phil's mind, he was already becoming the entrepreneur; the assignment became reality.

Jeremy refilled his glass, and with each sip, he opened up and shared more about his colorful past. He said he was living with his partner for many years, but when he passed a few months ago, life was just not the same anymore. They had a successful decorating business, catering to many society people in New York, and had lived in this apartment for more than forty years, with an actual monthly rent of 450 dollars. Phil nearly choked; he was paying the same amount for the shabby dorm studio! Jeremy planned to ask eight hundred but would really just like to have a trustful and kind person to live here. Phil thought about Albert, who could move in with him and share the rent, and they could start the business. He would bring the field experience and Phil the administrative brainwork.

When Jeremy detected the excitement, he leaned over and held both his knees tenderly; Phil felt his fingers moving in a gently caressing manner. He looked into the young man's eyes and said, "There is more. I don't know how you would feel, but I cannot take much with me, and since I want to sublet, I would like to leave most of the furnishings here."

This was getting better by the minute. Looking around at his things, Phil could already envision living here. His slow sipping of the sherry inspired the host to top off the glass, which Phil didn't care for, but at this stage, he wanted to please him. This was the perfect place! Phil asked if he could have his friend Alfred come right over, as he would probably be his roomy. Jeremy nodded enthusiastically.

Alfred picked up immediately, a little surprised to say the least, but he agreed and said he would be there in thirty minutes. Phil told Jeremy he was sorry, but they had to kill another thirty minutes until Alfred arrived. The older man didn't mind at all; on the contrary, he seemed very happy. They talked a bit more, and then he brought out a photo book and seated himself next to Phil on the sofa. The book featured many black-and-white pictures of him and his partner, taken all over the world; he was excited to share the many anecdotes that accompanied them. Phil could feel him moving closer and closer but didn't mind; he was quite charming, and Phil felt for this venue he did not mind pleasing him a little.

Time passed quickly, and before they knew it, the intercom announced Alfred was in the lobby. He entered the apartment with his mouth agape as he introduced himself to Jeremy, who beamed even brighter at this point. Alfred immediately received the grand tour of the place, and Phil could see in his eyes, with every new room he entered, his growing excitement. Phil whispered in his ear that the rent was very reasonable, even cheap. He couldn't understand why, and when Phil mentioned that Jeremy would like to leave most of the furnishings, he was sold. "You mean we could move in like this?" he said excitedly.

"I guess so, if Jeremy would take us."

Jeremy asked them to sit down and talk it over. He forced another glass of sherry on Phil and Alfred, but by now, they would probably have done anything to get his approval, even gulp down the sweet poison called Bristol Cream. Jeremy said he was planning to spend the upcoming holidays in Florida. He would pack up all the personal things and empty all the closets of clothing, but he wanted them to agree on a longer term, to which they happily agreed. As they raised their glasses, the toast was "Done!"

The two young men couldn't believe their good fortune, but here they were, thrilled to be moving out of the dorm into a super-classy Upper East Side apartment. The next step was to explain this to the folks, but not today; all in good time. They wanted to take Jeremy out for dinner to thank him, so they made plans for Friday evening. "I will be on my best behavior," he said, "even if this will be difficult in such charming company."

At the door, they held hands while saying good-bye, and Phil kissed him on both cheeks. He blushed, and when Alfred did the same, Jeremy beamed as if he were in heaven. Once they were out of the building, Alfred fell around Phil's neck, and the two jumped for joy on the sidewalk like stupid teenagers.

They stopped for coffee to talk things over. So much going through their heads. Phil was already planning to start the real business before he even turned in the business plan. Having achieved this first goal of securing a space, the work seemed more realistic. They had to start recruiting guys and find real capital to advertise. The enthusiasm was limitless.

Alfred asked, "Can I receive clients in the apartment?"

"Of course!"

Then he asked if Phil would consider having clients too. Until that moment, it had not crossed his mind, as he wanted to be the organizer, but if it helped the business, he would certainly consider it. They decided who would get which bedroom; since Alfred would probably entertain more, Phil offered him the master bedroom and settled for the smaller one. "All for the business" was their motto.

Suddenly Alfred looked up. "Any plans tonight?"

"No, why?"

"Well, I guess you should meet Jack. I think you would like him," he responded.

"Okay, now who is Jack?" Phil asked.

Alfred gave him a short description. They met in school; Jack was very good looking, intelligent, and always in need of money.

Phil soon discovered that Jack was, in fact, absolutely stunning—tall, well-built, with charm oozing out of every single pore. He was twenty-eight, seemed an eternal grad student, and had a great sense of humor. Jack spoke English, fluent French, and Spanish, another fantastic attribute for international clients. He was a perfect candidate for the business. Jack was also into computers and offered to make a web page as his initiation offering to the company. It had to be sexy but tasteful and should intrigue men of distinction, more than just advertise sex. They would take some pictures over the weekend, which he could include into the web page.

The evening was a great success. When Phil got back to the dorm, his head was spinning, so any attempt to sleep would be a lost cause. He sat down at the computer and composed an e-mail to Daniel.

Dear Daniel,

Well, I think things are progressing faster than I thought. I guess Good Times, Inc. will be up and running before I have to turn in my business plan. Thank you for introducing me to Alfred. He will be a partner in the enterprise and my roommate. We have a spectacular venue, perfect for in-calls too. I hope we will be able to welcome you and your friends soon at our new place. Operation in full starts with the new year.

Hope you had a good trip back to the West Coast.

All the best,
Phil

He pushed *send,* and the first promotional e-mail was on its way. *Wow, there is no way back now,* he thought leaning back in his armchair. While it was all still fresh in his mind, he began to list the expenses they would encounter; thanks to the very reasonable rent, they were below budget. He did, however, include a nice sum for advertising. Though in reality, the web page was free, there would be other things he would have to keep in mind. One expense was a gracious tip to the doormen, as he was hoping to host quite frequently. While Phil wrote the list, he heard, "You've got mail." Daniel had already responded.

Hey Phil:

> Now that is a surprise. I will certainly soon check out the place, and I will inform my buddies of it. Great that you can host! Many of my friends in New York cannot, and would certainly be happy to know of a decent place where they could spend some time in nice company and relax. Send me all the info once you have it, and I would love to do some introductory work. May be there could be a freebee with you for me. Hope to hear soon, and give my regards to Alfred.

> Love,
> Daniel

He could not wait! First they had to get their name out there, but discreetly. He wanted their place to be the best-known secret in New York.

Sunday, they met in the park; it was a cold but beautiful day. They needed some pictures for the web page. They joked around, and when Phil said, "We have to get some sex appeal into it," Jack offered to pose—but the shots should be from such an angle that he would not be recognized. He took off his jacket; underneath was a tight shirt that showed off his perfect physique.

"It's cold. Hurry up, I don't want to get pneumonia out here," he said.

They got several good photos, and then went back to the dorm to see them on the larger screen. Some were great, especially the ones of Jack; fabulous. Phil thought a little more skin was a necessity. They both looked at him questioningly, so he elaborated. "Guys, we are in a business where modesty is not an option."

They both started laughing, and Phil suggested we get some chest pictures, but he wanted to make it artsy. They agreed and started to take off their shirts. Both looked good. Phil suggested they embrace each other, but instead, he took pictures of them individually. When he said, "A nice butt shot would do the trick," he received another questioning look from them. Remembering the modesty lecture, they agreed and got naked. Phil was in voyeur heaven.

While taking pictures, he got a little excited. "I'm really starting to like my job!"

When there was sufficient material, Jack came over and started rubbing up against his future employer. "Now that we showed it all, what about you, boss? Don't you want to join the party?" he asked seductively. Heat rose in Phil, and when Albert started to unbutton the shirt, it was pure bliss. Soon Phil's pants dropped to the floor, and Jack licked him from his chest down to the erect penis, which he continued caressing with his tongue and lips. Albert moved in behind him, and caressed the nipples with his hands while his rock-hard penis was poking at Phil's rear.

He was floating on air as they moved to the bed, engulfed in a threesome of great ecstasy. They really knew how to please, and with offerings such as this, Good Times, Inc. was going to be a great success. After three incredible orgasms, they stretched out across the bed, exhausted. Jack laughingly confirmed Phil's former thought: "We are going to make this a success story with no comparison."

CHAPTER 4

T he following days were consumed with preparations for midterm exams, and whenever possible, Phil worked on the project. It was coming along well, and he was pleased to use real data. The only thing that worried him was how to find more high-class escorts. Considering his luck with Alfred and Jack, he hoped he would run into others in time.

The holidays were fast approaching, and Phil planned to spend most of the time in Westchester with family. Jack stayed in the city, while Alfred visited his folks in the Midwest. Jack promised he would work diligently on the web page and send his progress daily, and if need be, Phil could come down for the day.

Back home, the family gathered for Christmas Eve. The brothers brought their girlfriends, and it appeared their relationships were getting quite serious. Mother was thrilled to have everyone at home; Phil suspected she had a Christmas wish of becoming a grandmother one day soon. Then the questions began. They all wanted to know about the project, and the attempts at being vague made them even more inquisitive. They offered to assist their brother, but Phil rejected, explaining that they just didn't have sufficient knowledge about this particular line of business. This raised their curiosity level even higher, but Phil firmly requested the subject closed. He reminded them that it was not his choice to attend Business School in the first place, but since he had complied, they should as well.

Mother, in her diplomatic way, took her youngest son's side, as she tried to avoid unpleasantness in the house; she simply ordered them to let it go and trust his decisions. Phil's father and brothers accepted her verdict but were certainly not very happy about it. As they were on the subject, Phil told them he was moving out of the dorm. They were not thrilled, but they softened a bit knowing he would be in a safer neighborhood at the same cost. Since studio dorm rooms were always in demand, it was easy to vacate on short notice.

Jeremy sent a letter with the sublet contract, which Phil signed swiftly, afraid he might change his mind. He had packed up all his photographs and memorabilia and was already with his niece in Florida. The keys were with the doorman, who had instructions to distribute them upon arrival. Phil called Jack to say he was coming down to the city for the day and would like to show him the new place. Jack was excited and in return he had something to show: the nearly completed web-page.

Phil took the early train, dressed in a suit, as if he would to attend an important meeting. Jack was waiting at Grand Central Station; they took the number 6 train uptown to the apartment. When they entered the building, the older doorman approached them with an inviting smile and handed them the keys, introducing himself as David as he welcomed the two to their new home. Jack was impressed by the smart lobby.

"Wait until you see the rest," Phil replied. They took the elevator up, and as the new tenant turned the key, he said, "Welcome to Good Times, Inc."

Jack could not believe his eyes. He said he wanted to move in immediately, which posed a little problem, as the extra room was needed for possible clients. Phil gave him the tour, and in the process, checked the closets. Most of the personal belongings were gone, but Jeremy had left them a cupboard full of groceries. There was a letter on the dining room table, wishing all the best, explaining that he had canceled the phone and would cover the utilities until the end of the month. He would send them the bills in future by e-mail, and they should pay him. They were welcome to use whatever they found, but were asked to please be careful with the furnishings. Jack inquired about the Internet connection, which Phil had already arranged and would be up and running in a few days.

They wandered to the living room. The host, Phil offered Jack a drink, and they sat, looking around in awe of what they had, like kids in FAO Schwarz, laughing and joking around. Jack was thrilled and couldn't wait to start working. He opened his laptop and showed the progress on the web page. It was impressive, exactly what Phil had envisioned—stylish, informative, and sexy enough to appeal to a discriminating clientele. There was some skin, but very discreet. They registered the e-mail address and agreed the main number should go to a new cell phone.

"Okay, so what's next?" Jack asked as they leisurely sipped their drinks.

"Well, I guess I'll move in soon, get settled, and then try to become an entrepreneur/student."

They discussed the price structure for their services, the escorts' pay, and what would be a fair percentage for the company. For overnights, Jack had been paid as much as $1,500; however, most guys are only interested in fast and easy sex. They built a menu and agreed that Alfred and Jack, as partners, would be paid differently from future employees.

The cell phone buzzed, receiving a call from Daniel. "How is it going there?" he inquired. Phil told him they were at the place and talking things over, and asked if he could put him on speaker so Jack could listen in. "Sure, no problem!" Then he asked, "Are you operational?" He'd just had a call from a frustrated friend in New York who was there for the holidays and needed an escape. He had no place and didn't want to get a hotel room for a lousy trick.

Phil looked at Jack, who nodded silently. "Would you be able to have a guest over today?"

Jack nodded again. "Yes, I guess so. I have Jack here; he's very good looking and would love to accommodate."

"Can I give James your number so he can call you directly?" Daniel asked.

"Sure, no problem."

They exchanged some more trivialities, wished each other a happy holiday, and hung up. Phil went into the bedroom to see if the linens were clean and the bathroom in good order, when his phone buzzed again. The caller said, "Hello, this is James. I'm a friend of Daniel. He told me you could see me."

"Hello, James, I'm Phil. Yes, we would be able to host. Jack is here today. What are you looking for?"

Phil sensed James was brainstorming; he answered, "I just need a good time, to relax from the holiday craze here. I have to get out for a few hours."

"Well, you've called the right place. When would you like to come?"

Again, a small pause, and then a quiet voice said, "Very soon, if that's okay?"

It was, so Phil gave him the address and told him to ask for apartment 8A. He said he would be over in forty-five minutes.

Jack gave Phil a high-five and asked where he could shower and get ready. He showed him the maid's bathroom, because he wanted to keep the other one clean for the client. Phil went to the master bedroom and made all the preparations. Then he checked in the kitchen, what the fridge had to offer, and inspected the house bar.

Jack came out of the bathroom with a towel wrapped around his waist. "Get dressed. James will be here soon." They agreed on the rate and the scenario.

Phil was just sitting down when the intercom buzzed. "James is here to see you," David announced.

"Thank you, David. Please send him up." Jack went into the maid's room.

The bell rang, and Phil went to open the door. A very nice man in his mid forties was standing there; the host could sense he wasn't very comfortable and asked him in and motioned for him to sit down and relax. "Can I offer you a drink?" He gladly accepted.

He explained that he did not have too much time and just needed an escape. They agreed on the price, and Phil assured him that Jack would provide a memorable escape. He went to get Jack, and when the stud entered the room, Phil could see by James's face that he was pleasantly surprised. After a short introduction, the host excused myself and left the two alone. He could hear from the next room that they got along brilliantly, and after fifteen minutes, they had gone to the bedroom.

Phil quietly moved around the place, familiarizing himself with his new surroundings. It was wonderful, and he was tempted to light a fire but thought better of it, especially because he didn't know when the fireplace was last serviced. Then he called home and told them he ran into a friend and would stay in the city overnight and be possibly back the following day. Then he called Alfred and told him they were operational; Jack was with his first client, and so far, all was well. They chatted a little more when he heard the door to the bedroom open. Jack came out in a floor-length robe, with a huge smile on his face. He sat down and picked up his drink. "James is taking a shower," he said.

Ten minutes later, James appeared, fully dressed and much more relaxed. "Would you like another drink?" He readily accepted.

We all sat down, and James said, "This place is fantastic. How long have you been here?"

Phil told him they were fairly new and had no advertising as of yet, but they were thinking about it. James suggested they to keep it as low key as possible; he believed the best advertising would be by word of mouth from satisfied clients. They agreed and told him they would go on the Internet soon. Jack excused himself and went back to get dressed, and James told me what an excellent time he had. Jack was accommodating and wonderful, exactly what he needed. He asked if he could come back again,

"By all means, please do!"

"Might be sooner than you think," he added and asked how many rooms we had.

Phil told him two, but they also make house calls. He said for him, this setup was perfect; whenever he visits New York, he has to stay with family and could not have company there. This place is very sophisticated, not the usual dump, and therefore he was sure this venture was bound for success.

Jack came back, and Phil saw how James still lusted for him. He started feeling like a real "madam." This experience proved the school project would be great, and now he could defend all of the professor's possible doubts. He was aware that for school he had to keep this as an escort service only, and sex had to be kept out, but in essence did not think it would make too much of a difference.

James looked at his watch and jumped up. "Oh, shit! I have to go, but I'll be back soon," he promised, "and if I may, I'm telling a few friends with similar needs about you." As they moved toward the door, he handed Phil some bills, which he tucked into his pocket and wished him a happy holiday. He saw him to the elevator and returned to the apartment, where Jack was stretched out on the sofa with a huge smile on his face. Phil grabbed the bills and counted; he gave a tip of fifty bucks. He handed Jack his share and then stashed the rest in a drawer in the den.

"That was unexpected," Jack said, "but keep them coming."

While they were talking, the phone rang again, and Jack just glanced over and said, "I need some time to reload; not before later tonight."

They both laughed. It was Daniel, who greeted Phil with, "Congrats, I guess you have your first returning client." He told James called, very excited; said he had the best of times, that it was all so sophisticated, with no pressure, and before leaving New York, he would definitely come and see them again.

This was good news, and Daniel promised he would really help them in establishing a clientele. Phil thanked him and told him he hoped to see him soon.

Phil cleaned the apartment while Jack straightened the bedroom and cleaned the bathroom. They left, and on their way downstairs, Jack admitted that he thought Phil was crazy when he first told him about this, but now he saw that this could really be a great thing. Phil asked if he had an orgasm with James, and he promptly responded, "Sure, they love this! I feel if they pay, they deserve full attention, and with James, no problem. He was charming, very kind and very clean. What more can you ask for?"

Phil told Jack they had to get some business cards with no address, just a name and phone number; it had to appear plain and neutral. He would get the second cell phone, for business purposes only the next day. The phones needed to be answered correctly; what would happen when his mother calls and he answered, "Good Times, Inc., can I help you?" They both started laughing and pictured her face.

He began the moving process the next day, packing the books and all the personal stuff, and with one cab ride, he was out of the old and into the new. Phil decided to call home again and postpone his return for another day. It was the first night here, and it was a thrill. Getting all things arranged was easy: the books in the den, the personal stuff in the closet in his bedroom. He knew he might have to move out temporarily when they had clients, but was okay with this; business first.

Once everything was settled in its place, Jack said he was hungry and they should grab a bite to eat. Phil suggested that calling for pizza delivery to our new place would be much more fun. On his way in, he asked David if the fireplaces were functional, and was assured the building management kept everything in perfect order and that Mr. Jeremy had often enjoyed a fire in winter. Phil was inspired and ran out to the market for two bundles of firewood. They settled down and enjoyed a wonderful evening with pizza, red wine, and a cozy fire.

"What a life!" Jack exclaimed.

The phone rang, "hello, my name is Frederic. I am a good friend of James. We just spoke, and he told me about your place."

"Hi, Frederic. Thank you for calling. What can I do for you?"

After a brief silence, he said, "Would Jack be available this evening?"

Phil gestured to Jack, who swallowed a large piece of pizza. "One moment, Frederic, I will go and look; give me a second." He covered the phone and asked Jack if he wanted another client this evening.

"Sure," he said.

"What time were you thinking, and would you like to come here or have Jack at your place?" They agreed that he would come to their place at nine for some relaxation.

Phil closed the phone, and Jack just shook his head, saying, "We need more staff, with all these frustrated, horny men out there!"

At nine o'clock sharp, the intercom buzzed, and the night doorman announced that a Mr. Frederic was in the lobby. "Send him up, please," Phil said, and the routine of Jack's disappearance began again.

The doorbell rang, Phil went to open, there was Frederic, shorter than James, balding, carrying a few pounds too many. *Well,* he thought, *they don't all come out of magazines!*

He appeared shy and was very happy when Phil asked him in. The offered him to sit down, with the welcome drink they made the arrangements. He asked what an overnight would cost, but Phil could see he was uncomfortable with the price, so he settled for a regular visit. After everything was agreed, Phil went back to get Jack. "Wow, James was right!" was all he could say when he spotted Jack. Phil saw that Jack was not as enthusiastic as he had been earlier, but with a professional demeanor, he schmoozed himself into Frederic's heart.

After they warmed up to each other, the host excused himself and left the two alone. He noticed they stayed another few minutes on the sofa in front of the fire, and the silence in the room suggested they were already active. Phil heard Jack say, "You want to go next door where it's more private?" The pair then left the living room and disappeared into the bedroom. Phil opened the door to the living room to keep track of the comings and goings, and he saw Jack run in naked to pick up the two glasses they had left behind. He just threw me a big smile and was gone again. He thought to himself, *what a sport!* He cleaned up after them and went to work on his paper. Good progress was made; things seemed to come easier since the real experience gave him more confidence that a service like this could really become a prosperous enterprise.

Phil was deep into calculating a possible gain when Jack appeared at the door in his long robe. He had a huge smile on his face. "Wow!" he said. "This guy could blow a corpse back to life. Those lips and his mouth make him the Leonardo da Vinci of blowjobs. He's a genius!" Phil was very happy for him; he'd been concerned that Jack would be turned off by Frederic's appearance, but this proofed Jack was a real pro with a great sense of humor.

When Frederic emerged from the bedroom, he was very happy and gave Jack a kiss on the cheek. Phil asked if they wanted another drink; they both accepted and sat on the sofa, giggling. The man of the house was thrilled—another client who might recommend them! Phil kept the fire going; there was not much wood left, but for now, they were okay. Frederic told them he was friends with James from high school, and they had always kept in touch. He worked in Germany for an American pharmaceutical company and was responsible for acquisitions.

He usually visited his family for the holidays, but sometimes, he just felt like he had to escape. He said there were similar places in Germany but nowhere near this classy; usually the rooms were small, and one never knew if the sheets were ever changed.

"I wish you guys would open a place in Frankfurt!" he added.

Phil thought, *Let us first open this place, and then we'll see.*

He stayed another hour, and the two started to wonder if he would ever leave. Phil got up and walked into the office. Frederic followed, put the money on the desk, and gave him a seductive smile. Phil thanked him, and Jack, still in his robe, accompanied him to the door. Frederic put another bill in Jack's pocket and whispered in his ear that he would be back before heading back to Germany.

Jack closed the door and dropped himself into the sofa. "Wow!"

"This guy is an Olympian with his mouth. He's a born pleaser! Even if you don't want to see him naked, when you close your eyes, it all disappears."

After such a busy day, Phil was tired and told Jack he was going to bed. Jack asked if he could stay the night. "Sure, of course." Phil got undressed and stepped into the shower. While the hot water was running over his body, the curtain opened, and Jack stepped in. "Haven't you had enough?" he asked with a smile, but before he received an answer, Jack's lips pressed against Phil's, and they started kissing each other deeply. Phil didn't argue; just enjoyed the moment. He held tightly to Jack's beautiful body and felt a reaction between them. He couldn't believe Jack was still capable of an erection after this evening's activity. He looked into his eyes and saw a bright smile.

In a very soft voice, Jack said, "I am a sex machine!"

"That's good. At least I know I can book you several times a day!" They both laughed, and Phil turned off the water.

They toweled each other dry and got into bed, where Jack immediately covered Phil in kisses. He was very passionate, and it was now clear to him why James and Frederic were so pleased. His hands roamed everywhere, and his penis was hard and grinding at Phil's stomach. He could only surrender; Jack was orchestrating the entire scene. As their bodies rubbed against each other, he engulfed Phil with his extremities like a four-armed octopus. He was a master of pleasure, but the most amazing part was, Phil truly felt he enjoyed it as much as he did. The excitement grew steadily, and with every new touch, a spectacular orgasm was building inside him. Jack was also moving faster, and with an ecstatic outcry, Phil felt the warm shot of a large stream of semen between them, which brought him to an instant orgasm too. They held each other tightly and fell into a calm sleep.

CHAPTER 5

Phil awoke early the next morning, with Jack motionless, sleeping soundly next to him. Putting on the robe, he went to the kitchen for morning coffee and then sat in the living room, sipping his first cup, retracing the previous day. He was still in a kind of trance when Jack appeared in the doorway completely naked. His was one of the most beautiful bodies Phil has ever seen.

"Is there more coffee?" he asked with a charming smile. The host got up robotically, went to the kitchen, and poured him a cup. Jack took a large blanket and wrapped himself up, joining his boss on the sofa. "So, what's on the agenda today?" he asked.

"I don't know. I have to go back to Westchester later."

They discussed the many possibilities regarding the future of this company and thought about where they might recruit more escorts. Jack told Phil he would look into it and present candidates. Phil made a note to test the washing machine and dryer, realizing that they should do their first load and purchase a few more sheets and towels. It was very important that each client had the comfort of a fresh bed. What a luxury, to have your own washing machine installed in the kitchen and not have to run to the basement and comply with a schedule!

Phil returned to his parents later that day and spent New Year's Eve content in the company of the family. He knew that the following day, he would return to Manhattan and get ready for school and work. He had a call from James, who wished to see Jack on the third before he left town. Phil made a note in his date book and called Jack to confirm.

When he got back to the apartment on the first, David greeted him at the door, wishing a happy new year. He was still in the elevator when the phone rang. Jack asked if he could come over; he had some things to show him.

All seemed well in the apartment. Phil was working on installing his office and workspace when Jack entered. "Hey, guapo, happy New Year!" He greeted him.

"Same to you. May it be really a good year," Jack answered. Phil reminded him of James's appointment on the third and detected a bright smile on his face. "Okay with me," he said casually. Then he sat down, opened his computer, and started it up.

"I was just setting up a calendar to mark the appointments," Phil told Jack. He had made space for five escorts, but so far, only two with names, Alfred and Jack. Still, he was sure they would fill in the blank spaces soon.

Jack told him that Alfred called. He would be back on the fourth and move in, if that was okay.

"I guess so; that's what we had planned anyway. I think we should keep the master bedroom available for clients at all times. Alfred can move into the smaller one, and I'll take the maid's room. Alfred would have to entertain in his room, while the other would be free for outsiders."

"That's generous of you," Jack said.

For Phil, business came first, and for the little time he would spend in the bedroom, it would be sufficient.

Jack was ready, his computer up and running. He first showed the boss the finished web page. It was fabulous, and Phil suggested that once Alfred gave his approval, they should go online. Then he showed him designs of business cards, one with his name on, others with an empty line where the individuals could write their name in, but all went to my new cell number. Phil liked that; at least he could keep some control. He knew there would always be some private work, but he had to keep a firm hand on it. Phil thought Jack did a great job.

Then Jack put a handful of money on the table, which puzzled Phil. "I got another *wow* blowjob last night. I ran into Frederic in the afternoon, and he asked if he could come over. I hope I acted correctly. I believe, with him, we have more than a regular."

Phil thanked him. He liked his honesty and was sure Jack was as eager as he to see this succeed. He stashed the money in the box, enough to make their first month's rent. Very promising.

Jack said, "Well, I have this friend, and we fooled around a few times. He's from New York, and his parents are quite well known, so he can't visit the obvious places. He needs discretion, doesn't need the money, but is very intrigued by the concept."

Phil was skeptical. "Do you trust him?"

He immediately answered, "Yes, completely!"

Jack had him on the phone in a moment, and he soon asked Phil if the friend could come over in an hour. "You won't be disappointed. He is classy, speaks several languages, and is well traveled."

Phil was very curious how his first real interview would go, but they needed more "material," as they liked to call it. Jack, the computer genius of the group, helped create the database, which immediately transferred the data to the individual escort. They discussed provisional healthcare, if things really took off, and registering with Social Security. At first, they thought it was crazy, but in the end, it would make this all the more legitimate. Phil liked the idea, because he wanted to take this out of sleaze and into a real company. He had visions of going far beyond being an organizer of fun.

The intercom buzzed, and David announced Mr. Jeffrey. Moments later Jack walked in with a good-looking guy. He had sandy-colored, longish hair, and he was tall and well built. He walked up to the desk, stretched his hand out, and introduced himself with a firm handshake. *Good sign,* Phil thought, and asked him to take a seat. They started a casual conversation, which revealed that he was intelligent and well versed.

When the boss asked him why he would want to work here, he said it was kind of a fantasy for him, and he always wanted to do it but couldn't under normal circumstances. "When Jack told me about this place, I thought, *perfect.*"

Phil still wasn't sure he would work out; he was intrigued, but with high-profile parents, he might be a risk. He was charming and had a captivating aura, but would he stand the test? Phil was contemplating this when his cell phone buzzed. The caller ID simply said "Unknown."

He answered, "Hello?"

The caller asked, "Is this Phil?"

"Yes, who is this?"

"I'm Chris. Do you remember me? We were out the other night with Daniel and partied."

"Oh, sure I do. How are you?" He looked at Jack and Jeffrey, who smiled.

Chris told Daniel had called him, praising the establishment, and he wanted to see if Jack was available this evening, as he was looking to have some fun. Phil was surprised, not expecting a call tonight. He took his number and said he would call him back within five minutes; Phil had to see if Jack was around. Already, the wheels were turning.

"Well, guys," he said, looking to the two across the desk, "I have a client, good-looking and horny. He would like to meet Jack tonight; however, I've just decided Jack is not available. I would like to call him back in five minutes and tell him that Jeffrey, another very nice guy, would love to show him a wonderful time."

They were both speechless, but Jack agreed with the plan. Phil looked at Jeffrey and simply asked, "Are you ready?"

He was more than surprised. His response: "Is this part of the interview?"

Phil assured him this was a serious business! He needed a yes or no, and if yes, he needed to assess rather quickly what he was offering to the client. To his surprise, Jeffrey stood up and unbuttoned his shirt; then his pants and socks came off, and only his underwear remained.

He looked great. Phil could have left it at that, but he needed accuracy in his description, so he encouraged him to drop that last piece of clothing. Jeffrey did, standing in front of them completely naked. It was a very impressive sight, and Phil was proud to have such good-looking guys here. Phil could see Jack getting excited as he looked Jeffrey over. "No, Jack, we have a business to run here." Phil turned back to Jeffrey and tried to ask very professionally, "How much does it measure erect?"

He said it was seven and a half inches; that was good news.

"So, are you ready to start work, if Chris agrees?" He nodded in confirmation. "Okay, here we go then," he said.

Chris picked up the phone immediately. Phil told him Jack was not available, but Jeffrey would be very happy to see him. At first, Chris seemed disappointed, but he agreed to come over at eight.

The boss asked Jack to show Jeffrey around and get the room ready while he went downstairs to the market. Chris preferred Black Label, and he also got a couple of bundles of firewood. When he got back, David greeted him, and when Phil told him they were expecting a guest around eight, he gave him a knowing grin. He commented that they were quite a lively crowd, and he was impressed at their many guests. Phil told him they all wanted to see the new place and how much they love living here. Then he told him he should come up for a drink sometime after his shift, which he accepted enthusiastically.

"I like you boys. You are always pleasant and especially easy on the eyes," he said as the elevator door closed behind Phil.

When he got upstairs, Jeffrey was in the shower. He quickly checked on the room, and all seemed perfect.

Fifteen minutes early, the intercom announced Mr. Chris. It was Ivan, the younger night doorman, whose voice came through the speaker with his heavy Eastern accent. Phil greeted Chris at the door. "Welcome to Good Times, Inc.," he said, and kissed him on both cheeks. He walked in, looking surprised at the appearance of the place. Phil offered him a drink and suggested he relax in front of the fire.

They started chatting. Chris said this was a short trip, but since he was in New York, he wanted to take advantage of some extracurricular activities. They both laughed, and Phil told him, "Well, you've found the perfect place for that!" The host could feel his guest was anxious to meet Jeffrey as they sipped from their tumblers, so Phil summoned Jeffrey to come in and join them. Phil looked at Chris when Jeffrey entered the room and could see immediately by the smile on his face that he approved of his assigned companion. Jeffrey sat next to him; as soon as Phil sensed the chemistry was good, he excused himself and retired to the office.

There was some whispering outside the door as they moved into their love nest. Later, as he was engrossed in his work, a soft knock on the door broke the concentration. "Yes, come in." Jeffrey was standing there, wrapped in a blanket and with a big smile on his face. "Guess asking how you are doing isn't necessary," Phil said.

"Chris wanted to know, do we serve coffee in the morning?"

Phil looked up at him. "Can you do an overnight?"

"Absolutely," he answered.

Phil told him it was okay; he should just let him know what time tomorrow morning. He said 8:30, and Phil made a note of the time and wished him a good evening, then made sure they had enough milk and coffee in the house, finished some work, and then went to bed in the maid's room. The alarm set for 7:30, he was soon asleep.

The next morning, torn from a beautiful dream by the buzzing of his alarm clock, he got up, jumped into the shower, got dressed, and went to the kitchen to prepare some coffee. When he passed the master bedroom, he heard some action going on in there. Shortly after, two fully dressed, wet-haired men appeared in the living room. "Ready for some coffee?" He asked.

They simultaneously said, "Yes."

I went to the kitchen and returned with a prepared service tray. Chris was beaming. "Thank you for letting me stay," he said.

"No problem. We aim to please at Good Times, Inc. and hope to see you here regularly," Phil answered. He could see by the look in his eyes that this would be the case. Even more, he would be the best advertiser among his friends.

When Jeffrey excused himself for a quick bathroom stop, Chris came into the office and paid fifteen hundred for the night, saying it was worth every penny. He had to run, so Phil asked Jeffrey to accompany him to the door, where he saw that he slipped him an extra tip.

Jeffrey picked up his coffee and came into the office, threw himself into the chair and exclaimed, "Wow, what an awesome night! This guy is so nice. Did I pass the test?"

Phil looked up and responded, "Welcome aboard."

The phone rang; it was Jack on the line. "How did it go last night?" he asked. Phil told him Chris just left from his overnight. "Well, I guess that's good news for Jeffrey," he said with a laugh.

"Yes, we have another member in G.T.," as they started to call themselves internally. Jack then asked if he could come over early, and the boss told him he was always welcome. He had another appointment with Frederic later in the day.

"Yes, I've been dreaming of those lips all night," he said with a laugh and hung up.

Phil asked Jeffrey to go and clean up the room and make it available for Jack later. He showed him where the fresh sheets were and told him each person was responsible to ready the room for the next one. He gave him his share of the night's take, updated the new system, and stashed the cash in the piggy bank. "I have to open an account today," he said.

Very excited, Jeffrey left all his details, so Phil could call him if needed. They spoke a little more, and the boss learned that he had traveled extensively and was quite cultured. He was studying art history at NYU and loved attending the opera and theatre. Phil really liked him and was sure now he would be a great addition to the team. With business in mind he asked if he had friends he could recommend. G.T. would always be open, but it was very important they be good escorts, not hustlers. Looks were important, but here they needed more than just a pretty face; they wanted to be different, more refined. Honesty and cleanliness were paramount. He said he would think about it, gave me his schedule, and promised he would always keep me posted on his availability.

The business was off to a good start, with no major expenses, they were making money. They had already made the second month's rent, with money to spare for the sundries needed. They left the apartment together; Phil gave Jeffrey some money to buy lubricant and condoms, while he walked to the corner bank to open an account.

When he got back to the apartment, Jack was already waiting for him. He wanted to know all the details of the previous night, which Phil enthusiastically delivered. He told him he was working furiously on the paperwork for the assignment. He wanted to get it off his shoulders as quickly as possible; he had made great progress and within days should have the first printable draft.

Frederic was on time, and his lustful eyes suggested he did not require small talk with Phil. He wanted Jack. Phil showed him in and went back to the office. Before he left, he asked if he could talk about G.T. to a friend in Germany who might be interested in copying our concept. Phil wrote down all the details, along with the new business phone as well as the web page, which should be active within the next few days, upon Alfred's approval.

Alfred returned the following day and learned of the rearrangement. When he heard that the boss took the maid's room, for the prosperity of the business, he had no problem with the smaller bedroom. When they filled him in on the activity of the past few days, he was overwhelmed. "We're a real business, I guess," was his reaction.

"Yes we are, and all we need are more great phone calls." they were telling him about Jeffrey when Ivan announced via intercom that Mr. Jeffrey was on his way up. Jack went to the door to let him in, and Phil introduced him to Alfred. The two hit it off right away and seemed to have a lot in common. Alfred was happy with all the work Jack had done, so we launched the web page immediately. This called for a celebration. They gathered around the fire and toasted with a good bottle of French champagne. They were now fully operational.

Phil's private phone rang, and it was his father, checking in to see how he was doing.

The days ahead went well, as they all adjusted to their new schedules and lifestyle. They had a regular stream of visitors, and considering that they did very little advertising, they were busy and all made a good income. Most of the clients were married men who were looking for some "time out" from their regular lives. They enjoyed coming over to share a few laughs and some fun. They also made more and more house and hotel calls. Jeffrey was seeing an actor who was on a limited engagement on Broadway, usually in the afternoon. He said this was the perfect distraction while he played the straight heartbreaker on stage in the evenings. Extra tips were theirs to keep, but they had to deliver the share due to G.T.

Phil kept meticulous records of all transactions. They met on a regular basis to discuss their progress, other suggestions, and comments. Phil brought up the idea to invest in a healthcare plan. The others felt it was a good idea and asked him to look into it. Then the day came when the project was due, and Phil was proud to turn in a great and visually appealing paper, with a little help from Jack on several graphs. It would probably take weeks before he heard anything, so he devoted more time to the company in the interim.

One evening when Phil returned, Ivan greeted him at the door with a smirk on his face, prying for information. "You have quite a lot of visitors up there," was his opening line.

"Yes, we all have many friends. I hope nobody has complained," Phil answered.

He said no, but Phil felt he wanted to dig further. He was not in the mood to release any more information than necessary and wished him a good evening.

When he entered the apartment, he heard voices; someone must have a visitor, so Phil went directly to the office. There was a Post-it note on the screen: "Have Hank here, Alfred." Later, Phil was answering a call when he heard them coming out of the room. Alfred poked his face in and whispered, "Are you going to join us?" Phil signaled yes, shortly; he closed the door. Phil finished explaining to this new client how they work. He was very inquisitive about the various guys, and the boss assured him they guaranteed full satisfaction. He said he would think about it and likely call back later.

Now Phil went into the next room, where Hank got up and embraced him. They exchanged some small talk, and then he asked, "Would you also escort women?"

Phil looked to Alfred for a response. "Sure, why not? We don't want to be sued because of sexual discrimination." They all laughed at the answer.

Hank explained that his wife and a few girlfriends were planning a weekend in New York, attending the opera and dinner out. They would love to be in the company of a few charming young men, as they wanted to outshine some girlfriends.

"Wow, a new aspect of Good Times, Inc.," Phil said. "It certainly has possibilities."

He told us the date and how many guys they would need. He thought there would only be escorting involved, but he couldn't guarantee it. Phil explained to him that he would have to know up front who might want more than escorting, because he had to talk to the guys and warn them of the possibility, and he would also have to know if they could perform.

Hank laughed and promised to give me as much detail as possible ahead of time. He then asked if G.T. could organize more than just the guys, including a nice restaurant and possibly some dancing for the ladies afterward. He would be responsible for the expenses, transferring a good down payment, and they would settle up after the weekend. Phil was very intrigued; a new perspective had opened, and his business mind was racing. The boss was sure, if he could convince the other guys to collaborate, that they would enter a new chapter in their range of services.

They had another drink. Hank had to meet some businesspeople for dinner but said he would be in touch soon. Phil was excited about the prospect, and once Hank left, Alfred and he started fantasizing about the details. They decided to go out for a bite and discuss things further.

Ivan was smirking as they crossed the lobby, and as always, he commented on the friend who had just left. Ivan got him a cab and said the man gave him a nice tip. "Who is he?" he asked. "He is very nice-looking, as they all are, very nice men indeed!"

Alfred and Phil looked at each other puzzled and left the building. Over dinner later that evening, Ivan became part of the conversation. "He's kind of creepy" Phil said, sharing with Alfred about the earlier conversation. They agreed that they had to be careful with him.

When they got back to the apartment, Phil saw Ivan leaning into a car, talking with somebody. When he saw them, he immediately stopped his conversation, opened the door, and wished a good night. Phil made a mental note of the car but didn't think very much of it.

Life was good; G.T. was receiving calls now from leads on their web page. Businessmen from all around the world were calling, inquiring about the service and the individuals G.T. offered; almost all made a reservation. It was policy not to send men on hourly jobs, and amazingly enough, no one complained, as most of the bookings involved several hours. All the guys were happy with the arrangements;

they knew they weren't being sent to weirdoes and that most of the men were looking for more than just a quick orgasm. Most dates included dinner in a fancy place and the possibility of some interesting conversation with a mature man.

CHAPTER 6

When Phil walked into class and saw all the reports stacked at the front of the classroom, he knew his verdict was close. The professor picked up the pile and made some comments while returning the papers. When he approached Phil, he was afraid he would go into details, but instead said, "Now this was fascinating and a good read; interesting concept, quite realistic." He put the paper in front of him and said in low voice, "Can I see you after class?" Phil hesitantly opened the first page, was relieved to see an A and a comment underneath: *This feels so realistic. Good work and fun read.*

Phil waited until the others left the classroom, and when he approached his desk, the professor greeted him with a huge grin. "I know you think this class is boring and a waste of your time, but what you produced here was an absolute first, and I am very impressed. I would love to know how you got all the data and graphs. It all sounds so real." He looked at Phil as if waiting for an answer.

Phil finally, very reluctantly, asked, "Can you keep a secret?" He confirmed, so he told him, "While working purely hypothetically, I came across this apartment. Spoke to a friend of mine, and we decided to make it reality. We've been operating for nearly one month. I could give you a much more elaborate scenario today than the report, but I guess business is learning by doing."

He was cool about it and said, "Congratulations on the report. Not sure if you want to share all the details with your father, but he could be proud of you for your business savviness."

Phil left the class and headed home. When he got to the building, the car Ivan had been talking to was out front again. He entered the lobby, and there was David, with his professional smile. Phil asked him about Ivan, but he only knew that Ivan was Romanian, and would likely not be with the company for much longer, since there had been complaints.

Phil pointed out at the car and asked if he knew more about it. David shook his head but admitted that it was there very frequently. He thought it might belong to a resident on the block. "He's always in the car, driving around, checking on the neighborhood." David promised to keep an eye on it. Then he showed Phil his new cell phone and proudly added, "I will take a picture when he appears." Phil thanked him and went upstairs.

Alfred was sitting in the office, working on the schedule. There was an e-mail from Hank, giving them the date of the ladies' weekend in New York, with lots of details. They read it together.

> Hi, guys. Hope all is well. I spoke to my wife, and they will be in New York first April weekend, staying at the W Midtown. The plan is to have a good time. Saturday, three of them will go to the opera, while the other two are going to a show. They would like to meet for dinner afterward. They have all the tickets for the performances but don't know where to meet after, so awaiting a suggestion from you. All of them would love some fun company. I guess only one, possibly two, are out for more. I cannot make these predictions, since they would not tell me all. I trust you could book five very decent guys for the evening. If I learn more, I'll let you know. I know Jennifer would love Jack; she would be the one for more, if that is possible. Talk to you soon, Hank.

They looked at each other and just smiled. "Well, I could take one, I guess, one that doesn't want more," Phil said.

This could be lucrative and fun for G.T. First the boss checked to see which opera was playing that night, and he approved: *Ariadne auf Naxos* by Strauss. Phil asked Jeffrey if he knew of a good place where they could have a late dinner, somewhere between the venues if possible.

Everything was running smoothly. G.T. had more requests than it could handle, and there was a constant flow of locals visiting them, while out-of-towners often wanted to entertain in their hotels. In the meantime, the company had a stable of twelve guys, and all of them seemed to get along well with each other.

Later that evening, Phil received a call from John, one of the guys, saying he had to see him. The man he was with last night was nice, too nice, and wanted to take John to Europe for a long weekend. Phil knew this might come up one day. John said the man claimed to be working for a large software company in the Eastern Bloc. He had a convention and wanted to be accompanied, and he asked how much that would be, all expenses paid, of course. Phil asked if John wanted to do this and if his passport was up to date. Of course, he saw dollar signs and thought this would take them a step further in the right direction. Sergey, the client, seemed willing to spend major money for this service. John was intrigued and finally agreed. Jack seemed a bit envious but knew his turn would come too. Phil arranged a flat rate for the four days.

CHAPTER 7

The Lufthansa flight for Frankfurt was beginning to board; Sergey and John were holding two business-class tickets and approaching the security check at JFK when Sergey's cell phone rang. He looked at the display and motioned to John to go ahead. All the hand luggage was on the belt and going through X-ray. Sergey was very involved in his conversation but kept his eye on John, as security had removed him from the line for a more thorough scan. John assured the guard that he had nothing to hide, unaware that Sergey had planted a microchip under his lapel and he was now serving as a mule. But another quick pat-down finished the routine and left the small device undetected.

The moment John came out of the booth and collected the luggage, he saw Sergey ending his conversation, and with a big smile, passed trough security control. He too had to enter the booth but soon came out and joined John.

"What was that all about?" John asked.

Sergey just shrugged, saying, "It happens from time to time," and left it at that.

John could feel he was in better spirits, actually relieved, but he did not know why. They boarded the plane and were soon on their way to Germany. In the plane, Sergey joked with John, telling him that flying made him horny and he could not wait until they were at the hotel and able to spend some quality time together.

After some sleep, they landed early, passed through Customs, and went to collect the luggage. All of a sudden, John felt some tension in Sergey, picked up his suitcase, and walked toward the green exit. Sergey was fiddling with his suitcase, following John at a safe distance. He also passed the green exit, where a Customs agent asked him to step aside.

John was already through the electric door when he turned, surprised that Sergey was still not there. He waited a couple of minutes, and then the door opened again and a smiling Sergey appeared. "What happened?" John asked, and Sergey brushed it off by saying that with an Eastern passport, it was common to undergo these routine checks. They jumped in a cab, went into town, and checked into the hotel. John said he would take a shower while Sergey called the local office. John overheard Sergey say, "Yes, I am at the hotel, and all is fine. No, the trip was smooth." There was a period of silence and then, "Yes, I will bring all over in the afternoon."

He then heard some noise coming from the room. John thought Sergey would get undressed and join him in the shower, which he did, but it seemed to take a little longer than needed. They washed each other's backs, which made for great foreplay before they moved into the bedroom. They had hot sex; Sergey could not wait to put the condom on John, and he gave himself up completely. The room was filled with sex; the two men were moving their bodies rhythmically against each other, and John was deep in Sergey, who with every move, screamed louder with lust. They were both sweating, and soon Sergey started to shoot over his chest while John drilled into him. They finally collapsed onto each other, breathless and satiated.

In the afterglow, John cuddled up next to Sergey, and while caressing his face with one finger, he looked around the room. Sergey must have unpacked his case while he was in the shower; most likely the noise he heard. He got up and went into the shower to rinse off. When he came back into the room, Sergey was still on the bed. He said he had to go to the office and would meet John later for drinks. After they were dressed, and before leaving the room, Sergey searched with his lips for a kiss, which he received readily as he whispered, "Thank you for everything."

They went downstairs, and Sergey hopped in a cab while John decided to walk around for a while. It was unseasonably cold, but with the excitement of it all, to be in Europe was more than worth it.

While John explored Frankfurt, Sergey met with his partner in another hotel, not too far from his. There were four men sitting in the suite when he entered the room. None of them looked pleasant, and the only thing anyone said upon his entering the room was, "Do you have it?"

"Yes, I told you I have it, so relax." Sergey searched in his briefcase and came up with a small envelope, which he emptied on the table. An even smaller chip fell on the surface, and the man, most probably the boss, picked it up and gave it to another, who walked to the laptop and inserted the chip. The room went silent. All eyes fixed on the man at the computer, waiting for his response. It took some time and some programming, but finally his smile confirmed that the data was all there. The tension in the room immediately lifted, and boss offered drinks all around. Sergey told him they were stopped on both the trip out and upon arrival, but his hired companion was going through Germany with no problem. Then the boss asked if Sergey thought this escort might have suspected something,

"No, certainly not."

The boss was relieved and said, "I gladly pay for your sexual adventures, you fag, but be sure there is no suspicion. If you feel he might suspect anything, you have to inform us immediately."

Sergey nodded and assured him again that there was nothing to worry about. The boss winked at one of the goons and told him to get the small suitcase. He opened it, took out a large sum of money, and handed it to Sergey. He packed it into his coat and vest, and they continued to drink. The boss wanted more information about his escort and how they met. Sergey told him about the classy establishment, Good Times, Inc., where he hired the escort.

"You mean it is a bordello for gay men?"

Sergey blushed but nodded. The boss became inquisitive. Sergey didn't know anything more but promised he would find out. The boss asked how long he intended to stay, and Sergey said, "Until Monday morning."

It was obvious the chip was of great value, but Sergey didn't really care. At his age, it was all he could do to make enough income to cover his expensive lifestyle in New York by being of service to people like the boss. He thought it better not to question, and in his rather shallow way of thinking, Sergey was sure nothing too important could be on such a tiny chip. He felt living the moment was all he could ask for, considering his past in misery and poverty. He would never find out how many people he had made miserable with his work and was only looking forward to spending more hot time with John in the hotel. Sergey was eager to be free of the boss's claws, but his employer was not yet finished with him.

"Sergey, I want to know more about this escort of yours." When he flashed more cash, Sergey listened. The boss said, "I have a perverted nephew, a pansy like you, Sergey." The goons laughed approvingly. "I know there are places in this town where you pansies like to meet. My nephew can 'pretend' to run into you there. He can nonchalantly grill your escort and get more information about this bordello in New York."

Sergey was not happy; he wanted John all to himself for the duration of their trip. Now he had to trick him into a meeting with a clan member. He had no choice. "Tell your nephew to be at Planet around ten tonight. I can introduce them; but there's no guarantee John will talk about his employers."

The boss handed him a fistful of bills. "I expect answers, Sergey, and details!"

Outside the door, cash stashed carefully in his inner pockets, he found the stairs. Just as he passed into the stairwell, the elevator door opened. The two goons stepping out did not see Sergey, but he heard them knock at the boss's suite.

He was nervous when he reached his own hotel, and when he got to the room, he found John posing on the couch in a fluffy robe. "Get dressed," Sergey demanded. "I'm not happy about this place. We are moving to a better hotel."

John was surprised at the urgency but did as he was told. They went over to the Steigenberger Frankfurter Hof, a very luxurious five-star establishment. John questioned the move, but Sergey said he just wanted to show John how appreciative he was of his company and wanted to spoil him.

When Sergey felt safe, he fell on the sofa. "John, let's have a drink. Vodka on the rocks, please."

John happily obliged and sat next to Sergey, and as Sergey's nerves settled down, he told John his boss was very happy with his performance, and they would have a few days off. He loosened his tie and John slowly unbuttoned his shirt. After the second drink, Sergey became more involved, and the two started to make out on the sofa.

Finally spent, their clothing strewn about the room, Sergey asked about John's day. "I was off sightseeing this afternoon and saw a restaurant that looked good in the old town." They dressed and left, giddy in each other's company.

During dinner, Sergey asked John to tell him more about Good Times, Inc., but John only gave him cursory answers. "I'm really not at liberty to discuss the details with anybody." Sergey was impressed but diplomatically continued digging, to no avail. Dinner was good, they were satiated, and it was still only 10:00. They walked through the old town, and as they rounded a corner, they spotted a rainbow flag flying above a doorway.

Sergey looked at John and with raised eyebrows asked, "Are you game for a nightcap?"

"Sure, if you like, let's go," John answered.

They entered the place and were greeted by loud music. "Wow, a cultural shock after such a pleasant dinner atmosphere," John remarked.

Sergey scanned the room and spotted a quiet corner. They sat down, and a waiter sauntered over to take their order. Both men watched the waiter, in his very tight black leather pants head back to the bar, and as their eyes met, they laughed aloud. Sergey jokingly remarked, "Guess we landed in a gay bar!"

John was about to ask Sergey about his work when he spotted a tall, good-looking man smiling at him from across the room. Sergey recognized at once that this was the boss' nephew and asked John if he should invite him over. John was not that keen on the proposal but thought if Sergey would find pleasure in it, why not.

The young man sat next to John and introduced himself as Zurab. His English was very good, but when he learned Sergey spoke Georgian, the two were chatting in their native language, laughing with each other. John did not understand a word and politely sipped his drink when Zurab turned to him abruptly. "Oh my, please, forgive me, John. It is so rare to meet a fellow countryman here."

Sergey flagged down the waiter for another round and then excused himself. "Sorry, dear, have to make a pit stop." He left the two alone to give Zurab his chance.

Zurab bluntly asked, "Does he pay well?"

John was taken by surprise; he looked at Zurab, puzzled. "What do you mean?"

Zurab was thrown but eloquently recovered. "I was just wondering. I have seen him before, never spoke to him, but he is always looking for younger men."

John was surprised, since Sergey told him this was only his second time in Frankfurt. He said they were just two friends in town for the weekend.

Sergey pushed his way through the crowd, back to the table. John was happy to see him, as the bizarre line of questioning would have to stop. Zurab was charming, but John knew right away that he was fishing for answers, which he was not going to provide. Before the next round, John kissed Sergey on the cheek and whispered, "Let's get out of here. This guy is creepy!"

Sergey was relieved. He settled the tab as the three wished each other a good night. Back on the street, John felt an uneasiness rise in Sergey. He was nervous, constantly looking back; he seemed to be checking to see if they were followed. Three streets later, he finally could relax.

Back at the hotel, they jumped into the shower to wash away the foul smell of the bar and fell exhausted into bed. Sergey fell asleep fast, plagued by nightmares. John watched as he slept, restless and mumbling through the night.

The next morning, John awoke wrapped in Sergey's arms, happy he'd found some peaceful sleep, nevertheless. Lying there in close embrace, John retraced the events of the day before and thought something was strange, but he could not pin down what exactly. It was Sunday, and they had no agenda. John was hoping they could visit some sights, and maybe Sergey would open up a little. Still buried in thought, he suddenly was aware of Sergey's lips, softly kissing his shoulder.

"Good morning, sleepy." They both smiled as they shared a long and affectionate gaze.

"Call for some coffee and juice, would you please?" Sergey asked as he headed toward the bathroom. Upon his return, he grabbed his cell phone and was soon engaged in a friendly conversation. "A friend will be stopping by in a while, but we still have some time to ourselves," Sergey said with a sexy smile.

They enjoyed a morning romp and then decided on casual attire to walk around town. However, before they could leave, they had to wait for Sergey's friend. A few minutes later, a knock on the door made Sergey jump up. He grabbed a thick envelope, went to the door, and peered through the spy hole. When he saw his friend on the other side, he quickly opened the door. They exchanged a few words, and Sergey handed him a package.

Just as they were sitting down for lunch, Sergey's cell phone rang. He answered humbly in Georgian, and John could feel Sergey's annoyance—or was it fear? He didn't want to be too inquisitive. "Was that the boss?" John asked, and he felt from that moment on, Sergey became a different person altogether again. During the course of the afternoon, Sergey dropped a few hints, and John started to understand by what he disclosed that organized crime was involved. But it was the fear that truly gave him away.

John recalled the past few days, and things started adding up. Several security checks at the airports, the sudden move from one hotel to another, the chance meeting with Zurab the night before, but mostly the many mood changes in Sergey; it was definitively fear. John felt that fear now too. He told Sergey he was exhausted and suggested they return to the hotel. Sergey was very happy to oblige. Back in the safety of their room, they took a nap, and Sergey held John protectively in his arms.

Later, John thought it would be best to order room service, as they had to catch an early flight back to New York the following morning. Sergey agreed. John didn't want to be exposed in public in Frankfurt any more than he had to anymore.

John felt Sergey's relief as soon as the plane left the tarmac en route to home. At JFK, they separated at Immigration and met out front to share a cab back into town, where they agreed to call each other soon and get together again. John was happy to be home; he called the office to let them know he was back and that all was well. He was tired but would come by the apartment the following day.

CHAPTER 8

In New York, everything went well—school, work, and new clients calling daily, mostly through recommendation. In the evening, Phil thought a stroll down Madison Avenue and a little fresh air would do him good. A new doorman greeted him in the lobby. Phil inquired about Ivan, but he could give him no information. Ivan didn't show up for work and was nowhere to be found. He introduced himself as the tenant from 8A, and the doorman said his name was Fred. A stop by the bank's ATM, Phil made a deposit, and was impressed to see the balance.

He had earned a walk on such an expensive avenue, even if stores were closed and he could not spend. Just knowing that he could make him happy. After an hour out, Phil felt better and returned home. Alfred sat in the living room, reading. He put his book down when Phil told him Ivan was gone, but Fred the new doorman seemed very nice, an elderly gentleman with old-school manners.

Phil decided to make this an early night, but Alfred said they should organize their routine and find an outside meeting point to exchange the money so they could reduce the traffic here. Phil agreed and promised to give it some thought in the morning. He was just saying good night when the phone rang. "Good Times, can I help you?" The voice on the other end began to ask questions about the services. He said he would be in town a few days from now and would prefer an in-house call. "No problem," Phil said and told him to call when he arrived. He left the phone with Alfred, as he said he would be up for some time finishing his reading.

The list of escorts was growing fast, and Phil believed the reason for their success was the discretion. When John told about his trip to

Frankfurt, Phil became suspicious, and when Sergey called again the same evening to make an appointment, he knew there was more to the story. He must have felt his hesitation, but Phil assured him everything was fine.

He said, "I would like to meet at the house tomorrow evening, if that would be okay?"

Phil checked the calendar and told him yes, but John would not be available. I could have Alfred for him, if that was acceptable. He was hesitant at first, but he did agree. Phil did this deliberately; he wanted a new face for Sergey, somebody who could dig a little into his secret.

When he arrived the following night, he was first offered the obligatory drink and they chatted for a while. Phil inquired about the trip to Frankfurt, hoping that everything was to his liking, and then asked how his business was doing. His vague answers did not surprise him, but tension was felt. He may have thought John had shared the details. Phil assured him that discretion was the most important asset of their trade, and he seemed visibly relieved. Alfred came in and took him to his room, and for the next two hours they were busy.

The man who called earlier phoned again to make arrangements for the following evening. He said he would like to take the young man out for dinner, get to know him a bit, and then come back to our place. Phil thought this would be a perfect date for Jack. "Yes, I will have very nice young man waiting for you at the restaurant of your choice."

Phil called Jack and gave him the scenario. "Great," he said, "I'm looking forward to a decent meal."

Phil told him the client was very inquisitive, and he should stay sharp, as there may be some rather indiscreet questions.

Alfred and Sergey finally emerged, both seemingly in a good mood, and then Sergey's phone started to buzz. He began speaking in his language, and Phil could sense he got a little nervous. Even though he knew they could not follow his discussion, he spoke softly into the phone. When he ended the call, he seemed anxious to leave the place; he paid quickly, gave Alfred a generous tip, and out he ran.

"That was weird," Alfred commented after he closed the door behind Sergey. "He's a nice guy, but I think he has a shitload of pressure on him."

I wanted to know more when Alfred told me Sergey might have to go to Europe again, and inquired if he would be willing to accompany him on the next trip. This time, it was Berlin. Phil told Alfred about the guy he set Jack up with the next day. Jeffrey called and said that he was just leaving his client and wondered if they were still up and ready for a drink. He would be over in a few minutes.

The intercom buzzed, and Fred announced Jeffrey. "Any news on Ivan?" Phil asked him, but he couldn't tell him much more, only that Ivan had called in sick.

When Jeffrey came through the door, he asked if he could quickly shower. When he came out afterward, he just said, "I had to wash this off badly." He then told them that his previous client was a very nice man, but somehow he felt a rinse was not enough; he needed a good scrub.

"I understand," Phil said. "This is a risk we have to take in our trade."

He picked up the prepared drink and settled his account. "Fred is a nice guy. I like him much better than creepy Ivan," he said.

They sat and talked awhile. Jeffrey mentioned that he had to go south for a few days and G.T. should not count on him for a week. Phil made a note on the calendar.

Jack called the next day and confirmed his date with Joachim. He said he would call when they leave the restaurant; Phil assured him everything would be ready for them. Things went according to plan. Joachim and Jack came to the apartment and seemed to have a great understanding. Joachim, in his firm Prussian way, asked if he should settle the account now, Phil just said, "You have a good time, and we will see each other later." The two headed off down the hall, and from what I could hear, they had a *really* good time.

As the time drew nearer, we were all looking forward to the "hen night." I arranged with Claudia, Daniel's wife, to meet the ladies at 6:30 in the hotel bar. No further details were necessary, as a group of five young men would certainly be able to spot a group of five women. Claudia reminded me that Jennifer was the divorcee and might be interested in more than just an escort. I noted this and gave Jack—who was probably the best looking and the most bisexual in the group—instructions to give her special attention.

We were sitting at the bar, when five giggling, good-looking women entered the room. I looked up, searching for eye contact, when I saw the taller brunette headed straight toward us. We all stood and introduced ourselves, and when Jennifer grabbed Jack's hand, I felt the electricity in the air. She did not want to let go. I didn't even have to arrange the pairings; nature took its course. The initial awkwardness was very brief; they were all soon involved in chatter and laughter.

The women told them about their afternoon and the visit to the spa; they must have been sipping champagne the entire afternoon. Phil confirmed that he had made reservations at Ocean Bar and Grill, which was close to the Met, and since the show was over sooner, they would probably be there all at the same time. The two groups split up: those who were attending the opera and those off to a Broadway show.

The evening was an absolute blast. Phil loved the performance; the music and the ladies were fun and full of energy. Jennifer immediately grabbed Jack's arm as if to say "he's mine." When they all met again at the restaurant, the earlier banter continued until 1:00, when they finally left—the last patrons in the place. Phil observed Jennifer slipping a note into Jack's pocket. He inquired if they wanted to continue the party but was told it had been a long day, and they would like to go back to the hotel. Claudia asked if they could meet for late brunch the following day. Phil couldn't see why not, as he had blocked the entire weekend, as requested.

Alfred hailed two cabs for the ladies and kissed them good night. Then the guys stood at the curb, contemplating where they could go for a nightcap. They found a shady local bar, and Jack finally took the paper out of his pocket. Jennifer had left him her cell number and her room number, circled with a small lipstick heart. They all laughed their heads off and prosted to the new service provided by Good Times, Inc.

Forty-five minutes later, Jack placed his call, and Jennifer seductively told him she would like to know more about him and had a bottle of champagne ordered. Jack promised he would be there within twenty minutes. The party broke up, and the guys all went their separate ways.

The next morning, Alfred was reading the paper and drinking coffee, as was customary on Sundays. Phil went over the schedule and saw there was nothing for the entire day. He was happy and could relax; he even found himself hoping there would be no last-minute calls.

At 1 o'clock they all met for brunch, and the champagne flowed freely again. Jennifer had her head in the clouds, and they all knew the reason why: she couldn't keep her eyes off of Jack. When they finally said good-bye, Claudia whispered in Phil's ear, "This was a birthday gift from Hank. Just send him the invoice; I assure you, he will be generous."

Phil told her not to worry, that they all had a very good time. After long good—byes the guys headed back to the apartment and just hung out for the afternoon. Jack insisted on no more champagne; having had too much already, he was trying to sober up.

They were all in a giddy mood, and after some intercompany fun, decided to go out for pizza. Over their frugal dinner, Phil told the guys about how well Good Times, Inc. was doing and that dinner was on the house. They all cheered for him when he told them they had brought in well over a hundred thousand dollars so far, and there was a lot more where that came from. He thanked them for their good service, but they were just as thankful to him, because he made all happen. They drank to Jeremy: "May he have a great time in Florida!" Phil spoke to him on a regular basis, and when he mentioned he might come to New York for a weekend, Phil offered him he could stay in his old room. He just needed some warning, so they all could be ready for him. He appreciated this very much.

CHAPTER 9

T ime passed quickly, between school and work; the term was soon over, all exams were in place. Phil decided to speed up the process of his education and enrolled in a couple of summer courses, just to get it all behind him. He also had to have a good excuse to stay in town. One morning, he received an e-mail from someone named Horst, which read:

> Dear Good Times, Inc., I am very interested in meeting you. I have received spectacular reviews from a few acquaintances of mine. One is Frederic, the other Joachim. They have praised your establishment. I am not looking for service, though, just a meeting. I will be in New York early July on vacation. So you are aware, I am also a working man—escort. I hope to hear from you and see you soon in your city. Regards, Horst.

At first, this took Phil by surprise, but knowing that great patrons recommended this person, he wrote him back.

> Dear Horst: Thank you for your e-mail. I would be very interested in meeting you; I will most probably be around during your stay in New York. Where would you be staying? Please check the attachment for any further information. Look forward to meet you soon.
>
> Phil, Good Times, Inc.

In the attachment he included the website and phone numbers.

The summer holidays started slowly, and many clients left the city, headed for the beaches. They received more calls during the week from men who sent their families to the Hamptons or to other summer destinations, and only visited them over the weekends. It was a long, lonely time during the week, and these husbands were in search of charming company and some fantasy time, which G.T. graciously provided. It was amazing how many married men shared a desire for gay sex. With the family out of the house, it was a perfect time to explore these longings. The weekends were quiet, which was good, since many of the guys were escaping to Fire Island or similar resorts to leave the hot, unpleasant city behind them.

In early July, Phil received a phone call from Horst, who had arrived in New York and was eager to meet. Phil was home alone, with Alfred off visiting his parents, so he suggested they could meet at his place. Phil gave him the address, Horst said he would be over shortly.

A few minutes later, Fred announced that Horst had arrived, and when the elevator door opened, Phil nearly fell flat on his face. The most stunning, tall creature walked out, with a huge smile showing off his perfect teeth. "Horst?" he stammered, surprised, and the young man nodded. "Come in," was all he could get over his lips, still entranced by this Adonis.

Horst followed the host into the apartment; he asked him to take a seat and offered a cold drink. Phil was very anxious to find out more. "You have a wonderful place here," Horst said, looking around the living room. "I guess you would like to know why I am here?" he finally asked.

"Yes." Phil was eager to find out, as his fantasies began to wander, hoping the German guy might take advantage of him. Horst told Phil that he was escorting in Germany, and both Frederic and Joachim were regulars of his. They had both told him to get in touch with Good Times, Inc. when he was in New York. They said this was the classiest place they knew, and he should seriously consider establishing something similar in either Frankfurt or Berlin. This guy was not only an absolute looker, but he was so friendly, charming, and witty, Phil would have hired him on the spot! But they spoke business first. Phil told him how Good Times operated. He explained the most important factor was the men who worked there; they must be far above the average in every way—able to carry on a conversation, to make the client feel he is the most important person, not only for a quick fuck, but whatever else was requested. He told Horst many clients did not even require sexual favors, but were just happy to show off with a good-looking and intelligent man.

Phil continued, "We offer in-house calls, and we have two rooms where clients can spend private time with our men, and what happens in these rooms does not come out, not even to me. As long as the escort agrees and the client is satisfied, we are all good. Discretion is the one thing I preach to the newer guys on a daily basis. I am not interested how much over tip they make if they give special care; I am only interested in the rate. I am paying my guys very well, and everyone seems to be happy to work for me. I don't accept any bitching, and I am discriminatory when it comes to clients and assignments. I have five main escorts and approximately a dozen other good men to choose from."

Horst listened carefully and seemed to make very detailed mental notes. He asked if Phil could show him around the place. They got up, and the guest received the tour.

First Phil showed him the kitchen, which included an extremely well-stocked bar. Then they continued to Alfred's room, where everything was spic and span, ready to receive a potential client at any moment. Horst was very impressed, and when Phil showed him the master bedroom, Horst's jaw dropped. Phil opened the en suite bathroom, complete with fresh towels and all the amenities. "Now this is a beautiful room. No wonder Fred and Joachim were impressed."

Phil told him that it was always the escort's duty to clean up after a client and have the room ready and fresh for the next one. Some days, they have the room booked up to three times over, and he has to be sure it is always the same. Sheets and towels get replaced after every visit; he often has the laundry going the entire day, but it is convenient, as it is in the apartment.

Then Phil showed him his humble room. Horst stood behind him, looking in, but when Phil turned to leave, Horst blocked his way and stared deep into his eyes. The room was suddenly charged with lust, and like a mouse in front of a snake, Phil slowly parted his lips and Horst engulfed him with a kiss. The host's head got very light; he lost the equilibrium and fell backward onto the bed, and Horst landed in his arms. He was digging deep into his mouth, and their tongues began to wrestle. The kiss got Phil very excited, and when he felt Horst's hand moving down his chest toward the groin, he nearly lost it—especially when his hand grabbed the rock-hard penis through Phil's pants.

Horst sat up, and with a swift tug, removed his T-shirt and exposed to Phil the most wonderful chest. "Do you mind?" he asked. Phil was speechless, but his approving grin must have been sufficient confirmation for the guest. He started to work on Phil's shirt and pants, soon they were both naked, their bodies interlocked in hot and athletic man sex. Horst grabbed a condom off the bedside table, expertly put it on, and soon was poking at Phil's rear. He was very ready to give this gorgeous man complete access; never before did he feel the urge to be taken as strongly. Horst was a master. As he effortlessly changed from one position to another, with each adjustment, Phil felt him deeper and hotter in him. Several times he was very close to coming, but he tried to make it last until Horst asked "Where do you want it?"

"All over me please!"

Horst withdrew and a split second later shot the largest load Phil has ever seen all over the chest. One stream hit the chin and lips. Phil licked them clean; it was delicious. He was so happy, and completely forgot about his own orgasm when Horst fell on him. "Wow that was hot!"

They stayed this way for another few minutes, as all that sperm started to drip off Phil's body. He told him he had to go and clean up, and Horst followed into the bathroom, where they showered together. Phil handed him a fresh towel, which he wrapped around himself and went back to the living room.

The host joined him a few moments later. At first, they just sat there and kind of smiled at each other. Then Horst asked, "Are you okay? Sorry, I don't know what came over me, but you are so hot!"

Phil pointed his finger at himself and just said, "Me?" Horst nodded. "Thank you for the compliment, but have you checked the mirror lately?" He just laughed. Then they decided to take a walk in the park, and talk some more.

It was one of these typical hot New York summer days, but the trees in the park offered sufficient shade, making the humidity bearable. Horst told Phil it was his dream to create a similar establishment in Germany; Phil thought it would be a great thing, and his entrepreneurial mind already envisioned a transatlantic collaboration. He told him of a client who traveled to Germany on business frequently and always hired a guy for the duration of the trip. He was sure if they were able to have good people over there and make all the arrangements from here, it would not only be more economical, but a local escort could probably also offer a wider selection of entertainment.

Horst told Phil he had a friend in Berlin with whom he had this kind of arrangement, as he was based in Frankfurt. They were planning while strolling through Central Park and the new concept of going international was born. Since Phil was by himself in the apartment, and not much was happening at the time, he suggested Horst could leave his hotel and stay with him. He immediately accepted, and on their way back, they picked up all the belongings from the hotel.

When they got to the apartment, they relaxed and spoke some more. Phil showed him the computer program, booking schedule, and other tools of the business. Horst asked if Phil would be willing to share it with him, and was told that Jack would probably be able to copy all the basics for him. Things were off to a great start, as they enjoyed the few days together.

One evening, while Horst was still Phil's guest, Jack had an in-house client, so he came early to check on the arrangements. The houseguest and Jack immediately hit it off, and when Phil explained their plans, Jack thought this would be wonderful. "I could install a communication program," he said, "so international bookings could be done easily and efficiently. Most important, the data could be set up in one location."

When the client arrived, Phil asked Horst to sit in the office, leaving the door open, he could observe the routine. It was a first-timer, which was good. David announced him over the intercom; Phil opened the door and brought him into the living room, offered him a drink, and made some small talk until he felt the client was at ease. Then Jack was introduced and Phil excused himself, leaving them to become better acquainted. He went back to the office, where they witnessed Jack's impeccable skills and their imminent disappearance into privacy. Once they were out of sight, Phil and Horst went back into the living room. Horst asked if they could go back too and share some fun of their own while they waited.

Good Times, Inc. became busier and busier, and sometimes Phil had to delegate to others; between school and the organizing, he managed two full-time jobs. He knew he was very lucky, and when looking at the business plan after one year in operation, he realized the budget for advertising was much higher than needed. Most of the clients came by recommendation, and they had not spent a dime on printed ads.

CHAPTER 10

Alarge part of the success was the continuity of their clients. They had a growing number of regulars who knew and appreciated the quality of their services. Sergey was certainly one of them, and he was adventurous, meeting most of the escorts, but he soon selected a few as his favorites. Phil always tried to assign his flavor of the day when he put in the request. Carlos, a multilingual Hispanic man, became his favorite.

One day, when Sergey called and asked if he could have Carlos for a few days to accompany him on another upcoming trip, Phil made a note. He also told him he would have a very good escort in Frankfurt. It would be more economical, as he would meet him at the airport and spend the entire time with him, saving him all the travel expenses. Sergey said that would not work and gave weird excuses—he hated to fly by himself, for one thing. Phil agreed to talk to Carlos and make sure all his documents were in order. Sergey gave me his travel plans.

Carlos was okay and was looking forward to spending time in Europe with Sergey. In recent months, Sergey seemed more relaxed, but once he got the confirmation from Phil, he tensed up again. Phil was apprehensive and instructed Carlos to confirm by phone or text messages to him about his well-being while on the trip. If he felt anything was suspicious, Phil wanted to be told immediately. Phil informed Carlos of John's trip, so he would be well prepared and aware of the signs.

In the evening, he received his first call from Carlos from JFK, where he told his boss the security routine was exactly like John's experience. Sergey received a call just before going through security and asked Carlos to go ahead. Then they were both checked

64

thoroughly, but while Carlos was undergoing the check, Sergey was nowhere to be seen. Once he passed, he saw a relieved Sergey going through the same routine. *Weird. What is going on?* Phil asked himself. He shared this with Alfred, but he brushed it off by saying that since 9/11, security checks were much more thorough, especially for people of certain nationalities.

The rest of the trip was nearly a carbon copy of the previous one, first, more security checks in Germany; Sergey leaving to meet the boss; coming back to the hotel, where he decided he was not happy with the address. Carlos convinced him that another couple of nights there would be okay, and Sergey finally gave in.

Later, they decided on dinner outside in the old town and found a quiet restaurant not too far from the hotel. They sat down and had just ordered a drink when three men entered the establishment and were seated on the far side. Carlos felt observed; when he had to go to the bathroom, one of the guys followed him. When he returned, Sergey was apprehensive. They ordered, and when the food came, Sergey barely ate a bite. As they were getting ready to leave the restaurant, Sergey's phone buzzed; Carlos detected an immediate mood shift for the worse. He didn't understand what was being said but sensed it was nothing good.

Outside the restaurant sat a large, black limousine, and the moment they started walking down the street, the engine turned on. Carlos looked back and saw two of the guys from the restaurant jump in. Sergey noticed this too and guided Carlos into the pedestrian zone. At that point, one of the guys jumped out of the car and tried to follow them inconspicuously. Sergey became more and more nervous and was happy when he spotted a group of people smoking in front of a bar. "Feel like a drink?" he asked Carlos as he led him into the noisy bar. Carlos was searching for a quiet corner where he could write a short message to Phil in New York: *Weird, we are followed by three nasty goons. S is very nervous!*

When Carlos returned, Sergey was conversing with the bartender, who had given him the location of the back-door exit. They ended up in a small, dark side street, as Sergey tried to orient himself to get back to the hotel. The lobby was empty, and the concierge wished them a good night. When they got to the room, Sergey asked if he could use Carlos's phone to change the reservation so they could return to New York the following day. He told Carlos something was wrong, and he was afraid of his boss. He didn't inform the hotel of the change, since it was prepaid; he let them believe they would be still there until they were safely on their way back home.

Carlos was nervous now too, and they shared a sleepless night. Sergey gave his companion an envelope full of cash, and the following morning told him they would leave the hotel separately, taking two cabs. They would not have contact until they were both sitting safely in the plane.

At eight in the morning, Carlos took a small bag and headed downstairs, climbed into a cab, and was out of danger, but he saw two of the men from last night sitting in the lobby. He wrote a text message to Sergey, just saying, "Take back door."

A few hours later, they both sat in the comfortable chairs of Lufthansa business class. Seeing Sergey's relief once the plane left the ground, Carlos looked over to him and asked, "Is there something you would you like to tell me?" But Sergey just told him the less he knows the better.

When they landed in New York, they separated again. Sergey said they would meet outside, again explaining that he gets detained, and he thought it better that the customs agents did not know they traveled together. Carlos had waited more than twenty minutes before he finally saw Sergey come through the automatic doors with a wide smile. He felt truly safe for the first time in forty-eight hours. He gave the cab driver an address, and when they reached their destination, Sergey asked Carlos to come up. He wanted to talk to him in private, and he was sure this place was not bugged.

They entered a small studio apartment in a walkup building. Sergey explained that this was his safe house when things got too scary. Then he asked Carlos for his bag and took out another larger envelope. Carlos was surprised, seeing this for the first time. He had the first envelope Sergey gave him in Frankfurt tucked in the inside pocket of his jacket.

Sergey said, "I am very sorry to have taken advantage of you, but I could not meet with my friend in Frankfurt anymore. Since I knew I would be searched, I had to make sure the money got through safely." Carlos, as an American, was less likely to be searched, and Sergey thought it was his safest bet. He opened the envelope, took a few bills out, and gave them to Carlos. He then asked Carlos to sit down and listen carefully. He told Carlos his boss was a very disagreeable person and was involved in blackmail, money laundering, and smuggling. He was ruthless and saw people as disposable objects.

Besides the business Sergey was doing for him, his boss was very interested in Good Times, Inc. He saw this as a way of using the escorts as mules, and prostitution was always good for money laundering. Both times, he was very inquisitive about the operation, and this time he went so far as to request that Sergey spy on the establishment. He knew the operation was very well run and profitable. Carlos just listened, and at this point wanted to leave and put this Sergey episode behind him. Sergey told Carlos to be cautious and to warn the men of suspicious characters, mainly with Eastern accents. Carlos took the money, said good-bye to Sergey, and took a cab home, where he called Phil immediately and asked if he could come over.

Phil was astonished that he was back already, but after Carlos's detailed account of the trip, he was happy he was home safe. Phil promised he would keep his eyes open and told him he had felt for months that the man he had seen in the parked car was observing the street. At one point, he thought Ivan, the former doorman, might also be involved. Once Ivan was gone, Phil was less attentive, and although he saw that same car from time to time, he never saw anything suspicious.

CHAPTER 11

Weeks went on. Phil was more attentive and noted carefully each time he left or returned to the building if there was anything out of the ordinary. He saw nothing until one warm March afternoon, when he came back from school. Upon entering his block, he was stopped by yellow tape closing off the street and reading "Crime Scene." A young policeman asked where Phil lived; he gave him his address, and he let him pass. When Phil entered the building, he saw David, who looked distressed. He sat on a chair, and another young policeman was next to him. Phil walked up to him and asked if everything was okay. David raised his eyes and told him they found Ivan killed in a car across the street.

Phil looked at the policeman, and he confirmed and added that there were two bodies in the car. One was Ivan, the other not yet identified. When the policeman saw Phil's astonished face, he asked if he would like to talk to a detective. When Phil told him he knew Ivan only as a doorman and had little contact with him, he let him pass to the elevator. In the apartment, Phil turned on the local news station NY1, and sure enough, it was breaking news that an execution-style double murder was committed on the Upper East Side. The camera showed their entrance, but the reporter would not release any detailed information. He pointed out that the two bodies were found in the afternoon, but police suspected that the shooting took place in the early morning hours.

They asked for information on the two victims, anything that would lead either to their names or any observation that could help solve the case. When they showed the picture of the second victim, Phil knew that he was the one sitting in the car and observing the house for a very long time. He was the one Ivan once talked to; maybe he had just been a friend.

They interviewed the chief of police, who released only very vague information. However, he did mention that this kind of execution-style murder was often linked to organized crime, and the police also suspected that both victims were Romanian. Phil's head started spinning. He was afraid that Ivan was involved with a clan; his constant remarks about their frequent visitors and his questions and observations started to add up. Phil was unsure if he should tell the police about all this; he was afraid they would start asking too many questions.

Phil left the TV running and at first watched the repetitions every thirty minutes. The commentator announced that new information had been released by the NYPD on the Upper East Side murders. It was confirmed that the two victims were members of a Romanian crime organization, and the investigation would concentrate on feuding crime organizations, mainly based in Brookline. While Phil was watching attentively, the intercom buzzed, and David asked if Detective Summers could come up and see him. Phil said yes and turned off the TV and went to the door.

The elevator opened, and a heavyweight, unpleasant-looking person walked out in the company of a younger, attractive guy. Phil asked them in, and Summers introduced himself and his colleague, Detective Kors. Phil automatically offered them a drink and asked them to sit down. They looked around and must have been astonished how students could afford this apartment. He explained that it belonged to a friend who moved to Florida, and they were subletting the place fully furnished.

They both accepted a glass of water, and Summers immediately started the questioning. Phil told him again that he did not know Ivan very well. He decided it best to tell them about the other person who had parked his car out front and was always waiting for him. As he was finishing his sentence, the business phone buzzed. He looked at the screen and excused himself quickly to go into the next room.

"Hello, Sergey. How are you?" Sergey was obviously nervous and said that he just had a visit from somebody who inquired again about their establishment. He said that he told them that he only had a phone number and usually met the men in restaurants or at his place. Then he said the visitor mentioned that the Upper East Side murders should not be repeated, and therefore the more information he could give, the safer everybody was.

All of Phil's blood rushed into his head, and for the first time since he started G.T, he felt fear. Phil thanked him and said he would love to see him if possible. They agreed to meet later at a coffee shop. Phil went back to Summers and Kors, who were waiting. He sat down and expected more questions from them. Alfred entered, and Phil introduced him as his roommate; Summers asked if he would join them. Alfred asked for a few minutes to go to the bathroom before.

Kors took a piece of paper out of his inside pocket, a photocopy of handwritten notes. He handed it to Phil and asked, "Does this mean anything?"

Phil looked at it and thought his eyes would jump out of their sockets. It was a list; the first column was dates, the second was the time of day, and the third a description of men. It read like a visitors' book for Good Times, Inc. Date, time of entering the building, and then description: *"Tall, gray hair, glasses, expensive suit. Same person was here a few days ago, staying in building for little over two hours."* There were many of these notations. Phil and Alfred immediately knew that somebody must have checked them out, but when detective Summers asked if they had seen this list before, both shook their heads. When he asked if Phil could think of a reason why this was made, he hoped to sound convincing and told him no. Then he showed the list to Alfred again, who looked at Phil and shook his head too, returning the paper to the detective.

Phil told him that he watched NY1 news before they came, and the reporter said that the police were convinced that this was an act of organized crime. Detective Kors nodded in approval. They asked again if they ever had any suspicion that Ivan was involved in any such activities, but they both assured them that apart from his inquisitive behavior, they never assumed anything like that. Phil told them that when Ivan called in sick and was replaced by Fred, they did not miss him. He made no secret that he didn't like Ivan very much. When they asked why, he couldn't really think of a reason; he just felt that Ivan always wanted to find out private details, and they as students have a lot of friends who come visit, but they never had complains from any other tenants.

They were both given a business card, and the detectives told to give them a call if they remembered anything else. They all got up, and Phil showed them to the door, where he caught a very friendly smile from Detective Kors before he closed the door behind them. When Phil returned to the living room, he met Alfred's scared, questioning eyes, as he waited for an explanation from Phil, who was almost as baffled, then Phil told Alfred he received a rather frantic call from Sergey, who wanted to meet him. Alfred asked if he should join, Phil gladly accepted.

They were going through all the possible scenarios when the phone buzzed. A heavily accented voice told Phil, "We have to talk. We do not want any more blood on the street. You can stop this" he asked who was calling, but the other person did not reply and just continued, "We have a lot of information on you, and we do not want to harm anybody, but you have to agree to meet." Phil asked again about his name, and the voice said, "You can call me Dmitry."

Being paranoid Phil said he couldn't meet him today, Dmitry didn't seem happy about this. Phil got the feeling that this was not going to be a pleasant business conversation. Dmitry requested a meeting at ten tonight and told him if he had made prior commitments he should seriously consider changing them for his benefit. He told Phil where to meet, and when asked how he would recognize him, Dmitry just said not to worry; he knew who he was.

The calls made him very anxious. He was nervous and sensed trouble but could not envision the magnitude yet. Alfred and Phil left to see Sergey. When they arrived at their meeting place, he was already there, and they could see in his face that he was nervous too. They sat down, and after a few seconds that felt like an eternity, Sergey started by apologizing. At first Phil didn't understand why, but then he told them that he used the escorts as mules during his trips to Germany. He assured them that they were never in real danger. He explained that he was always thoroughly checked at airports, because of his past and his nationality, and therefore needed inconspicuous subjects to get the microchips through security and customs. His employer requested more and more of these transports, but he felt less and less comfortable using their service, because he really started to look at the escorts as friends, and he did not want to jeopardize their relationships.

His boss, however, had no sentiment, and for him, humans were material and easily replaceable, especially if they were paid companions. Sergey continued by telling them that the organization was getting more powerful within the United States, especially in New York, and he was convinced that the killing on their block was initiated by them.

Phil's heart started pumping harder, and he became very nervous. He asked if he knew someone named Dmitry. Phil could see fear in Sergey's face, but he just said that there were several by this name, and none of them was good news. Then he asked Phil why he would know this name, and he told him of the earlier call and the requested meeting later this evening. Phil told Sergey about Ivan, the former doorman, and that he was one of the victims.

When Alfred asked him why he thought they would be interested in their activities, he just shrugged and said that he could think of reasons ranging from blackmail to mule service, but money laundering was also an option. He added that his boss in Frankfurt wanted him to spy on them, and after Sergey would not release sufficient information, he tried various ways to find out all the details.

Phil looked at Alfred, who seemed equally shaken up. From all they learned, they became more and more worried about the meeting with Dmitry. Phil asked Sergey if he would be willing to meet with the police, in a safe place, of course. At first, he ruled this out completely, but when Phil told him that Detective Kors seemed nice, he said he would think about it. Alfred asked if they had to be afraid and if any of these goons were clients of them. He wasn't sure, but he couldn't rule out that they had guys sent to the place.

Phil was now concerned that the apartment might be bugged. He didn't want to voice this suspicion, but made a mental note to talk to Kors. Phil asked Sergey how he should behave later, and he suggested that he should be as vague as possible. He was sure that this Dmitry was only instructed to have a first meeting with him, mainly to scare and make him insecure, but at this point, things would not go much further. Dmitry would certainly make some requests and ask to think about them and then suggest another get-together. He also said that the proposals would probably be only to their benefit, and they would leave them little negotiation space. Sergey wrote down a phone number and just said that this was only known by very few people. If they needed to contact him, they could call anytime.

Phil thought this was more than he could take for his first Mafia meeting, and he said he would inform him of the outcome with Dmitry. When Phil tried to pay, Sergey waved him off and said that they should leave; he would leave in a little while. They said good-bye, and with leaden feet of fear left the coffee shop.

Outside, Phil looked at Alfred and said, "Sorry to get you into this mess," but he just shook his head and said that they were all in this together, and they would make the best of it. Phil asked him about Kors and if he thought it would be a good idea to inform him of the new circumstances. At first, Alfred was hesitant, but then suggested that Phil calls Kors prior to the meeting with Dmitry.

He took out his cell phone and dialed the number. After two rings, Kors answered the phone. Phil simply told him he would like to meet him, very soon if possible, because he had some new information. The detective wanted to know more, but Phil told him that he couldn't speak over the phone. That must have sounded very suspicious, but Kors agreed to meet immediately. He asked if he should bring backup, and Phil said no. He told him that he was off duty and was therefore dressed casually. Phil really didn't care; he just wanted to see him as soon as possible. They agreed to meet in Central Park at Seventy-Ninth Street in thirty minutes.

At this point, Phil thought it was best not to return home, since he didn't know if he would be followed. He started seeing ghosts at every street corner; constantly turning around to make sure no suspicious characters were following him. Alfred said that he would go back to the apartment, so if they were followed, they had two leads, and it would probably confuse them.

Phil entered the park a little early, but soon Detective Kors walked up to him, wearing extremely tight jeans, a very fashionable top, and a baseball cap. He wanted to sit next to Phil, who suggested they stroll, because moving around calmed his nerves. At first he was very professional and immediately wanted to know why he had to meet so urgently. Phil thought he should give him a short synopsis, but first he asked if he had an open mind. This made him raise his eyebrows, and a vague smile appeared on the detective's lips.

Phil told him he was gay, and Kors said he knew. Then Phil told him about Good Times, Inc. now he had his full attention. He told Phil that after leaving the apartment, Summers, the older guy, went on and on about "the spoiled fags in the great apartment," and as always, he just had to sit there and listen. Then he looked at Phil and said with a bright smile, "I am not married, I do not have a girlfriend, and I guess it is nowhere in the stars that I will be hitched to a female real soon."

That statement made Phil feel more comfortable, since he knew he had somebody within the NYPD he could talk to and trust. Phil told him that they were a very classy escort service, and sometimes offered in-house service. The clientele was mixed, but most of them were wealthy, if not rich, and some of them were important figures in politics and the business world. Phil said that one of the secrets of their success were the far-above-average escorts, most of them graduate students. Clients were safe with them, and discretion was a priority.

Then Phil told him about Sergey, never using names, of course—about the trips to Europe and the smuggling he had learned earlier this evening. Sergey was telling him all of that, and he was convinced that his boss in Frankfurt had something to do with the killings in front of their building. He also told Kors that earlier, he received a call from somebody named Dmitry who summoned him to the Apple Café, a small coffee shop on Third Avenue. Phil told Kors that Sergey stiffened up when he told him about this meeting but said that most of the goons are called Dmitry, and they are replaced constantly.

Kors listened more carefully, and after taking a note pad from his inside pocket, wrote down the address of the meeting place. Phil told him he wasn't sure if they surveyed the house; they probably knew him, but he just said that Phil should relax. Then Phil told him he was afraid their place was bugged. Phil told the detective how the routine usually works and that the clients spend some time alone in the room to shower and get ready. Kors smiled and remarked that Phil watched too much TV. He reassured him that with everything going on in his life, TV was rather scarce.

Kors promised he would come the following day to check the place, if that would make him feel better. Yes, he told him, it would. While they were walking, he asked if he could make a quick call. "Sure, go right ahead," Phil said.

The detective dialed a number from his call list, and two seconds later, Phil heard him say, "Jeff, have a fun birthday party at Apple Café tonight around ten. Be yourself, and take lots of pictures of you, and try to get as many of the other guests too, especially the guy who will be sitting with a young, good-looking dude wearing," he looked at Phil and continued, "a dark blue sweatshirt and glasses. He has wavy, longish, dark hair." He then said good-bye and hung up. He smiled at Phil and said, "I hope you didn't mind me calling you a good-looking dude, because you are."

Phil blushed and asked him how it felt to work in the police department with all these macho guys. Kors told him it wasn't always easy, but he liked his job, and what he did in private was nobody's business, even if they always bugged him. He then told Phil that his first name was Kevin, and he would be on top of it. If ever Phil wanted, he would come by and check things out, and he promised he would scan the apartment the next day, to see if the bug fear would hold. Before they said good-bye, he requested to call him later, to tell him how the evening went. Phil told him that he could wait at their place; Alfred was there, and he would certainly return immediately after. Kevin said he would think about it, but Phil should call Alfred to tell him that he might be over later.

They went their separate ways. Phil was intending to grab a bite to eat, but somehow his appetite was not there; his stomach was all cramped up from nervousness.

Phil returned home to see if everything was okay, and Alfred told him that he'd had a call but thought it was better to send out then receive here for the time being. He arranged for Jack to make the outcall. Jeffrey was out on a call too; he was booked in the morning. Everything seemed fine. I told Alfred that Detective Kors might come by later to get the news of the meeting. He just smiled and said that he would entertain Kors until my return.

When Phil got to the Apple Café, there were only two elderly couples there. He sat in a remote corner and ordered a soda. The waitress was just putting the drink down when a tall, bearish-looking man entered the place. He came straight toward the table and sat down. "I am Dmitry," was all he said as he waited to give his order. He asked for a beer but no glass, just the bottle.

Once he received his drink and felt unwatched, he started talking. His accent was even stronger now than over the phone. "My boss has observed your business, and he wants to control it." Phil just sat there speechless as he continued. "He is asking to get monthly payments of 10 percent at first and wants to get a copy of the books."

Phil's brain went wild, and he thought this guy was crazy, but when he lifted his jacket and Phil saw a gun he knew that the Dmitry was not joking around. It was then when the door of the calm coffee shop opened, and a group of young people with funny paper hats came storming in. They were laughing and fooling around, which was a wonderful distraction, and Phil had a little breathing time. Dmitry was rather annoyed by the commotion.

The partygoers sat down not too far from them, and when the waitress went to their table, they all showed an ID and ordered beer. The most mature said that it was his friend's twenty-first birthday, and they were celebrating. The waitress threw a quick glance at the IDs and then went back to get the order. They were laughing and kidding around, and Dmitry became more and more pissed and wanted to leave. Phil watched them over his shoulder and saw that two of them took out small cameras and started to take pictures of each other. They tried hard to make funny faces and pretend to have been drinking all day long.

Dmitry tried to continue the conversation. He said that Jeff, one of your employees, was presently with one of his partners, and if Phil didn't agree to the demands, they would do him harm. Phil was quickly thinking who Jeffrey was with; it was a new client, one who came with Sergey's recommendation. It all started to make sense. He got very scared and just wanted to get him out of there. While he was thinking, the guys in the birthday party continued to drink their beers and take photographs. Then he saw one of the guys raise his cell phone and take pictures of Dmitry while he was concentrating on my answer.

Phil asked what he needed to release Jeff. Dmitry said there was not much he needed, just that Phil had to agree to the first step, that his boss would be partner in Good Times, Inc. He said that this was only to show that they could intrude anytime, and if Phil didn't comply with the demands, worse things could happen.

The kids at the next table finished their beers; one guy paid for the round, and with even more noise, they left the place, making us believe they would continue somewhere else. Dmitry seemed relieved. He took his cell phone out of his pocket and in broken English said, "Let him go. All okay here." Then he asked for the check, paid, and stood up. Phil followed like a sheep, and out on the street, he said, "You better do as we say. Remember the shooting in your street? We do not want to do this again." He turned and left, but before he disappeared, he turned around and said, "You will hear from me again real soon. Have a nice night."

Phil stood there for what felt like a very long time before he was able to move. He was in shock, and his head was spinning. As he walked back, he was praying that Kevin Kors would be at his place. He had to talk to somebody; he had to know if this was a bad dream—or worse, reality.

When Phil got to the building, Fred the doorman greeted him with a big smile and remarked that he should get some rest, because he looked exhausted. If he only knew! When he entered the apartment, he heard Kors' voice and felt immediately relieved. Phil went to the living room, where the detective sat on the sofa, talking on his fancy cell phone.

"He's just coming in. Okay, I'll tell him. Thank you. Talk to you soon." He closed the phone and motioned Phil over, but he first went into the kitchen, got some ice cubes, and poured himself a stiff drink. Only then did he sit down.

Alfred came in and with questioning eyes wanted to get all the details. Phil was even more paranoid than before and told him to turn the music up. Then he went into the office and called Jeffrey, who answered immediately. Before he could say anything, Jeffrey started talking. "That was so weird. When I got to the Hyatt, a rather unpleasant-looking guy opened the door. He asked me in and offered me a drink. Then he sat down with a large glass of vodka—not his first, I was convinced, and he started asking me questions. Most of them I couldn't even understand. His English was so bad."

Phil listened and was happy that he was safe, but he didn't stop talking. "Then he started to scratch his crotch, and I was afraid that this was the sign that work would start, but he just sat there while I sipped on my drink. Nothing else happened until the phone rang. He got up and said he changed his mind, and I should go now."

Phil took a deep breath of relieve and told him that everything was prepaid and he got his share nevertheless. He said that he would come by the next day, and they hung up. When Phil looked up he saw Kevin Kors in the doorway, with a curious expression. Phil told him that he spoke to Jeffrey, one of the escorts who was held hostage at the Hyatt while this Dmitry guy was making requests. "When he told me that he was holding Jeffrey, I had no choice but to agree to all his demands." Was all Phil said.

Kevin came over to the desk and showed the pictures on his phone and asked if this was Dmitry. "Yes, this is the weirdo," Phil confirmed, "but what does that do to me? They are after me and don't fear any collateral damage." Phil told him about Dmitry's requests. Kevin listened carefully, and when Phil mentioned that Dmitry more or less confessed that they were responsible for the murders outside, the detective really started to pay attention.

He must have sensed that Phil was afraid. He walked over, took Phil by the arm, and guided him back to the living room and to his drink. He put his arm around Phil's shoulder and promised that he would do all he could to get this settled. Phil told him that his biggest fear was the safety of the guys. How could he send them out to meet anybody without being afraid they could be harmed?

As they were sitting there, the phone rang. I looked at the screen, but it was a blocked number. That wasn't unusual until now, but everything had changed so much within the last twenty-four hours. Phil pushed the talk button and just answered with, "Hello?"

When Phil heard Dmitry's voice, he stiffened. He looked at Kevin and motioned that it was him. Kevin leaned over and tried to listen to the conversation. Dmitry said in a very firm tone, "I am sure that you are clever enough not to tell anything about our deal to the authorities."

Phil didn't react, didn't know what to respond, but Kevin just shook his head, which made him timidly say, "Sure." Then he just wished a good night, but before hanging up, he asked if Jeffrey was okay. Phil said yes, and Dmitry laughed and ended the call. Phil just looked at Kevin, who must have felt the fear and put his arm around Phil's shoulder again. Phil wanted to ask him what he should do, but he felt it was unfair, since at this point there was no answer.

They were just sitting there, and Kevin tried to comfort Phil by saying that Joe, the guy who took the pictures, thought he was cute. Phil smiled; it felt good to get a compliment. He said that the pictures were already sent to NYPD, and they would know more about this Dmitry person the next day. He added that Joe was waiting outside the coffee shop hiding, and when he saw you leaving, he returned to get Dmitry's empty beer bottle so they could try to lift fingerprints. With immigration records, they would soon have a real name.

The day had taken its toll on Phil, and he started to get very tired, his eyes became heavy. Phil told Kevin he would take a quick shower and then go to bed; the detective said he would go the office to see if there were any results and would call him in the morning.

Phil woke up early, stumbled to the coffeemaker, and got his first brew running. With the mug, he sat down at the computer and started opening the e-mails he had neglected the night before. There was nothing out of the ordinary, just the customary ads and a few requests for company. Phil was answering them when Alfred came walking in.

"Good morning," he said. "How are you?"

Phil assured that everything was okay, but he knew that things would not be the same. He was afraid to send anybody out to new clients who did not come with good recommendations.

Alfred also seemed hesitant, and they started to discuss new strategies when the phone rang. It was Kevin, who told Phil that he spoke to his boss, who was initially pissed that they had acted without his permission. But when he saw Dmitry's pictures and all of Kevin's notes from the day before, he was satisfied and calmed down. Kevin received the go-ahead for a bug search in the apartment; a crew would be over around ten, if that was convenient. He then asked if they could meet for coffee at a neutral place. When Phil asked why not here, he said he would explain later.

Just before 10:00, David announced some men from NYPD over the intercom. They came in, unpacked their gear, and started walking around the entire apartment. At first, nothing seemed suspicious, until they reached the master bedroom, and Phil heard one of the guys say "Bingo!" He found one bug in the bedroom and another one in the bathroom. They all laughed, amazed at the old-fashioned devices. But they were there; they couldn't have been planted long ago, and Phil was trying to think who could have put them there.

Phil went back to the books, but none of the guests in the past weeks seemed suspicious. Then he remembered a shy European guy who only came once, and after he came out of the room, he seemed extremely anxious to leave. Phil was convinced that the name in his records was not correct, but he still wrote it down on his note pad, to give to Kevin, along with the date of his visit. After the successful search, Phil offered the guys some coffee while they were giving him some hints and advice. They said they would take all the evidence with them, to check the origin.

After they left, Phil got dressed and headed over to meet Kevin at 3 Guys, a large Greek coffee shop not too far away. He was already sitting there, a large mug in front of him, looking very tired. "You must have had a rough night," Phil commented, sitting across from him in the booth.

He told Phil that he was spending his free night and day at the station. "At first, I took a lot of shit from my superiors because I met you and spent time with you without informing them, but when they saw the results, they mellowed and even congratulated me," he said, between yawning and sipping coffee. He continued that they found the details on "Dmitry," who entered the country two weeks ago. His real name was Gregory Amoff, and he was a Romanian citizen; he had an impressive rap sheet with Interpol for his affiliations with organized crime. As of this day, they could never really prove anything.

What came next left Phil speechless. Kevin said that he was appointed as an undercover agent at Good Times, Inc. Phil guessed his astonished face made him a little nervous. "I won't see clients, but I should move in with you and give the clients the impression that I'm part of the organization. The department already made appointments at the hairdresser; they insist that I change my hair color and get a new look."

Phil was finally recovering and could only say, "But I like the way you look now."

He laughed and just responded that he liked his new boss. He said that somebody would drop off some personal items of his this afternoon, since they wanted to avoid any of the spies seeing him move in with luggage. He said he would probably just be sitting around, monitoring the incoming calls. He assured Phil he would be very discreet and only report suspicious characters. Kevin also added that he would be armed for our protection.

Phil didn't mind him moving in, but the rest was making him very nervous, and he told Kevin so.

"So I guess I have to get some groceries for tonight. I imagine we'll be eating in," Phil said with a nervous smile.

"Yes, I'm looking forward to it. Candles would be nice and a good night's sleep."

In his head, Phil was trying to organize the sleeping arrangements; he thought he would set up a bed for him in the office. Before they left, Kevin said he would be over in the afternoon, and Phil should record all the activities until then; later he would take over.

CHAPTER 12

Back home, it was business as usual. At this point, they had more house and hotel calls, which was fine. The fewer people entering the door, the better, at least for now. Phil made a couple of bookings for the night and the following days. At 4:30, the intercom buzzed, and David announced Martin. Then he whispered into the receiver, "He looks like Detective Kors' younger brother. Weird." Phil asked him to send him up.

He went to the door, and when the elevator opened, a very blond, short-haired version of Kevin emerged. He had to laugh and could just say, "Don't you have a mirror at home?"

Kevin laughed and said that this was the most expensive haircut he'd ever had, and it was all paid by the department. "What did the doorman whisper into the phone?" he requested.

Phil told him, "He thought you were your own weird younger brother."

He asked if Kevin was okay with the sofa bed in the office. He looked at Phil and said, "Well, do I have any other choices?" They sat down, and he started giving instructions. He wanted to attach a device to the phone that made it easy to record and listen in on conversations. Phil had no problem with that, but he told him that with certain clients, this was not necessary. Kevin respected this and said that he could push the button when he thought it was important for the case. Then the detective asked where he could stash his few belongings, and which bathroom he was to use. Phil suggested he share with him, so they would not intrude into the daily routine of the place.

As they made all the arrangements, the phone rang. It was Dmitry, and he asked if Phil had slept on his proposal. He wanted to meet again soon and would need the confirmation. Phil wanted to hang up, but Dmitry said, "Wait, wait." Kevin pushed the recording button. "I need a boy to travel to Germany on the weekend. He has to be reliable, and he has to meet a guy there. Not sure if there will be sex; possible, but not sure. Tell me tomorrow his name. He just has to deliver a package." Then he hung up.

They listened to the recording again, and Kevin looked at me and suggested that this would probably be an undercover job. He said he was sure that nothing would happen here while they had somebody in the field doing a job for them. Phil didn't like this at all, but he had to agree. Kevin said he had to call the department and took out his safe phone.

He called Summers, told him about the call, and then asked if he was permitted to make this trip. Phil sensed that Summers was unhappy, but after a short silence, Kevin said "Okay, call me back and let me know. I have my passport and everything here, but you would have to get the approval from above."

While he was still talking to Summers, Phil's phone rang again, and this time it was a very angry Dmitry on the line. Phil pushed the button and signaled Kevin to hang up. "Didn't I tell you not to call the police, and keep this business between us?" Dmitry screamed through the phone. Phil had to move the receiver away from his ear. "You asshole, you called the police and told them."

Phil tried to calm him down by saying that the police interviewed all parties in the building after the shooting; they were just asking if they noticed anything different, just routine questions.

He was not satisfied, and Phil knew he must have noticed that the bugs were removed but couldn't bluntly say so. He insisted that they did more than just routine questioning and wanted details, but Phil was firm and said that the only thing they did was go through the apartment, interview them, and leave. He tried to sound as innocent as possible, but he knew that Dmitry was not buying it. He slammed the phone down. Phil was shaking and trying to calm down by covering his eyes; Kevin started to massage his shoulders and softly said, "Just relax; I am here to protect you."

Yes, it felt good; Phil felt safe and was slowly loosening up. "I'm just a business major from Westchester. Shit, why me?"

Kevin started laughing. "Well, I guess you picked the wrong line of business."

While they were talking, Kevin's phone rang, and Phil watched him sit up straight. He guessed his boss was on the other side. "Yes, sir, I will do that tomorrow morning first thing. Yes, I will send you all the details tonight. Saturday it will be delivered here?" Then he hung up and said, "Guess we're in. I have to have pictures made for a new passport, which will be ready by the end of the week, so if Dmitry calls, try to stall him until Sunday." He seemed cool about the whole thing, or at least he didn't show any nervousness. Phil was much more agitated about the entire thing, but for Kevin, it seemed fun to work undercover.

The phone rang, and Frederic was on the line, telling Phil that he just got in for a two-day meeting and was horny as hell. He asked if it was too late to come over, and Phil told him to call in ten minutes; he promised to try to arrange something but couldn't guarantee it.

"I guess that's not somebody we have to tape," Kevin said.

Phil told him about Frederic and got up and went to Alfred's room. He knocked on his door, Phil told him about the call, asking if he would still be interested. He just looked up from his books and said, "Well, a great blowjob after all the studying can't hurt. Sure, let's make some money."

When Frederic called back, Phil told him that Alfred would be available. He could imagine how he was beaming on the other side as he excitedly said, "I'm on my way!"

Phil and Kevin heard Alfred get into the shower, when he came out wrapped in a towel he asked. "Can I use the master room? All my books are spread out."

"Sure, no problem."

Kevin was intrigued and started asking questions. Phil told him that the guy was not really good looking, but from what he has heard, he must give the greatest blowjobs ever. Kevin laughed, and with his head shaking, he said, "And he pays for this?"

"Yes, very well, and I haven't seen any of the guys come out with a disappointed face yet."

Alfred looked at Kevin and said, "You want to take him?"

Kevin blushed to a crimson red and said that this was not in his undercover contract, but it sounded tempting. They all laughed, and Phil said if he wanted to take a quick shower, we would just wait here for Frederic and let him make the decision. He could sense that Kevin was intrigued but also nervous, but nevertheless, he went back and took a shower.

When Frederic arrived, they were all comfortably lounging in the living room. Phil introduced him to Martin, Kevin's undercover alias, and he could see in Frederic's face that he was all crazy about him. He asked if he could talk to Phil in private for a second. They went into the office, when he asked how much it would be if he wanted to have a good time with both of them. Phil made a price, and Frederic said, "Deal." Phil told him that Martin was new, and he should probably be patient at first, but he was sure he would loosen up fast. They went back, and Phil told the guys that Frederic would like the company of both of them. They looked at each other and smiled.

They had another short drink together; Phil knew this would loosen Kevin up a little. Then they disappeared into the master bedroom. Phil had finally some quiet time to dedicate to his studies. Carlos called and said that he was home and everything went well with his client. Phil made it a new rule that all the escorts had to call in after their jobs. He told them that this was not to check on them, only to make sure they were home safe. He always made a note of the time when they called. For the first time in quite some time, Phil felt relaxed. He knew that the guys in the next room were probably having a great time, and he was listening to some soft music and getting prepared for the next day.

Phil must have dozed off over the books when he heard the two guys coming out of the bedroom. They whispered and giggled, and he went out and told them to go and put on robes. For the first time, he saw Kevin naked; it was a very pleasant sight. He had a beautiful, hairless body; he could see that he worked out regularly. His equipment was above average. They were all sitting in the living room when Frederic came out freshly showered and with a priceless smile on his face. "Can I have a drink?" he asked, sitting down with them. Phil could see that he was a very satisfied client.

After a little while, he said that jet lag was forcing him to leave now, but he would probably be back before flying back to Frankfurt and would love to repeat tonight's experience. He quickly came back into the office to settle his account, and on his way out, he gave both guys a nice tip. Kevin blushed again; guess he had not yet realized that he was entering the career of an escort. Phil told him that it was an absolute rule that nothing of this ever leaves these rooms, and discretion was one of the main rules of the house. Phil could see that Kevin wanted to tell him about what happened, but the boss simply told him that he hoped he enjoyed it, but preferred not to know too many details. Phil gave him and Alfred their shares, and when Kevin saw the cash in his hand, he was amazed.

Phil opened the sofa bed in the office, said good night, and went to his room, hoping he could get a good night's sleep.

The next morning, everything seemed perfect. Phil had given little thought about all that was troubling him in the past days, until he was confronted with the bitter reality by Dmitry's phone call. He was informed that the person would have to fly on Sunday; he would be handed an envelope at the airport, and he would have to deliver it on the other side as instructed upon his arrival. He asked about the details of the escort, and Phil told him that it would most probably be Martin, but he still had to ask if he was willing. He then asked what else was requested of him, but Dmitry said that these details were not yet available to him, but he would let him know.

Phil was just finishing the call when Kevin appeared in the door with a mug in his hand. "Any news?" Phil told him that he would be traveling on Sunday with Lufthansa to Frankfurt, but he was still awaiting further details. He had to deliver an envelope, content unclear, probably very important, since they would not trust it to any other courier.

"Is there more expected of me?" Kevin asked, and Phil told him that this was not yet known, but asked if it would be a problem. By Kevin's reaction, he figured he was pretty relaxed about it. He sat down across from Phil, and the boss felt that he wanted to tell him something.

"What is it?" he asked when Kevin said he was aware that it was company policy not to talk about work, but he had to talk about it, and he was the only one he could talk to.

"If NYPD ever found out about last night, I would be done, but I have to admit that it's been a fantasy of mine, and it felt good."

Phil promised him that he would never request him to do anything he didn't feel comfortable with, but he knew from the others that Frederic was a perfect gentleman and probably his best introduction to the trade.

Kevin got dressed and left for his appointment with the photographer. Phil stayed behind, hoping the phone wouldn't ring too frequently; every time it rang, he was afraid it could be one of the goons, making new requests. Things seemed to calm, and everything was pretty normal. Saturday afternoon, Frederic called and asked if he could have a repeat of the other day. Phil asked him to hold for a minute while he asked the two guys.

Kevin beamed and said, "I'm fine with it if you are, Alfred."

It was a go, and Phil confirmed the date with Frederic. In the evening, the new passport was delivered in the name of Martin James Hopper, all the other data was authentic. Martin sat down and started to experiment with possible signatures. The guys got ready for Frederic while Phil tidied the place a little. At 8:00, the intercom buzzed. Phil's first thought that the 9:00 must be early, but when he heard Fred say that Mr. Dmitry wanted to see him, he nearly dropped the receiver. Phil ran into the bathroom to tell Alfred and then Kevin to stay out of sight. Then quickly hid the phone recording gear and tried to put on a relaxed face. He went to the door, and the goon was already standing there. He walked in without invitation and dropped himself on the sofa.

"Nobody here?" he asked.

Phil looked around, shrugged, and said, "I don't see anybody."

"Don't be smart-ass, boy. I want to know who is going to Frankfurt tomorrow. Give me name and what he looks like."

Phil told him that the person was Martin Hopper; he is six feet tall with short, blond hair. "You will tell him I meet him outside check-in and give him the package. There will also be a letter with instructions. He has to read it only in the plane."

"What is in the package?" Phil asked, not really expecting an honest answer. Dmitry just looked at him and gave him a dirty smile. "I just wanted to know if it was anything dangerous and if he would have problems taking it through security." Dmitry shook his head. He gave the impression that their business was completed and then got up and handed a bundle of cash, saying that should cover the expenses.

Phil thanked him, and as they walked toward the door, he asked, "How big is the package?"

He just wanted to shut Phil up, but he was faster and said, "Just so I know what kind of luggage he has to take with him." This sounded like a genuine request, and he said it would just be a large Jiffy bag; he motioned with his hands the approximate size.

On the threshold, he turned around. "Don't fuck this up. It would be very bad for you and all your guys. If this Martin guy does all we request, he will be back safe by Tuesday afternoon."

Phil pushed the elevator button, and when the door opened and the goon was inside, his knees nearly gave in. He rushed back into the apartment, where Kevin was hiding behind the door. "This is one unpleasant fucking dude," he noted. Phil couldn't disagree at all. He showed him the stack of cash he left for expenses, and Kevin quickly grabbed it and declared it evidence.

Phil looked at him with amazement and said, "It's probably me who is paying for his ticket tomorrow in this case."

He smiled and said that G. T. could easily spring it, and he would invest his share of tonight's take to the trip.

"I need a drink badly right now," Phil announced. He went into the kitchen and came back with a hefty scotch on the rocks.

Phil was still relaxing on the sofa when Frederic was announced, but the two guys were sweet and said they would greet him at the door, and he should just stay calm. Phil loved how Kevin was going along with the situation; he had the impression he started enjoying his new role. Phil certainly loved his company, and he sometimes lusted after him. When the three guys walked into the living room, Frederic came up to Phil and greeted him with two kisses on his cheeks. Phil asked him to sit down, and Alfred served drinks. It was Saturday night, and nothing else was on the books, so Phil thought some company would be nice; but he felt that Frederic was anxious to enjoy his adventure, so he was again left alone with his problems.

He went into his room and turned on the TV, but it was hard to concentrate. He was constantly thinking about the people in the next room, and for the first time, he experienced a kind of jealousy. Phil sat there watching something of no importance and thinking of Kevin having fun. He got angry at himself, involving him in the game, and especially thinking that he was so removed and superior. Phil felt sorry for himself, angry and restless. He was sure that they would be busy for some time and decided to cool down by walking around the block a couple of times.

He got dressed, left a note where he knew Alfred would find it, and left the apartment. When he got to the street, a cool breeze welcomed him. It felt great; he felt free. He started walking toward the park, but in his head, he couldn't forget what was going on in the apartment right now. Phil was unhappy and jealous, he was afraid that he was falling in love with Kevin. And what was worse, he knew that he was going to send him off the next day to do something dangerous. Phil was miserable. The cold air helped, until he had the distinct feeling that he was being followed. He turned another corner and waited in a dark doorway when he saw Dmitry pass by. He must have thought that he lost him; Phil saw him walking faster to catch up. Once he saw him disappear, he continued at a leisurely pace.

Phil knew he would catch up with him, but in the meantime, he probably had a shitty time. Phil was aware being watched, this didn't make him feel good, but he hoped that once Kevin returned from Frankfurt, things would be normal again, at least for some time.

Phil returned home and didn't feel his shadow following him anymore. When he got upstairs, the note was still in the same place, and the guys were still in the master bedroom. This did not make things any easier, but at least he was feeling better. Phil went into the office and did some work; later, the door opened, and Kevin came walking in, dressed in a robe. He walked around the desk, grabbed Phil by the shoulders, and said, "Are you okay?"

He nodded and continued his work. Soon after, he heard Alfred and Frederic in the next room. Kevin was still with me, and when Phil tried to get up, he held him down, lowered his face, and kissed him on the cheek. Phil fell back in his chair, not knowing what was happening to him. Kevin left the room and joined the party next door. Phil felt as the host, he had to join them, and when he entered the room, Alfred and Frederic were joking together. When Kevin's eyes met Phil's, his bright smile made him feel like a million dollars.

They all sat down, and Frederic told us he would fly back the next day. It went through Phil's head that he might be on the same plane as Kevin, which was not good. He didn't want any association at the airport, but luckily he was flying with Singapore Airlines, while Kevin was on Lufthansa. Kevin sensed that he shouldn't mention his trip, and when Frederic got up, they wished him a great trip and hoped to see him soon.

Alone again, and after a few confirmation calls that all the guys were safe, Phil was exhausted and decided that he would be bad company anyway, so he left and went to bed. He heard Alfred and Kevin cleaning up and soon fell into a blissful sleep. He had a dream from which he didn't want to wake up. Kevin was next to him and whispering in his ear, "I think I love you," and he felt strong arms holding him. Phil was very happy, and he was convinced he saw himself smiling in his dream. He felt comfortable and protected, and he was sure that this was the most wonderful dream he ever had.

He woke up the next morning alone and sad, but the memories of the dream made it a great morning. It was late, but Phil knew the others were still asleep, and tried to be as quiet as possible. Pouring his first cup of coffee he noticed Kevin standing behind him wearing a big smile. When he asked how Phil slept, the boss blushed and told him it was wonderful, and mentioned that he had only good dreams. Kevin produced an even wider smile and helped himself to a cup of coffee. As Phil walked to the living room, he looked at Kevin and suddenly wasn't sure anymore if it was only a dream, but he didn't want to spoil his hopes.

They both sat down, holding their mugs and pretending they weren't in the mood to talk, but there was tension in the room. When

Phil got up for a refill, Kevin grabbed his leg, and when Phil looked down, the detective said, "I think I love you."

This isn't a dream anymore. What's going on here? Phil was confused, but robotically he leaned forward and started kissing him. "I have to get a refill," Phil said, blushing as he quickly left for the kitchen. He was confused, torn between reality and the dream. He couldn't determine what was more real, and he wanted to run back to the living room and tell him that he felt the same, but couldn't. He was here to protect them; he was not here to fall in love with him. He was scheduled to go on a dangerous mission later today, and if all went according to plans, he would probably move out, get his natural hair color back, and soon forget the days they spent together. Phil was holding on to the counter, staring into a kitchen cabinet.

"This is wrong," Phil said softly to himself. When he heard, "What's wrong?" He tensed from shock; he was sure he was alone. When he turned around, Phil saw Alfred standing there.

Alfred just smiled and said, "No, it's not wrong; let go and accept. I feel it'll be wonderful, so don't fight it."

Phil handed him a cup and left the kitchen. When he got out, Kevin was gone. Phil was disappointed but also relieved that he didn't see him at this confused moment. He heard the shower running in his bathroom and, remembering Alfred's words, he walked in, got undressed, and stepped into the shower. Kevin greeted him with the most welcoming smile he had ever seen. They held each other while the water ran over their naked bodies. Phil searched for Kevin's lips, which were ready to be found; they kissed and kissed until their skin started to wrinkle. Phil turned off the water and said, "Now I know." He looked at him questioningly but didn't get the expected response. No more was said; they got dressed and decided to have brunch somewhere in the neighborhood.

On their way back to the apartment, Kevin held Phil's shoulders and looked him in the eyes, saying, "When I was holding you last night in your sleep, I felt better than ever before. Can I see you again when I get back from Frankfurt?"

It was a real dream, Phil thought, and he could only nod and give him a faint kiss on his cheek in the middle of the street. They arrived home, and the tension was unbearable. Phil wanted to kiss him, to hold him, certainly not to send him off on his mission, but he knew that he had no say in the matter.

Kevin threw a few things into his bag and with sad eyes said, "I will grab a cab for the airport."

They hugged, and Phil felt compelled to say, "I am waiting, and I hope you will be here with me on Tuesday. I think I love you too." They kissed again, and he left.

CHAPTER 13

Comfortably dressed, Kevin arrived at JFK with only one bag. When he opened the door of the cab, Dmitry was already standing there. Kevin had received complete instructions from Summers: first, he had to play ignorant; Dmitry was to approach him; then he would take the Jiffy bag so that one of the other undercover agents could take a good look at it before he put it in his carry-on bag. Everything seemed smooth so far. Dmitry, in his humorless voice, told him that in the separate, smaller envelope, he wrote down all the instructions, but these were only to be read once the plane was airborne. Kevin put this in the inside pocket of his sports jacket. He felt that there were more people watching him but gave the impression that everything was peanuts and he had it under control.

When he proceeded to the check-in counter to get his boarding pass, he noticed that the man behind him in line was holding a Romanian passport. He got his desired seat and proceeded to the security check. He was told to forget to remove his belt, so when he passed the scanner, it would alarm the security officer. He dropped off his bag on the belt and proceeded. As intended, the buzzer went off, and the man in uniform asked him to step aside. Since it was one of the busiest periods, he asked him to collect his bag and then step into the small cubicle for additional scanning. He pulled a curtain.

Kevin knew that Summers would be hiding in there and exchanging the Jiffy bag with a similar one. Everything went very swiftly; when he left the booth, the Romanian passenger was there, but he seemed satisfied seeing Kevin leave the compartment with his bag and all cleared by the authorities. Kevin moved quickly away, hoping that his shadow would follow him and Summers could leave the booth unseen.

The flight was announced to be delayed forty-five minutes, due to late arrival of the plane. This was arranged to give the FBI more time to inspect the envelope before returning it. Kevin sat in a quiet corner of the business-class lounge and took out a book from his bag. He did it so obviously that he first had to take the Jiffy bag out for all to see that it was there, taking his book and replacing the envelope and zipping up the bag. He was not exactly sure where his shadow sat, but he was convinced he was not far.

Finally the flight was called for boarding, and Kevin proceeded to the gate. When he entered the plane, with the goon three people behind him, he asked the flight attendant if he could use the bathroom quickly and moved uncomfortably to indicate that he felt tremendous pressure. Before he proceeded to his seat, he disappeared into the toilet. There, as instructed, he found the original Jiffy bag stashed in a small storage cabinet used for the replacement toilet paper and put it back in his carry-on. He then left the replacement there for somebody to clear out soon.

When he opened the door, he saw the goon checking him out, but Kevin just smiled at him. He was not surprised to find this unpleasant man to be his neighbor for the next few hours. Kevin took out his phone and typed a message: *Hi, Phil. sitting in the plane. Very nice here in business class. Guess I have a pleasant neighbor. See you soon, love, Martin.* He clicked *send* and closed the phone. After the plane was finally airborne, the flight attendants started to serve drinks, and it took a large vodka for Martin's neighbor to finally loosen up and introduce himself as Dmitry.

Oh, another one, he thought and introduced himself as Martin. After the plane reached cruising altitude, Kevin got up and went back to the bathroom to read his instruction letter. He opened the white envelope and started reading the typed page.

> *I hope you still have the package. Upon arrival a driver with a sign with your name on will be expecting you in the arrival hall. Have him take you to your hotel. Check in and wait for further instructions.*

"That's it?" There was nothing more; Kevin was disappointed. He took another paper out about a second hotel closer to the airport where he was supposed to move after the delivery. He was not allowed to go back to the original place. He was supposed to let the flight attendant know where he would go, so Interpol could make arrangements on the other side. He scribbled on a piece of paper, *I don't know name of hotel; will be met at the airport and dropped off there.* When he left the restroom, the goon was outside, waiting to go in. Kevin gave him a smile, which was not returned. That was good timing; he could slip the flight attendant the note and return to his seat.

Kevin awoke from a short snooze by the captain's announcement that they would be landing soon and that they were able to make up the delay thanks to a great tail wind.

Upon arrival, everything was smooth. Kevin took his bag and exited the plane. The attendant wished him a good stay in Frankfurt. Passing customs was easy; Dmitry was always close. When he stirred toward the green exit, an agent asked him over and inquired if he had anything to declare. Kevin shook his head but then was politely asked to open his bag for a quick inspection. Kevin did as asked, and over his shoulder saw how Dmitry had put on a nervous and angry face. They browsed through the contents, closed the bag, and wished Kevin a nice stay. Dmitry's face relaxed, and he followed at a safe distance. Outside was a large crowd of people awaiting other passengers. Kevin saw a number of dark-suited limo drivers holding name boards. When he saw his alias's name, he approached the guy with a smile. "Are you Mr. Hopper?" the driver asked politely with a heavy German accent.

Kevin nodded, and the two left for the exit. "Can I carry your bag?" the man asked, but Kevin told him that he could manage very well himself. A large, black BMW left the airport, heading toward downtown Frankfurt. Kevin turned on his phone and wrote an SMS to Phil: *Hi, dear. Safe in Frankfurt. All is well. Talk soon.* When he turned around, he got the feeling that he was being followed, but this time it was not Dmitry; the guys looked like German secret agents. He was hoping that they would be from his camp and felt a little more relaxed.

The chauffeur was trying to make polite conversation, and Kevin had the impression that he was just a hired driver who had nothing to do with rest of them. He concentrated more along the way and tried to read as many street signs as possible. Bleichstrasse, a busy main road, led into Konrad Adenauer Strasse, where the journey came to an end in front of the NH Hotel.

"We have arrived," the driver said with a smile. Then he inquired if Kevin would need transportation back soon. Kevin asked him for his number and promised to call when he knew his plans.

In the lobby, he walked up to the reception desk, and the clerk asked him if he had reservations. He gave his name and was checked in without being asked for any ID. He took his keycard, walked toward the elevator, and went up to his room. There he threw his bag on the bed and headed to the bathroom when the room phone rang. *They're not wasting any time,* he thought and picked up.

"Hello, Martin. Welcome to Frankfurt." The voice was American, which was a wonderful relief for Kevin. "How is your room? I just wanted to tell you that James and I are in the lobby bar; you're not alone." Kevin thanked him and hung up. He felt better knowing that he was not all by himself.

He heard a knock at the door, and a voice called out, "Room service!" He opened the door, and a woman handed him some towels. While unfolding one, she showed him a recording device and asked if everything was to his satisfaction. Kevin nodded and thanked her. He placed the towels in the bathroom, left the door open, and went back into the bedroom.

"Okay, guys, I'm ready. Let's get this over with," he said to himself. After a few minutes, he thought that a nice shower would be appropriate, and since he was just waiting anyway, he might as well go ahead. He opened his bag, took the Jiffy envelope out, and deposited it in the room's safe. Then he went into the bathroom and checked out all the amenities, he had to leave his things home, traveling only with a carry-on. All he needed was available to him, so he undressed and let the water run. He carefully placed the bugged towel on the side and was soon relaxing under the stream of hot water. *I wish Phil were here with me,* he thought, putting gel all over his body. The thought of Phil gave him an erection, and while soaping his chest, he started rubbing himself. His imagination became very active, and soon he was so excited that he squirted a large load against the shower stall. His entire body shivered with excitement, and he felt much better now. He rinsed off and walked out to hear the phone ring.

"We are coming up. Do you have it?" a very unpleasant voice demanded.

"Can you give me a minute? I'm just getting out of the shower," Kevin answered.

The reply was, "I don't give a shit," and the line went dead.

Kevin rushed around, trying to assemble some fresh clothes; he heard a loud knocking on the door. "One minute, please." He rushed into the bathroom and grabbed the robe. Then he opened the door to find three men standing there. One was Dmitry, who looked at Kevin as if he was seeing him for the first time.

They walked in without waiting for an invitation, and the boss went over to the armchair and sat down. "Where is it?" he asked in a determined voice that made Kevin aware that these guys were not playing around.

"I put it in the safe. One moment."

The boss asked, "Any problems?"

Kevin looked at Dmitry and said, "No, but I am sure you know that." He could see that the boss was not in the mood to socialize, and he would be happy when they would be gone again. He tightened his belt and walked to the safe, where he pushed the four-digit code and took the envelope out. He walked over to the boss and handed it to him.

The goon looked at it first and then ripped it open and peeked into it. Kevin couldn't see what it contained. The boss handed it over to one of his guys, who made it disappear into his briefcase. Kevin was hoping that this would be the end of it, but the boss said that Dmitry would like to spend some time with him. The other two got up and left the room. Kevin was very uncomfortable; he considered telling his guest that a few minutes ago, he had masturbated in the shower, hoping the guy would lose interest, but Dmitry was not showing any signs of leaving.

"I just want a good blowjob. I'm not gay, just very horny, and people say men give good blowjobs."

Kevin wasn't sure if he should feel relieved by this development, but when Dmitry stood up, opened his belt, and dropped his pants, he knew there was no escape route.

"Take off your robe," he ordered. Kevin, in a state of shock, obeyed. Dmitry waved him over and pushed Kevin onto his knees. "I have washed after trip," he said, and Kevin could still smell the scent of fresh soap.

At least there's that, he thought, and he slowly started licking the growing penis in front of him. He was trying to think only of nice things as he worked fast and furiously, hoping that would bring all this to a swift end.

Dmitry seemed very close when he yanked Kevin's head back. "Not so fast. I want to enjoy this," he said.

Kevin was starting to be okay with it, but when Dmitry told him he couldn't make a mess and therefore wanted Kevin to swallow his full load, paranoia came back. Now he wanted this over and done soon, so he could go on with his life. He engulfed the large penis again and promised himself not to let go until he finished this guy off. Dmitry was very excited, and the wet lips around his manhood and the furious tongue movement soon made him gush out a tremendous flow of semen, which filled Kevin's orifice to the rim, but he tried to keep all in there.

Dmitry was breathing heavily, and for the first time, Kevin thought the guy had a smile on his face. He took a towel and emptied his mouth's contents into it; he was too revolted to swallow. Dmitry didn't notice or care anymore; he was satisfied and soon stood up and pulled his pants up and went toward the door. On the threshold, he turned and said, "I might be back for more. That was good."

After the door locked, Kevin rushed back into the bathroom and started brushing his teeth like never before, gargling with mouthwash until the bottle was empty. Then he took his cell phone and typed a message: *Dear Phil, Just had a lousy experience but will get over it. At hotel. I will call your friend, but if you can, call me want to hear your voice. Love, M.*

He started to look for Horst's number, which Phil had given him before leaving. He thought it would be better to call from downstairs.

The phone rang. "Hello?" he said timidly, but when he heard Phil's voice, he was ecstatic. He didn't know where to start, but it was unimportant, since it was just the voice and the banalities that counted at this very moment. When Phil asked about the bad experience, Kevin just said that it could wait until he was back. He didn't want to talk about this now; time was too precious. Phil told him that he had called Horst, and he would be at the bar downstairs in forty-five minutes. At the end of their conversation, Phil begged, "Please be back soon. I miss you."

They hung up, and Kevin felt miles better. He looked around and thought of not coming back here, but how would he do this?

He got dressed and went downstairs. The elevator door opened, and the third goon, the one who never said a word, was sitting there, throwing a smile at Kevin, who walked toward the bar. He sat down on an empty stool and ordered a much-deserved drink. He was staring at his glass when a guy in his forties, sitting there alone as well, asked, "Are you American?"

Kevin looked up and nodded. "Just arrived today, but I'll be leaving again soon."

The other guy got up and moved closer, making it look like two compatriots meeting abroad. He stretched out his hand and introduced himself. "Hi, I am James."

Kevin looked up and smiled, saying, "I'm Martin." They got involved in some casual bar talk; then James said he really disliked this hotel, and if he were Martin, he would move soon to a safer place. Kevin got the hint and said he would, but there was somebody in the lobby trying to prevent this from happening.

"Oh, forget your stuff. Just go out for dinner and never come back."

Kevin told James he was expecting a friend, and they would probably go out together, and he might just do that. Then James said that Ed was at another hotel in suite 1304, and he would certainly let Kevin crash there for a night or so. They always laughed in between, so the goon who was trying to pick up some of their conversation just thought they were making stupid small talk. Soon after, a stunning guy walked into the bar and went straight up to the two.

"Martin?"

Kevin beamed. "Yes! Horst?"

They shook hands, and Kevin introduced Horst to James, a fellow American. They ordered more drinks and soon were laughing and having a good time. James then said he would suggest they have dinner in a restaurant close by. It was convenient to get there, and the specialty was a perfect back door. They all laughed again when James got up and said that he had to meet friends, but they might meet later again. Kevin and Horst stayed a little longer and then agreed to go to the suggested place.

Kevin said he would get his jacket from upstairs and be back in a minute. Horst lounged around until Kevin came back, dressed to go out. The two left the lobby, quickly shadowed by somebody else, possibly another Dmitry. Kevin felt safe telling Horst a little about his reason for being here, and when Horst tried to suggest another restaurant, he told him they had to go to this one, because after dinner, he would have to escape. He would not return to the hotel but stay at another place at the airport, all arranged by the FBI and Interpol.

"Wow, that is exciting!" was all Horst had to add to this.

They arrived at the restaurant, which was pretty empty, allowing them to pick a table that gave them some privacy. Kevin was convinced that very soon they would have company, but before he sat down, he excused himself to go the men's room. He wanted to check out the situation before the other guys arrived. Horst sat down and started studying the menu. Kevin came back and sat across from him.

They were making small talk when two men entered, two new faces, Kevin noticed, and when the waiter went over to them with the menus and grabbed their attention, Kevin took a quick shot with his camera phone. They ordered typical German dishes; the portions were huge, but Kevin finally found his long-lost appetite. The place started filling up, and soon no table was vacant. They talked a lot, and whenever the name Phil came up, Kevin got all sentimental. Horst had to smile, and when they ordered dessert, he said, "I think you have to rush back and talk to Phil. He is a great guy."

While Kevin and Horst had a lot of fun, the two men who sat across the restaurant seemed rather annoyed and were hoping that they could get out soon. Kevin also started contemplating how they could disappear. The waiter came up to them and said that in a few minutes, a large group of guests would arrive; there would be a lot of commotion in the place, and they would offer a great shield for an escape. Kevin looked up in amazement, but the waiter just blinked and said that everything was taken care of.

"That's a first—being treated to dinner by the FBI," Horst said with a big smile on his face. Sure enough, first three, then five, then even more people came in. They all gathered around the large center table and shielded the goons from Horst and Kevin. They looked at each other and then searched for the waiter, who gave them the go-ahead. They got up, and seconds later, they were on a dark back street. Horst tried to get his direction and then motioned to the left, where he knew they could easily catch a cab.

The entire escape took less than three minutes, and the two were safely speeding toward the Sheraton Hotel, at to the airport. They walked in and went straight to the elevator and up to the thirteenth floor. Kevin knocked on 1304, and a tall, good-looking black guy opened the door. "Ed?" Kevin asked. "I'm Martin, and this is Horst. We were told to come here."

Ed opened the door for them to enter. The TV was on in the living room; two doors led to bedrooms. "Welcome. Glad you made it. We were waiting until you two were safe before we wanted to close the trap," he said. "The two guys from the restaurant are already in custody, the one in the hotel too, and now we are working on the others."

"What did I take over?" Kevin asked.

Ed said, "There was very important information on microchips and some less-important papers about the research on a pain medication that went wrong in a lab. It has tremendous potential to become a new, powerful hallucinogen and possibly a very dangerous designer drug. The production is easy and inexpensive, once you have the components. If this hit the streets anywhere, it would lead to disaster. The company that created this poison thought it had all destroyed, but somebody must have been faster, and they were able to recover nearly all the data, which is now in the possession of this group. They were only missing the last bits of the formula, and you delivered it to them. If we don't act fast, this shit could hit the market in a few weeks, and once it's out, there would be no way to stop it. One of the very possible side effects is that it will create internal bleeding, and no cure would be available. The victims would rot with tremendous pain from inside."

"These guys don't care, and they know that there would be enough junkies out there who would take the risk for an extra kick. Circulation would be very easy, since they could make it look like an ordinary aspirin."

Horst and Kevin sat in disbelief. Questions arose in Kevin, "Why didn't they just overnight the stuff? Why use me as courier?"

Ed explained that the X-ray machines at these shipping companies were sometimes very strong, and it could destroy the data.

"Why didn't they change the formula I took over at the airport?" Kevin asked.

"Two reasons. For one, they didn't have enough time between the find and your takeoff, and second, if they found out there was some manipulating done, you and everyone around you would have been in very serious danger." He then added that the reading of these chips required very sophisticated software, which was certainly not available at JFK. Ed told Kevin that he knew all about Good Times, Inc., and they were not interested in the little organization, but they knew that the clan had been spying on them for some time and thought they would be the perfect tool for the distribution once they had the pill.

"It was good that this Phil Sherwin contacted you and that he had sufficient trust to give you all the details. Oh, by the way, we are holding a few guys in New York too, and somebody called Sergey is singing like a bird.

"I've heard about this person," Kevin said, and added that he was a regular client of Good Times, Inc.

"Yes, this was probably why the boss, who we don't yet know by name, had him under wraps," Ed finished.

At this point, Kevin had nothing more on his mind than going home. He was told that they had changed his flight to Singapore Airlines early the next morning. They wanted to get him back before anyone could find him.

Ed looked at Horst and asked, "How are you, are you okay?"

Horst was a little taken by surprise and said this all sounded very scary. Ed said that there was a group of Interpol guys in the hotel too, and he should talk to them, because they were tailing him for his protection since he returned from New York a few months back. Horst became very nervous, but Ed just said not to worry; they were fully aware of everything that was going on and had no interest in his activities, but they were interested in talking to him.

"You want me to call them and go and see them or have me ask them to come here?" This was pretty definite, and he had little choice, but he decided that he would like to remain here and have somebody talk to him in the now-familiar surroundings. Ed went to the phone and dialed a four-digit number and in accented German told the guys that Horst was ready to listen, but they should come to 1304. While they were waiting Ed offered them a beer, which was greatly appreciated.

Just a few minutes later, they heard a loud knocking on the door. Ed got up, peeked through the spy hole, and then opened the door. There stood two tall, very German-looking guys. Kevin saw a wide smile on Horst's face, and when the guys approached, he said in German, "Nice seeing you again."

The other guy laughed and blushed a little. To keep everyone in the game, they agreed to converse in English. Ed nodded appreciatively. Gunter explained that they were following Horst for the past few months, and once they ended up in a gay bar and started a conversation, they had a very nice time and lots of laughs. While he explained this, he looked at Horst, who approved of everything he heard.

"Okay, enough sweet talk here," Ed interrupted. "Gunter told us that at this very moment, while we're having a beer, they are very busy in the main station. They've arrested sixteen goons, all with fake papers and long records. They call it the bust of busts at this point, but so far they're still not sure if they erased the entire organization. We have the name of the killer in New York, thanks to the wimp who asked you for favors at the hotel."

Gunter looked at Kevin, who felt the bad taste in his mouth coming back. He took the bottle and rinsed again. Gunter thanked the FBI for their help; they established that the main branch of the organization was in Germany. The New York clan was only providing the material but wasn't really organized within. All the information came from the person they called the Boss, who was now in a high-security cell downtown. Interpol suspected that there were still some on the loose and therefore gave Horst the option to leave with Kevin the next day for New York until they felt safe that all of them were deactivated.

Horst looked at Kevin, who started to feel the magnitude of all this. Gunter said that he had talked to the FBI heads in New York, and they would like to keep Martin, the undercover man, alive for some more time. Kevin wasn't sure if he liked this or not, but at least he could stay with Phil, which was all he cared about at this moment.

Horst said that he had nothing with him to leave town, but Gunter made clear if he was taking the option to go to New York he would have to leave the following morning and could not return to his place. "I'm sure you can get everything in New York. You will have some credit to buy clothes and other things."

Horst was thinking hard. "Okay, but this is a return flight you are giving me?" Then he remembered that he had no passport, and said that they would never let him through immigration in the US. Gunter suggested that he give them an apartment key and tell them where he keeps his passport, and they will send it to him in a couple of days, when the coast was clear. What concerns the immigration Ed would organize to have them both picked up at the plane and bypass the immigration routine.

Gunter looked at Kevin and Horst and said, "Do we have a deal?"

They looked at each other and simultaneously said, "Okay!"

Gunter took two tickets and boarding passes out of his pocket and gave these to them. "You have to be there at 7:45 tomorrow morning. Flight leaves at 8:20." He seemed relieved, one less problem in Frankfurt. "I guess you should get some sleep now. Departure is just across the walking bridge downstairs; it takes you ten minutes." He then got up to leave. He said to Ed, "Will I be seeing you tomorrow in town?"

Ed nodded, and they left. Kevin finished his beer while Horst went next door to get ready for bed. When Kevin entered the room,

Horst came out of the bathroom freshly showered, with a white towel wrapped around his waist. Kevin was very tired after the trip and all the adventures, so he took a shower and jumped into bed himself. He wished Horst a good night and immediately drifted into dreamland.

Horst was still nervous and thinking about what would happen while he was gone, but he came to accept the idea of going to New York. He looked at Kevin and suddenly had the strong urge to touch him and to find comfort with him. He positioned himself so that he could hold him, and with an incredible erection, fell asleep as well. They were still intertwined when Ed knocked on the door and called them to get up.

When they got out, Ed had some coffee brewed and gave them final instructions, saying that they would be met on the plane in New York by Sarah. Kevin was still not fully functional, and in his state of confusion asked if Ed had more information on the arrests. Ed said not really, but they should get the newspaper; he was sure they made headlines.

They said good-bye and left. After crossing the footbridge that linked the hotel to the terminal, they spotted the sign for Singapore Airlines and proceeded through security. They were asked to go directly to the plane, because Interpol was checking if anybody was following them. When they got to the gate, one of the staff members came up to them and asked if they were Martin Hopper and Horst Schreiber. "Please follow me," he said. On the way to the plane, the flight attendant turned around and said that they were probably exhausted from the past days. Kevin and Horst looked at each other in amazement not knowing that they made already headlines in the papers.

"Now, everything is safe, no worries, but Singapore Airlines would like to make your trip as relaxing as possible, and has therefore taken the liberty to upgrade you both into first class."

That was a nice surprise. There were only eight places; you couldn't even call them seats anymore. It was luxurious, and the attention given was overwhelming. They were the first on board, and immediately a very delicate-looking flight attendant wanted to serve them a glass of champagne. "Could we have coffee instead?" Horst asked politely.

Before he finished the sentence, the girl was gone, and seconds later, she appeared with two beautiful settings and a silver pot of coffee. They sat down, and another person brought them a large selection of newspapers. Kevin quickly grabbed the *International Herald Tribune,* while Horst picked the *Frankfurter Allgemeine.* Both had similar headlines. "Organized crime busted by FBI and Interpol" read the English paper, while the German version read *"Internationaler Verbrecherring durch Interpol und FBI zerschlagen."* The guys were immediately deep in the articles. There was little they didn't know yet, but the English paper was more hesitant and feared that there were still some cells operational, while the Germans were pretty optimistic that they got to the core. Both papers agreed that the criminals were not very sophisticated, but they didn't hesitate to brutally eliminate anybody who was in their way. The proof was the Upper East Side murders.

The plane left on time, and Kevin and Horst felt like kings as they enjoyed the pampering by the crew. They were very disappointed when the captain announced their imminent arrival in New York; this treat was making up for so much they had endured over the past few days. Upon leaving the aircraft, a female agent greeted them and asked them to follow her. She knew that Horst had no passport and simply slipped him a piece of paper that he had to sign and return when leaving the country again.

CHAPTER 14

A black Lincoln Town Car brought Kevin and Horst to
Manhattan, where Phil was nervously anticipating their early
arrival. David greeted them at the door and asked if they read
the paper today. "They caught the guys from the shooting," he said
with some pride in his voice, as if he had been part of the procedure.

Upstairs, Phil ran to the door when he heard the keys, and when
he saw Kevin standing there, there was no stopping him. He went over,
embraced him strongly, and kissed him passionately. Kevin was very
happy that the ice was broken and responded with equal vigor.

"Hey, you two lovebirds, can't you just let your guest pass before
you make out in the hall?" Horst said with a laugh, pushing himself past
them. They let go of each other, but from this moment on, it was clear
that this has developed into more than just an undercover arrangement.

They all went to the living room, where Kevin and Horst told Phil
about the great trip back and gave details of the past couple of days in
Frankfurt. After things started to calm down, Horst said that he would
probably be here for some time, which made Phil look at Kevin and
said, "If Kevin wouldn't mind, you can have his bed, and I would share
mine with him!"

A wide smile came to the detective's face, and without awaiting any
further comment, he picked up his stuff, went into Phil's room, and said,
"I'm moving in." He dropped himself on the bed, and Phil was quick
to join him. Horst said he would take a shower, just before the door to
what was now *their* bedroom closed. The two were soon continuing the
kissing they had started in the hallway, and Kevin whispered into Phil's
ear how much he had missed him, and that he was thinking about him
all the time. And so a wonderful friendship with all the extras began.

They started to undress each other, piece by piece, until they were both naked and soon engaged in passionate lovemaking. Kevin was lubing Phil with his saliva and started to penetrate him carefully. Phil. screamed from lust and pleasure, so loudly that even Horst under the running shower must have known or suspected what was going on in the next room. Meanwhile, the two young lovers continued, and with every move, Phil got closer to climax. Kevin started moving faster and soon filled him with all he had stored in him. They enjoyed their first simultaneous orgasm.

When Phil's breathing normalized he told Kevin that this was the first raw sex he ever had, and it felt so good, so complete. He was now part of Kevin and would treasure this moment for the rest of his life.

"So I can stay for now?" Kevin asked.

"You can stay for as long as you want," Phil immediately replied. They just lay there without saying another word, in a very close and loving embrace.

It was late afternoon when they finally got up, and after some needed cleanup, they went up front, where Horst and Alfred were talking in the living room. "I'm so happy that you are back and safe," Alfred said, looking at Kevin. "Oh, Summers called. He said that you should activate your phone, and when I see you, I should tell you to call him immediately."

Kevin realized that he had never turned on his phone since he touched US soil, and he went back to the room to get it. He dialed Summers, and after two rings, the chief detective picked up. One could read in Kevin's face that the man was not very happy about the lack of communication, but he finally asked if they were all there. He wanted to come by and give them the updates. Kevin covered the phone with his hands, threw a begging glance to heaven, and said, "He wants to come here and talk to all of us. Is it okay?"

"Sure," they all said.

"But tell him to loosen up and make this unofficial so he can have a drink with us," Albert added. They were all laughing while Kevin communicated their request.

Less than forty-five minutes later, Fred was announcing him over the intercom. When he stepped through the door, he looked exactly as Phil remembered him: same trench coat, same suit, same tie, and the same miserable look on his face. Phil could sense that he was not very comfortable in this company but nevertheless he accepted a beer and sat down.

After the first gulps, he got some color in his face and started to give them an account of the arrests made in New York and New Jersey. They were sure that Dmitry was the head in the US and organizer for "the Boss" in Frankfurt; he also killed the two guys in the car outside the house. With him, there were probably fifteen others who got arrested during a stakeout; five were let go because there was no proof of involvement. They were free out there somewhere, the young men could see that Summers wasn't happy about this. He said this is why he would leave Kevin in the undercover position for the time being, because a vendetta by one or the other could not to be ruled out.

He said that the real purpose of the clan was terminated, however, one of these creeps might just start with the know-how to blackmail people. Kevin looked at Phil with a smile, trying not to seem too obvious that he was more than happy to continue working at the apartment. Summers asked what Horst's plans were and suggested that he should stay here for some time, since he'd heard from Frankfurt that there were also some loose ties there. Until they could be sure they'd cleaned out the entire organization, he would not be safe. The detective assured us that they were shadowing all the suspects, but it was possible that they were not aware of all of them. He ordered Kevin to monitor incoming calls whenever they saw a reason to do so.

The longer Summers talked the more human and relaxed he appeared, and soon he accepted a second beer. He advised that they should still be alert but could continue with their normal lives, but he also suggested they keep a low profile and be aware that they might be followed and monitored. He then asked if they thought it necessary to have the apartment searched for new bugs, but Phil told him that they hadn't had any suspicious visitors in the past days.

As he was getting ready to leave, he said that the police were aware of the activities here, but since they cooperated so well and they believed that it was for the NYPD's benefit as well, they would not take any action. He also added that they should not put any advertising out there, and keep the place as low key as possible. Phil told him that he never felt advertising was necessary and that they would operate as they had in the past.

Phil closed the door behind him and went back to join the others. They agreed to go out and have a bite to eat.

The days passed as usual. They had many bookings, and Phil started to look around to recruit new escorts. This was not an easy task. In the meantime, they had fifteen escorts, who mostly did hotel calls. Phil was still trying to keep the apartment calls as limited as possible. It also came in handy that Horst was staying with them and was willing to take over clients whenever he was available for some extra cash.

CHAPTER 15

It was a regular Tuesday afternoon when Phil received a call from a younger-sounding guy with an Eastern accent. He inquired about their services and said that he would be interested to come and see one of the men, but he lived outside New York and therefore requested an apartment call. Phil booked him for 8:30 that same evening and asked if he had any preferences. He seemed open, as long as the guy knew what he was doing. Phil was not concerned about that and first thought of Jack, who wanted to come by anyway. Because of the accent, he taped their conversation, and when Kevin came into the office, he asked him to listen to his last conversation.

"That's interesting. He sounds very determined, not shy or insecure; he's asking questions that usually aren't asked over the phone."

As they sat there, they both had the same thoughts, and Phil asked "Is this shit not over yet?"

Kevin hesitantly answered, "Well, this might be one of these side products, who will be more into blackmailing than anything else." He came over to Phil's chair and embraced him. Then he said in a rather sad voice with little conviction, "I guess I have to do what I'm paid for, if that's okay with you. I will take him."

Phil was a little shocked and surprised that he would offer himself, and felt jealousy was overcoming him. Kevin must have sensed his feelings; he kissed him on the cheek and said, "This is only a job, but if we do not root these guys out, we will never see the end of it."

Phil knew he was right, but his feelings for him grew steadily, and the thought of him pleasing a client in the next room was painful. When he told Phil that it could not be worse than his encounter in Frankfurt with the goon, the boss agreed. Kevin promised that this would not mean anything to him, just a trick, but he had a distinct feeling that they were on to something.

There was still plenty of time, and Kevin put in a call to Summers' office. "I think we're on a lead. Can I have a bug detector?"

Phil heard the person on the line requesting more information, which Kevin delivered. After a few minutes, they agreed and promised to have somebody deliver the device with some groceries to the apartment within an hour. It made Phil feel better to know that Kevin was really doing this as his job, but it didn't change much for him.

The bags were delivered, and one of the younger handymen in the building brought them up. Kevin went immediately to work; it looked pretty easy, and Phil was happy that his new lover thought of it. Phil received some more work requests for the evening and the days to come and thought to himself that it would be a real pity to let this business go. They really did very well. They were able to expand into different services, and more and more women called for escorts to take them out for dinner and cultural events.

These were frequently Phil's dates; he loved being taken to Carnegie Hall or the Met, and once he was asked to go to a formal dinner at the Metropolitan Museum with a wealthy heiress. She was a little kinky, and since the tabloids always made her look like a lesbian, she thought she would prove different and give the press something to speculate. She told Phil everything up front, and there seemed to be no secrets between them when he picked her up at her place on Park Avenue. They had a drink there before leaving for the museum. It was a very interesting evening; Phil was introduced to many celebrities and even saw a few familiar faces that had come to his place in the past.

What a stuck-up society we are, he thought. Phil was drilled, and they all wanted to squeeze details out of him about their relationship. He made it a sport to give them meaningless answers. When the evening was over, she kissed Phil good night at her door and asked if they could do more than just dinner. Phil told her that he had very good-looking guys who were willing to please her further. It must have worked on her, because only a week later, she called G.T. and asked for a "full" date. Phil told Jack about it, and he was very willing. The two now meet regularly at her place. After each date, they always got flowers delivered and a wonderful thank-you note, and Jack gets hefty tips and pricey gifts.

Evening approached, and Kevin got ready for his date. When Jack came in, he told me that on his last Park Avenue date, he was asked if he could arrange a couple of guys in the near future for a hen party. Phil asked about the date and looked through the list.

"Yes, I think with Frank and Horst, we would have a great group."

Jack was fine with the selection. They talked some more, and Kevin entered the room. "Hi, how are you two lovebirds doing?" Jack asked, looking at Kevin and Phil. He must have felt the tension in the air. Phil told him about the guy they were expecting, and at first he wanted to assign him to Jack, but Kevin felt that he was here for a reason, and it would be his duty.

Jack raised his brows. "Hey, no problem. I'm sure I could take him down, but if you're doing it, I'll stay here with Phil to give some backup, just in case."

Phil felt much better, but Kevin suggested that he shouldn't be around when the guy comes; if there was anything behind it, he would probably be intimidated and not come forward. They all agreed that Kevin would pretend to be here alone and that the others would hide somewhere until the two were in the room.

The intercom buzzed, and Kevin responded. Soon the guy was in front of the door. Kevin—or now Martin again—asked him in. He was a short but nice-looking guy smelling of strong cologne. He surely wanted to give the impression that he was clean and showered. Martin offered him a drink; vodka was his beverage of choice. They sat down, and while the guy nervously looked around, Martin tried to make conversation. He soon found out that his visitor was not very experienced but had fantasized for years about having sex with another man.

Martin, as casually as possible, tried to make him comfortable. He asked where the man was from and where he lived at the moment—superficial small talk. At first it seemed that the young client didn't want to release too much information, but with his second drink he loosened up and became more talkative. Once he appeared more relaxed, Martin suggested going into the bed room.

When Jack and Phil heard the door shut, they came out. Phil wasn't very happy, knowing that Kevin was pleasing this guy, but Jack's company was diverting his thoughts a little. Phil was very relieved when after only thirty minutes, Kevin came out of the room in his robe and said that Dmitry was taking a shower. "That was weird and nothing to be jealous of," he said. "We were just there naked, and he wanted to touch me, wanted to feel my hard cock. Then we jerked off together, and after he shot his load, he embraced me and kissed me. That's it." Kevin shook his shoulders, came over, kissed Phil, and said, "It's all okay, but he wants to come pay and talk to you. I'll turn on the tape recorder."

Kevin quickly went into the office, pushed the record button, and hid the small device behind a pile of papers, and then left the room. He asked Jack to come with him while he got dressed, thinking it better if the creep believes that he's not surrounded by too many people.

It took the new Dmitry nearly fifteen minutes before he appeared in the living room. Phil offered him another drink, which he accepted, and he asked him into the office. He sat down and introduced himself again. Phil laughed and said, "Do your mothers have no imagination when they name their boys?"

He didn't seem to get the joke, and just stared at Phil, trying to look serious. He opened his wallet and put a number of bills on the table, which Phil picked up and put in the drawer. "Thank you. I hope you are happy with the service."

He looked up, and Phil could sense that he wanted to compose correct sentences in his Eastern brain when he started. "Today I came as a client, but we want to be partners with you." He looked the host straight in the eyes and tried to read his reaction.

"Partners? Sorry, we are not looking for partners here. We're just fine the way it is," Phil answered with a smile, but Dmitry didn't think that this was funny.

"My former boss made you a similar proposal some time ago, but unfortunately he will be detained from doing any business soon, so we, the ones who are still active, have promised him to continue his work."

While Phil was looking at him in amazement, the door opened, and Kevin peeked in. Dmitry turned around and gave him a smile. Kevin said, "All clean again and ready."

Wow, the little prick was planting bugs, Phil thought. *Well, they will never work, or even better, he will be probably take them back home.* Phil asked Kevin if they should make the gentleman a farewell present, but Kevin shook his head and disappeared again. "Sorry, where were we?" Phil asked.

Dmitry seemed a little confused by now; first it seemed that he was not taken seriously enough, and trail of negotiation. "Well, we want to be your partners," he repeated. "We want to share your profits and would give you protection from other people who want to harm you."

He appeared proud and must have thought he was back in the game, but when Phil told him that they were not really interested in their services, he tried to regain his tough composure, and with a less amicable voice said that it was not really Phil's choice, that they had already made the decision. At first, they would ask $5,000 per week in protection money. They were monitoring the business, and if they could see that G.T. was in a position to give more, they would raise the amount.

"Now listen to me," Phil said. "This sounds like extortion, and if you believe this will fly, you have to go back to your people and renegotiate with them."

He seemed astonished by this reaction, and when he moved toward his pocket, Phil was afraid he might draw a gun, but he felt safe, knowing that Kevin was ready on the other side of the door. He pulled out a pack of Kent cigarettes, but when Phil told him that this was a no-smoking place, he put them back. It was obvious he was nervous, and when he rose from the chair, he said, "You will hear from us soon. Better consider our offer, because we are not known to be playing games."

Phil looked at him and said that he appreciated his warning, but he had doubts they would be interested to have any further business together. Phil thanked him for his visit and told him that he would tell Martin that he enjoyed his company. With that, he got up and decisively pushed Dmitry toward the apartment door, where he handed him his coat and made him leave. Phil could see through the spy hole in the door that it took him some time before he pushed the call button for the elevator. He appeared very angry, and Phil wouldn't have been surprised if he buzzed the apartment again to finish the conversation to his benefit.

When the elevator door opened, he boarded, clearly furious. Jack had already gone downstairs, and when Dmitry came out, he walked across the street and got in a waiting car. Jack could see that the driver and Dmitry had a heated argument, until the engine started and the small car sped off into the street. Jack copied down the license plate and came back up again.

"What an asshole," he said when he walked through the door. Kevin was already on the phone with Summers, playing him the tape. Summers commented that this was exactly what he was afraid of: this guy was a little nobody, but since he had nothing to lose at this point, he was probably trigger crazy and for a few bucks would do anything.

"Thank you, guys," Summers said. "I don't think there's anything happening tonight, but we have to sit together and make new plans tomorrow. These guys are not organized and have no fear, which is more dangerous. We have to get them soon, before they start getting desperate. Have a beer on me." Summers ended the conversation and hung up.

Kevin appeared in the room with four bugs he had harvested in the bedroom and bathroom. Then he suggested that he would scan the office too; the guy might have planted one while I was unaware. "Go right ahead," I told him while I poured myself a drink.

"I'll have one too," Jack said while Kevin started to work on the office and continued to the hall. He was successful in the office; the jerk had stuck a little microphone under the rim of the desk, this would have given them most of their booking information.

They all sat down and enjoyed the drinks. The phone rang, and the creep Dmitry, with a very angry yet frightened voice, screamed through the phone, "You assholes! You will hear from us soon, and next time, it will not be pleasant!" He then slammed the phone down. They all guessed this guy got a good beating from his superior after returning with no results and a few hundred dollars lighter. There was no time to record the last call, but it was so loud that everyone in the room was able to hear what he said.

Alfred walked in; he looked tired but said that he was off tomorrow and looking forward to sleeping in for once. "So I can go to classes tomorrow?" Phil asked, having missed quite a few lately. He was scheduled to graduate in May but still had to get a few credits out of the way. It came in very handy that he did all the extra credits in summer school, and he was looking forward to turning his back to the books for a while. His parents were still hoping that he would move back to Westchester after graduation and occupy a desk at Sherwin & Sons. This certainly won't happen, not as long as he can be entrepreneurial in the Big Apple.

The routine seemed to return. They had little out of the ordinary for a few days, and the NYPD decided to call Kevin back into the department by the end of the month. Horst was also told that he was free to return home. He was a great help and soon had a nice following of guys. He was sorry to go but said that anytime G.T. needed support, he would be here.

Then the luck seemed to change. Summers called on a Friday, late in the afternoon, and said that he had to talk to them at the precinct; Kevin and Phil should come down at six.

When they entered the very busy station house, Kevin, who was very familiar with the complicated layout, guided Phil directly to Summers. On the way there, they heard many macho guys whistling and calling out, "Hey, Kev, you look great in blond!" which earned some laughter from the others.

When they reached the office, Kevin knocked on the door and waited for the loud, "Come in." Summers was behind his desk, hidden by piles of files and folders. Behind him was a large board with very graphic pictures. He asked them to sit down and then turned around and gestured toward the picture wall and said, "This is the last surprise."

Phil looked at the pictures and remembered similar scenes from the series *Law and Order.* "What is it?" Kevin asked.

Summers made them get up closer and then asked, "Do you know this guy?"

Phil looked hard; he felt like He had seen him before, but couldn't really pin down where and how. "I'm not sure. Why?"

Summers told them that his body was found on the Lower East Side, badly beaten, and when he finally died, they dropped him in a junkyard in the Bowery. It is believed that he was hustling or escorting. "Wow, yes, now I remember," Phil said. "He came for an interview once, wanted to work for us, but I didn't feel he would fit into the team. I told him that we were not interested."

Summers asked if Phil could remember when that was, but he just speculated it was six to eight weeks ago. Phil remembered he could not leave the house at the time and asked him to come there. Phil told Summers that he'd been a nice guy, but unfortunately we have to keep our high standards, and he was not educated and refined enough. They parted amicably, and there were no hard feelings.

"You remember his name?"

"No, but I can check at home."

Summers said that it looked like he was the victim of one of these groups who were involved in the case too. "It could even be one of the many Dmitrys."

"Oh, shit, that is scary. Guess I have to start with the confirmation system again." Summers looked questioningly at Phil, and he explained that during the rough times, he asked all the guys to call in after the jobs, just to make sure that they were safe. Phil was now speculating that the goons might have seen him leaving their place and followed him.

Summers calmed Phil by saying that they would most probably not have waited that long to act, which sounded reasonable. But then Kevin added that the recent calls and the extortion demands came from a lower tier of gangsters, who were only out for a quick buck and not into any sophisticated scheme or organization.

CHAPTER 16

Things seemed to normalize again, and the business continued to prosper. The regular clientele grew steadily, they all tried to forget about the recent past, though being more careful with any new client.

It was early afternoon when the phone rang. At first, the person on the line seemed very afraid to speak, which Phil was used to. After a few calming words, Tim—as he introduced himself—became more relaxed. He started with the obvious inquiries, wanting to know about the establishment, and he was extremely worried about discretion. When the first hurdles were past, he wanted to know more about the men who were available. Phil told him about a few, but he needed to know what day or time Tim was looking for. He said that he was free this evening, if that was possible. Phil told him yes, and he could meet two or three of the guys, and make his selection, he would match him discreetly with his dream date.

It all sounded a little suspicious, but by now Phil was used to the insecurities of the first-timers. Since Alfred and Jeffrey were around anyway, he asked them to be present for Tim. At 8:00 sharp, he was announced by the doorman. Phil went to the door, and when the elevator opened, a nice-looking man in his mid forties walked out. Phil greeted him with a friendly handshake and showed the way to the living room.

When Tim spotted the guys sitting on the sofa, he froze stiff. Jeffrey and Alfred got up and greeted him. Jeffrey asked if he could offer Tim a drink, which he immediately accepted. "Sorry, this is new for me, so I'm a little nervous," he said while looking deep into Jeffrey's eyes.

"Hey, no problem, Tim. I'm sure you'll feel much better after a nice scotch on the rocks," Jeffrey said and walked into the kitchen to prepare the drink.

When Phil joined him for a refill, Jeffrey took a note pad and scribbled *Tim is my father's best friend and his name is Charles, WOW.* Jeffrey returned to the others with the drinks. Phil observed from afar, but Jeffrey behaved very professionally, and he noticed Tim relaxing. They were all getting along well, and Phil saw how he tried to build a connection with Alfred, who got up only to move closer to Tim.

After the second drink, Tim finally gathered his courage and asked where he and Alfred could have a little privacy. Alfred got up, took Tim's hand, and ushered him into the master bedroom. When the door closed, Jeffrey produced a huge grin on his face and said to himself, "I knew it all along."

Phil was very curious but thought it better not to ask; I was sure Jeffrey would spill it all in due time. The wait was shorter than anticipated; Jeffrey got up and asked Phil to join him in the office. When the two of them were in there, Jeffrey threw himself into an armchair and started laughing. Phil sat in his chair and just waited for what was to come. "I knew it. I always had a crush on Charles, but he was always secretive, and when he announced he was getting married to another socialite a few years ago, I thought all was lost, but I guess not." He sat there with a huge smirk on his face and then added, "There is, however, something wrong. He is just such a control freak, and coming here is very odd for him. There has to be more than just sex."

Phil looked at him, a little puzzled. "What do you mean? He seems like a very nice guy who just wants to escape his routine; perfect for a regular."

Jeffrey agreed hesitantly, but it was obvious that he was not happy with the answer. They were making small talk when Kevin entered the room and said, "Hey, how is it going?"

Phil looked up with a longing smile, and Kevin walked over to him placing a nice kiss on his lips.

"Wow, this is getting serious here!" exclaimed Jeffrey with a loud laugh. They all decided to go into the next room and have a drink.

Shortly after, Alfred appeared in the room and just whispered, "Nice, but weird." Five minutes later, Tim came in, and a strong negative tension filled the room. Phil could sense that the situation was awkward for him, but nevertheless, Tim or Charles went up to Jeffrey and asked if he could have a word with him in private.

"Sure, go ahead; take the office, but have a drink first," Phil suggested.

The two disappeared into the adjoining room, and Jeffrey closed the door behind them. The others stayed back and thought that this would be a personal talk, but then the door opened, and from the threshold, Jeffrey asked them to join. First he looked at Kevin and inquired if this room was clean. Kevin nodded, while the others were rather surprised by the question.

Then Jeffrey took over. "Guys, this is Charles. He's just told me something I believe you should hear from him directly."

Charles turned to the newcomers in the room, and with a blushing and nervous face started. "Well, I guess it is no secret in here that I am gay, and probably you know that we, Jeffrey and myself, are from rather well-known families. I had to get married a few years ago, but from the beginning, my wife and I have a good understanding, but of course my private life cannot go public." He stopped for a moment, took a large sip out of his tumbler, and continued. "In the past, I regularly met with a nice guy called Oscar. We had an affaire; he was discreet, and I paid for his apartment and tried to make his life a little easier. One evening, when I visited him, he was very nervous, and I could feel something was up. He asked me if it would be terrible if we would not have our regular routine, but just a drink, because there was so much on his mind, and he would be a dreadful lover. I agreed. We sat down, and he told me that there were guys after him requesting protection money. I could feel that he was not joking; he told me that he was considering moving back to the West Coast. I tried to calm him down, but when he told me that they knew of our arrangement and they knew my name, I got nervous, and the worst-case scenarios shot through my head."

Kevin introduced himself to Charles and asked if he could take some notes. He briefly explained his undercover work and Good Times, Inc. were partly responsible for the raid and the elimination of the Romanian clan that killed two people in front of this building. Obviously, this didn't help Charles to calm down; he got even tenser but gave Kevin permission to do his job. Then he continued by explaining that he was approached with an anonymous letter containing the number for Good Times, Inc. and the instructions to go there and plant a couple of bugs in the place. The instructions gave exact locations, which made him believe that they were familiar with the establishment. Included in the envelope was a bad picture of a body lying near a container. His eyes started to get glossy when he said that he suspected that this was Oscar.

Kevin immediately asked if he still had the picture. Charles nodded. He grabbed in his inside pocket, took an out envelope, and handed it to Kevin. He opened it and with a quick look confirmed that this was the body they found only a few days ago. Kevin then asked if he would identify the person at the morgue. Charles again nodded. The letter that was also still in the envelope gave a very detailed description of the apartment and very precise locations where the bugs were to be planted. In the last paragraph, the author of the letter made it very clear that if Charles did not follow the instructions, they would release information about his life with Oscar to the press, and he might end up like the person in the picture.

Kevin asked if he could keep the letter; he wanted to run it by the lab and check for prints. He had little hope of finding anything usable but still didn't want to rule out the possibility. He stashed the picture and the letter into a larger envelope and set it aside. They all sat there in silence, not knowing how to continue, when Kevin suggested that in order to protect Charles, they should plant the bugs and make them believe his mission was successful. This made them all exchange looks, because they knew that this would limit their freedom drastically.

Alfred suggested that they would receive more clients in his room, and he would use the main room if he was alone. This sounded like a plan, but how could they know that clients were safe, since one bug was also planned to be placed in the living room and one in the office? Jeffrey suggested that they would mainly do outcalls at this point, and if the client needed a place, it was cheaper to get a hotel room than be blackmailed. "This will only be for a short time," Kevin said. "Now that we can go after the guys for murder, the NYPD will be much more efficient."

Kevin took out his cell phone and said that he had to call Summers to run this by him. After a few rings he picked up. Kevin explained the situation and told him that he had a person here who could identify the John Doe from the Bowery. Summers agreed to Kevin's plan to plant the bugs and suggested that Charles should stay with them until he could arrange for protection. He promised to call shortly, to give further details. Kevin hung up and reported back to them.

Jeffrey asked Charles if he should call his wife, Daisy, but Charles said that she was visiting friends in Paris, and there was nothing to worry about on this side. Phil got up and said, "The show must go on. Shall we give our audience some work to do?"

Kevin asked for the bugs. When he saw them, he whistled through his teeth and remarked that these were more high-tech than the previous ones. They all agreed to keep to meaningless chitchat, and no names would be mentioned. Another round of drinks loosened Charles more; he seemed able to forget the pressure for a short time.

Summers called, and Kevin nodded professionally and said that he had to go into another room; Phil followed him and closed the door behind them. Kevin asked if he could put the call on the speaker, so Phil could listen in. Summers explained that they located a van in front of the house, but the two guys inside were not known to them, and therefore they would prefer to trail them back to their place, rather than arresting them down there. Summers believed they could lead them to the core of the organization when they deliver the tapes. Phil thought this was clever, even if he knew that this would inconvenience his business, but another heavy police action on the block could be suspicious.

Summers continued, telling that a Detective Connors will soon be at the apartment. He'll pick Charles up and leave through the back door. Then he told Kevin to ask the gentleman if he would mind going with the officer to the morgue to identify the John Doe. Phil went to the door and waved Charles into the kitchen. Kevin asked him if it was convenient for him to go to the chief medical examiner's office with an officer to see if the body was really Oscar. Charles sadly nodded in agreement. Kevin related the message to Summers, and everything seemed to be settled. It was around 11:00 when the doorman announced a Mr. Connors. He came up, and soon Charles and he left for the Milton Helpern Institute of Forensic Medicine.

Outside the building, another car was ready with two officers to follow the van. An officer in street cloths was strolling up the street, taking a small dog for his night walk. The dog walker pretended that just behind the van, he needed to pick up the dog's droppings and at this occasion fixed a small bug with a magnet on the car, just in case the following officers would lose the van.

Once Charles was gone, the guys upstairs called it a night. Everyone returned to their rooms, and Jeffrey went home. Down on the street, the two guys knew it would be boring from now on, and after another hour sitting there and listening to nothing, one of them made a call on his cell. Soon the van slowly left the parking space. The two officers in the car around the corner saw the movement on their small GPS screen, and the driver put his car into gear. Traffic was still busy enough to be covered by other cars; one of the officers was in constant contact with central station and reported all activities. They were heading toward the Fifty-Ninth Street Bridge that brought them into Queens.

Traffic got thinner, and the officer asked for a replacement to follow the van, since he felt that the trail could be discovered. They were given the location where they would have to take a right turn, and another car would continue. A few miles down the street, the van turned left into a large parking lot. The two guys got out, locked the car, wished each other a good night, and jumped on bikes and rode off.

"Now what?" exclaimed one of the officers. He reported the status and was ordered to park nearby and observe the van. They over heard the good-night conversation and speculated that the two men were students making some money on the side; they didn't appear to be of Eastern European descent. The two policemen were ready for a long, boring, cold night. One took out a thermos and poured two cups of steaming coffee.

CHAPTER 17

In Manhattan Charles and Detective Connors were driving over to 520 First Avenue. Connors parked the car in the private parking lot. He seemed a very nice man, and Charles felt at ease, even if all this was very new to him. He reflected on the evening; strangely enough, he felt good that Jeffrey was part of it. At least he had a confidant he could talk to.

The two went through a back door and down long, fluorescent-lit corridors until they reached a large elevator. Charles's heart started to beat faster when the door slid open and they entered the spacious cubicle. When the door opened again, they were in front of a large reception counter with a haggard-looking woman seated behind. The officer went up to her and inquired about John Doe 3-122.

Without looking up, she pointed to her left and said, "Room five." The closer Charles got to his destination, the heavier his feet felt, but he knew he had to get this over with. They entered a room with lots of stainless-steel furniture. Dr. Ramsey greeted them; then he looked at Charles and said that the victim was badly beaten, and what he was going to see would not be pleasant. "Are you ready?" Dr. Ramsey asked in a somber voice.

Charles nodded, and the white sheet was pulled down. The face of Oscar became visible—what was left of it. After a split second, Charles had to turn around and hold his hands in front of his eyes. He whispered, "Oh my God."

Detective Connors walked over, and with the friendly gesture of holding Charles's shoulders asked, "Is this Oscar?"

Charles nodded, sobbing. Dr. Ramsey covered the corpse again, and the two left the room. Outside, Charles dropped into an armchair and buried his face in his hands. Detective Connors was very compassionate and sat down next to him. The few minutes of silence were interrupted by the opening of the elevator door; a man in white was pushing another covered body into one of the rooms. Charles seemed to recover and slowly rose from the chair; Connors followed. The two men walked toward the elevator and silently left the building the same way they entered.

Back in the car, Charles finally looked at Connors and asked, "Who could do such a thing? Who are these people?"

The detective told Charles in very low voice that they believed these were ruthless dilettantes, the bad survivors of a larger, international group. He then explained that with the help of Good Times, Inc., Interpol and the FBI were able to crush the top, but when the little guys saw that the bosses were gone, they started their own chapter and were now trying to get into the protection business. He let this sink in and then continued that the greatest worry was that they were not really organized, but just trying to get money however possible. This didn't make them any less dangerous; they were brutal, and murder appeared routine to them. This didn't make Charles feel any better, and when Connors asked if he could assist them in the matter, Charles agreed immediately and promised he would do whatever possible.

"Okay, do you know where Oscar lived?" was the first question Connors posed.

"Sure, I have a key to his place. You know, Officer, Oscar and I had a very nice arrangement, and I was very fond of him."

Connors asked if he would like to show him the apartment, and Charles agreed. The detective picked up his cell phone and called in. "The body is positively identified, and we're now going to the victim's apartment." He closed the phone, and Charles gave him the address. It was past midnight, but Charles knew that sleep would be not possible anyway and was actually relieved to be in company of a protector.

They parked the car in front of a hydrant on a tree-lined street in Chelsea. Connors put an official police sign on the dashboard, and the two men left the car. "Can I have one of these?" Charles joked.

Connors, happy that he seemed to recover, answered, "I'll look into it," and followed Charles up the stoop of the brownstone building. It was a nice dwelling; the hall was neat, with a withered bunch of flowers. On the second floor, Charles opened the back apartment with his key, and what greeted them was not a pleasant sight. The usually very tidy place was ransacked and in complete chaos. A broken notebook was lying in the corner of the living room, and papers were all over the floor. Connors asked Charles not to touch anything and slipped a pair of latex gloves over his hands. Charles stood there in complete shock, tears pushing through his eyes.

"Oscar was such a neat freak; he was the one who always bought fresh flowers for the entrance hall."

Connors walked around the place. In the bedroom, he found broken picture frames and photos next to them showing Oscar and Charles standing below the Eiffel Tower. He raised his eyes to ask for an explanation, but by now Charles felt he had little to hide. "Oscar accompanied me several times on trips. We were lovers. I was aware that he saw other men, but we had something very special." He fell into an armchair to recollect his thoughts and then continued. "I love collecting art, and we often traveled to Paris to visit galleries and museums. He could not get enough; he was like a diamond in the rough who tried to make up for the basic education he had. He always asked questions and was desperate to suck up any information he could get."

Connors saw that Charles was running through his memories and thought best just to listen to what he had to say. "When we were in Madrid once, we went to the Reina Sophia, the modern art museum. When we stood in front of the famous painting *Guernica* by Pablo Picasso, he changed his expression, and I could sense the pain and fear he experienced. He became obsessed with the work; he tried to get hold of any information, and I am sure somewhere in this mess there is an album of all the collected articles and pictures he has amassed since then."

Connors started to develop a sincere liking for Charles. As he was feeling sorry for him, he realized that Charles lost far more than just a sexual adventure. Both men were in their own worlds when the harsh ring of the cell phone brought them back to reality. Connors opened the phone and listened, nodding from time to time. He finally said, "I have to ask. I don't want to inconvenience at all." He turned to Charles and said, "This is my boss. He's afraid of leaving you without protection, but at this hour he can't find a replacement. He wants to know if I could spend the night on your sofa until he gets everything organized."

Charles was surprised but said that he had no problem and actually would feel much better having him around. Then Connors received the order to close the apartment and go back with Charles and call it a night.

They drove uptown, and as usual, it was difficult to find parking close to the building. Charles suggested that they should have the doorman park the car in the garage. Bill couldn't leave an official police car in anyone else's hands, so the doorman suggested going down with him and showing him where to park. In the meantime, Charles was waiting in the luxurious lobby. The two came up the elevator, and when the doorman left, Charles and Bill Connors went up to the penthouse.

It was a very classy place, filled with wonderful art. Charles went ahead, and Bill followed him into a spectacular living room with large windows, offering an incredible view over part of Manhattan. "Can I offer you a drink?" Charles looked at Bill and saw that he was contemplating whether he was on duty or not but then decided a beer would be wonderful. The host left for the kitchen and returned with a beer and two glasses, one filled with ice cubes. He set the beer on the side table and went to a cabinet to get a bottle of scotch to pour himself a hefty drink.

They raised their glasses and sat down on one of the sofas. Charles saw the little light on his phone blinking and excused himself for a second while he listened to the message. It was Daisy, his wife, calling from Paris, telling him that she would extend her stay a few days if that was okay and that he should call her in the morning. Charles looked at his watch; it was past two in the morning, which was after eight in Paris, and he decided to get the call over with. He dialed the long number for Paris, and when the other side answered, he asked in perfect French for Room 806. He was immediately connected and after a few of rings Daisy picked up. "Good morning, dear. How is everything?" He listened to her, and from time to time, a smile rushed over his face.

Bill guessed that she wanted an account of his doings. He told her that he spent the entire night with the police, and when he said that Oscar was killed, Bill was struck with amazement. Charles then told her that he was here with the police; they thought it best that he have some protection until they knew more about the murder. "Yes, dear. I feel it is much better if you stay in Paris until all this has calmed down. I'm sure you're safer there. Enjoy your time."

After the usual good-byes, he hung up, took his glass, and went back to join Bill on the sofa. Charles could sense that Bill was very curious and offered the explanation that his marriage was more or less arranged, but he was always very open with his wife, and she seemed to be handling the situation extremely well. The two men were getting tired, and Charles suggested that Bill could sleep in one of the guest rooms. He showed him the extra bedrooms and said, "Pick one!"

Bill chose the one closest to the master bedroom. The host gave him all the necessary toiletries, a comfy T-shirt, and a robe. When everything was settled, they said good night. Bill walked over to Charles, gave him a nice hug, and said, "Thank you. You're a real champ." They went into their rooms and both were fast asleep within minutes.

The two policemen watching the van in a Queens commercial parking lot were sitting there without any results. The van sat idle, and by six in the morning, the yard came alive. Drivers picked up their vans and went to work, but the blue one was not going anywhere.

In the Good Times, Inc. apartment, the morning began as usual. Kevin got a message on his phone that the surveying car was gone, which was good news for the guys; they could move around freely and not concern themselves with any word they were saying. Coffee was made, and the day was planned; everything was running smoothly.

In Charles's penthouse, things didn't go as easily. At eight in the morning, Charles went to the living room, where Rosa the housekeeper served him juice and coffee, like every morning. She started at seven and cleaned the kitchen from the night before. Bill entered the kitchen dressed only in the T-shirt Charles loaned him before they retired. Rosa was not only surprised by the new face in the kitchen but also by the attire. Bill, surprised himself, went back to the bedroom to get showered and dressed.

Charles was reading the *Times* and starting his morning routine when Bill entered the room. "Good morning," Charles said, looking up from his paper. "Want some coffee or juice or breakfast?"

Bill was eager to get some coffee. Charles called Rosa, and when she came in, he introduced her to Detective Connors. Bill mentioned that they met earlier under strange circumstances. Rosa blushed a little, but in immediate self-defense said, "I didn't see anything."

This made Bill laugh, and he said, "Now, that is *not* a compliment for a man."

She turned crimson, and her head looked like it would explode any moment. She laughed and left the room to get coffee. Bill told Charles about the earlier embarrassing encounter in the kitchen, which made both men laugh. When Rosa recovered, she returned with the coffee.

Bill told Charles that he spoke to Summers, the detective who was in charge of the investigation, and he asked if he could come by around ten to ask him some questions. Charles replied, "Sure."

The phone rang. Charles answered and was happy to hear Jeffrey's voice. He told him that he was here with Detective Connors and about everything that happened the night before. He spoke about Oscar and how sorry he was that this happened. When the name Oscar was mentioned, there was sadness in his voice, which made Connors look up and see Charles's teary eyes.

Jeffrey asked if he wanted some company, saying he could come over if Charles would like, but Charles responded that Detective Summers was expected for some questioning. "Give me your cell number, and I'll call you when we're done here, okay?" He took a pencil and wrote the digits on a piece of paper and hung up. After a long shower, he got dressed and returned to the living room, where Connors was reading the paper and awaiting his boss's arrival.

Just after 10:00, the doorman announced Mr. Summers. Bill and Charles were in the living room when Rosa came in with him. She asked if she could bring some beverages; they all gladly accepted more coffee.

Summers then asked if Charles knew Oscar's full name, "Yes, his family name was Fuentes, and as far as I know, his father died, and his mother lived in Lansing, Michigan." He told the detectives all he knew about the family, at least what Oscar had told him over the period when they were close. He told them that he signed the lease for the apartment in Chelsea, telling the landlord that he did this for his nephew, who studied at NYU. Oscar was not really going for a degree at this point, but he was very keen to improve his lifestyle.

With a sad voice, Charles said that just a few days ago, Oscar mentioned that he aspired to a BA, which made him very happy. Summers, with some hesitation and a cough of embarrassment, asked if Charles was aware that Oscar also saw other gentlemen for money. Charles lowered his eyes and nodded silently. After a moment of silence, Charles said, "Yes, this is how I met Oscar nearly two years ago, but in recent months, and with my financial help, he was only seeing a few other men. He promised that he would soon stop, but at this time, he had to send money to his mother, and he was too proud to ask me for more."

Charles told the detectives that he tried to find some part-time work for Oscar, but things were not easy. He added that they were together an average of two nights a week, and the times together were very good, not only sexually, but Charles felt like a mentor and sometimes looked at Oscar like the son he never had.

Summers took a copy of the blackmail letter out of his briefcase and asked if he had any idea who the author might be. Charles just shook his head. Then Summers produced a second letter and said it was found in Oscar's apartment this morning, folded in a copy of Ayn Rand's *Atlas Shrugged*. It was a threatening letter, and it came from the same printer as the letter to Charles, written in the same bad English; but the content was bluntly clear. "Did Oscar ever mention this to you?"

"No!" was Charles's answer, but he seemed shocked. "He was behaving strangely and nervous last time we met, but wouldn't tell me the reason."

Summers made notes in his little black book and then pulled another little notebook from his briefcase. "I guess this is a small bookkeeping record of Oscar's. He must have paid some protection fees to them." He placed the open book in front of Charles, who could only read *Dmitry 100, Dmitry 80,* and so on. "We think the Romanians were protecting him for some time, and Oscar was forced to go along with them."

"Why had he not told me?" Charles murmured, shocked by all these revelations. "I could have helped him, I would have sent him away for some time," he burst out.

Summers then inquired when Charles received his letter and was surprised to hear that it only came to him a couple of days ago. "Why would they wait so long to target you? I guess they wanted to suck Oscar dry first, and when they saw a better opportunity and wealthier victims, they intended to go for the big bucks." Summers packed up all the evidence he'd displayed on the table and continued. "Good Times, Inc. has been a target for some time. For weeks we've had an undercover agent in there. You met him—Kevin. They've tried to bug the place multiple times, but they must have found out that the guys were warned, and they started looking for a serious victim to do their job, because they knew the moment a shady character entered their establishment, once he left, they would scan the place."

After closing the briefcase, Summers inquired what Charles's plans were for the coming days, and when he learned that Charles didn't intend to go anywhere, the detective seemed relieved. He said that they were getting closer to the core of the organization, and he believed that within days, everything would be back to normal, or as normal as it could be. Charles told them that he spoke to his wife and encouraged her to remain in Paris for a few days more; he didn't want her to get involved. Then Summers said he would feel much better if Detective Connors could stay with him until everything was over. Charles was a little surprised, but he was starting to like Bill's company, and he accepted. Bill said that he would pick up some personal items and a change of clothes at his place and be back for dinner. "What do you like to eat? I will send Rosa out for some grocery shopping."

Bill beamed and said "Steak would be great."

"Okay, steak it will be."

Summers got ready to leave. On his way out, he said that they had the two eavesdroppers from the van; as suspected, they never saw any of the Romanians. They were two unemployed electronics freaks who got some fast money. They were only asked to set everything up; from today on, the listeners would likely be from the organization. Summers asked Charles if he was okay being alone for a few hours, he responded that he would call a friend, who would come over.

Once they left, Charles dialed Jeffrey's number and immediately got him on the line. "Hi, the police just left. One of the detectives will move in here, but for the time being, I am alone." When Jeffrey offered he would come over, Charles gladly accepted.

Thirty minutes later Jeffrey entered Charles's penthouse and walked into the den. Charles sat behind his desk doing some work, but concentrating seemed difficult. He got up and for the first time embraced Jeffrey and gave him a kiss on the cheek. "Let's go next door; it's more comfortable there," Charles suggested.

They sat down on the sofa, and Rosa came in and announced that she would go out now to do the shopping. Charles told her to get good steak at the butcher shop and some vegetables; he would be eating in tonight. Then he looked at Jeffrey and asked "Want to join us?"

Jeffrey thought about it and responded, "Why not; could be fun." Rosa then noted that she had to buy three steaks and suggested that she would go to Loebel's on Madison.

Soon the two men were alone, and though it was early, they decided that the hectic day called for cocktails. They filled their tumblers with ice and added hefty portions of good scotch to it. It seemed that the circumstances had brought the two closer. Charles told Jeremy all about Oscar and how he really liked the guy. He was also very curious to find out how Jeffrey got involved with Good Times, Inc., who had no problems telling him.

He said he wanted to move away from home, but a job was not really possible, because he wanted to finish grad school. A friend introduced him to Phil, and he thought since he liked sex very much, this would be the perfect solution. He told Charles that it was very lucrative and he never felt like a hustler. Most of the men seeking their services were well-educated and very nice. "It must have been a shock when you saw me there," he said.

Charles admitted with a smile, "I wished that you were not who you are, because I would have picked you. I have to say, I always had a crush on you, but I wasn't sure if it would be proper to have sex with the son of my best friend." They both laughed, and the early cocktails did their share too.

Charles wanted some juicy details from Jeffrey's experiences, and as he provided him with sexy anecdotes, he felt that Charles was getting more and more excited. He felt how accidental touches brought him closer and closer. Jeffrey, who also felt a strong attraction, decided to go with the flow. It took only a few more moments until Charles set his lips on Jeffrey's, and his tongue slowly moved the lips apart and entered Jeffrey's mouth. The two men were soon engaged in furious kissing, and Charles's hands caressed Jeffrey's chest and neck. He answered with his hands moving up and down his Charles's back and soon felt that excitement was growing fast in their pants.

Charles broke loose, looked and Jeffrey, and said, "Is this all right? Should we do this?" Jeffrey gave him a soft kiss and said, "Hey, we're both grownups. We know whatever happens, we can't reproduce, and frankly I am as hot for you as you are for me. So does that answer your question?"

They both laughed, and Charles suggested that they go to the bedroom. Jeffrey picked up his glass and followed. Once the door was closed, they fell in a hot embrace and continued the steamy kissing from the living room. Now they started to work on their shirts. They unbuttoned each other, not letting go, and soon reached the pants. They both dropped to the floor simultaneously, as if it had been choreographed.

Still kissing, they moved over to the bed, where they fell heavily on the soft mattress. Now Jeffrey took things into his hands. He freed Charles from all the remaining textiles and shed his too. Once they were both naked, they fell in a tight embrace. They kissed ferociously, and their naked bodies rubbed against each other. Jeffrey discovered that touching Charles's nipples made him very excited. He slowly broke from the kissing, and his tongue started wandering down to Charles's chest. Sucking a little on the nipples produced an extreme reaction. The nice, cut penis was rock hard, and Jeffrey could not resist caressing the head with the tip of his tongue. There was already some liquid oozing out, which Jeffrey licked off carefully.

Charles was in absolute ecstasy, bending his back up and moaning loudly. Jeffrey opened his mouth and took hold of the entire shaft. His saliva lubed the beautiful penis, and he knew if he didn't slow down, his Charles would soon be having a very intense orgasm. He decided to hold on a little longer and returned to kissing. The host calmed a little and welcomed Jeffrey with an open mouth. Charles turned around, and soon they were in a 69 position, pleasing each other orally. Jeffrey let his tongue wander down Charles's shaft; he licked his scrotum and continued to the anus. It tasted very good, and the reaction was unexpected. Charles freed a cry of ecstasy when the tip of the tongue slightly entered his orifice.

Jeffrey added sufficient saliva and then slowly introduced his finger into the well-lubed hole. He could feel how the excitement grew, and it took only a few more moves on the shaft with his open mouth until Charles released huge streams of sperm deep into Jeffrey's throat. Charles lay there exhausted while Jeffrey laid a hand on himself and soon shot all over Charles's hairy chest.

"Wow that was intense!" Charles said, still trying to regain his normal breathing. Jeffrey smiled at him with a boyish smirk. They both grabbed their drinks, and Charles admitted with a satisfied smile that this was the best sex this bed had ever seen. Jeffrey got up and asked if he could jump in the shower quickly.

He was standing under the strong stream of water when Charles entered and asked if he could wash his back. They both stood there and were soon locked in another passionate kiss. They dried and got dressed. On the way out, Charles rearranged the bedding so Rosa would not immediately suspect what had happened while she was running her errands. They returned to the living room, and for the first time since they met the night before, Jeffrey felt that Dad's best friend was relaxed.

Back in the old comfort zone, Charles said that his father should probably not know how well they got along. Jeffrey just laughed and promised to keep it their secret, but he certainly hoped that this would not be the end of a wonderful friendship with some extra perks.

When Rosa returned from shopping, she walked into the living room and handed her boss an envelope. She said that a young man gave it to her on the street and asked her to deliver it to her boss, and then he ran away. She didn't question anything and just returned to the kitchen to stash away the groceries. Charles got pale in his face and looked at Jeffrey, wanting to know what to do. Jeffrey suggested leaving the letter where it was and letting Detective Connors take care of it when he arrived. This again brought nervousness into the room, and Charles was happy that Jeffrey was keeping him company.

Connors returned just before six o'clock. When he entered the room, he could sense the tension, and Charles immediately pointed to the letter. Connors went over to the table and turned it over with a pencil. There was nothing on the reverse, so they had to open it. He pulled a pair of latex gloves out of his pocket and asked for a sharp letter opener. Connors called Rosa and inquired about the bearer of the letter, but she could only say that he was wearing dark clothes and a helmet. He appeared young and approximately "this tall," and she held her hand at around six feet. "He spoke strangely, but it could be the helmet," she added.

"You mean like an accent?" Connors asked, and she nodded.

He sat down and flipped the letter over again with the opener. "Guess we have to find out what it says," looking up at Charles. "By the way, I'm Detective Connors," he said, holding out his hand toward Jeffrey.

"Sorry, I'm Jeffrey, a friend of the house."

Once the introduction was finished Connors slid the tool into the envelope and cut the top open. He pulled a piece of paper out, unfolded it, and laid it flat on the table. All three pairs of eyes stared at the text:

It was sad that your friend didn't want to talk, but we found you anyway. Convince the guys they need our protection, first payment 10,000. We will tell you soon where you have to deposit the cash. If you want to be safe, do not call the police, this is an arrangement between us. We are sure that the press would love to know about your life.

Your protectors.

"What a bunch of fucking morons!" Connors exclaimed. "I have rarely seen such amateurs. The way they act, it should be easy to get them, only they have no fear of killing or getting killed. They're ruthless, stupid, and brutal." Connors packed the letter into a plastic slip and set it aside. Charles asked if anyone was ready for a drink. Jeffrey helped himself to another scotch while Connors agreed to a beer.

CHAPTER 18

A few blocks away, Phil answered the phone, and a weak-sounding Carlos asking if he could come by. "Of course. I'm here, and so are Alfred and Kevin."

A few minutes later, Carlos stood at the door, and when Kevin opened it, he had a hard time recognizing Carlos. His face was disfigured, completely bruised, his left eye swollen to the size of a baseball. "Oh my God!" was all Kevin could get over his lips as he helped the injured Carlos into the living room. Alfred and Phil were equally shocked when they saw Carlos, who obviously was in great pain.

"We have to get you to a hospital immediately. What happened?" Phil asked.

Carlos could only speak very softly. He told them that three guys with helmets came out of nowhere and started beating him up and then left him in the alley. But before they walked away laughing, they told him that this was only a warning, and if they didn't follow instructions, worse things would happen.

Phil had heard enough and asked if Carlos felt strong enough to go the emergency room at Lenox Hill, which was only a couple of blocks away. "Please just give me a couple of aspirins first against the pain."

Alfred hurried to the bathroom to get the pills while Kevin filled a bowl with hot water in the kitchen to clean off the worst around the bruises and cuts. They all pampered over Carlos, who shrieked at every touch. Kevin and Phil decided to take him to the clinic while Alfred stayed back in the apartment.

They were able to walk the short distance, and when they entered the emergency room, a nurse helped lay him on a bed. She returned seconds later with a doctor, who asked Phil and Kevin to step out. They sat in the busy waiting room, and every time the door opened, they hoped for Carlos's doctor to come out. After nearly two hours he finally appeared, he said he was able to fix the cuts to the face, but Carlos had to stay in the hospital, because they were afraid of internal bleeding.

"I have to contact the police," the doctor said when Kevin got up and showed him his ID. The doctor asked them to step aside, where they had more privacy. Kevin explained in a few sentences what they knew and told the doctor that NYPD was very active in the investigation and hopefully close to solving the case.

The doctor said he believed Carlos was lucky, but the injuries were pretty serious, and he should know who to contact in Carlos's family. This was more difficult. Phil knew that his mother lived in New Jersey and his last name was Santos and he was enrolled in the engineering department at NYU. The doctor made some notes and then said that they gave him something to help him sleep, they could do nothing at this time and should go home.

"Can I come and visit tomorrow?" Phil asked.

"Sure, but make it in the afternoon. We will have to run some tests in the morning. I want to get him through a scanner."

Phil and Kevin thanked him and said good night. On their way home, Phil spotted two guys with helmets in front of the hospital and immediately got scared. He pointed them out to Kevin, who must have noticed them too. They returned to the emergency room and told the doctor about the possible suspects outside. Kevin asked if he could stay with Carlos overnight until he could make arrangements the next day. It was past midnight, but Kevin thought it necessary to keep Summers informed and dialed his number.

The chief detective was annoyed at first to be woken up at this time of night, but when he realized the seriousness, he was very appreciative of Kevin's handling of the situation. He said he would put a call into the department and send a squad car by to check on the two individuals. He ordered them not to leave the building but said they should survey the guys until they were checked out or taken in. Kevin went over to the nurse and asked if there was a room facing the street that he could use for a short while.

"There is this storage room with cleaning supplies just over there. Go check if that would do."

Kevin went over to the room, opened the door without turning on the lights, and approached the window. "Great view, thanks!" he called back to the desk. From up here, he could see the two guys; they were talking to each other and seemed to disagree on something. One looked like he wanted to leave, while the other one didn't. While they were still arguing, a black-and-white police car turned the corner slowly, as if just cruising the neighborhood. When it was in front of the two guys, the officer opened the door and got out. The guy on the back seat wanted to jump off the bike and run, but the officer already had him firmly by the jacket sleeve. The other was holding on to the bike.

Kevin saw how the second officer got closer and said something, but when he didn't get an immediate response, he took the driver by the arm and forced him off the bike. They were asked to remove the helmets, and then he saw that one took out a wallet and handed an ID over. One officer made them sit on the stoop of a brownstone building, where he could keep them under control; the other got into the squad car to run the ID on the computer. After a moment, he came out again and must have ordered the guy to lock up his bike. Once it was safe, he handcuffed the bike's driver while the other officer did the same to the second guy. They dragged them over to the car, sat them in the back, and drove off. Everything seemed very smooth from behind the first-floor window. Kevin pushed the redial button and told Summers, "They just picked them up. Can we go back now, or should I stay with Carlos here at the hospital?" He listened to instructions and then replied, "Okay, will do," and hung up.

Phil was trying to stay in the background while Kevin was doing his job. Kevin went over to the reception desk and started talking to the nurse. After a few minutes, he came back to Phil and with relief in his eyes said that they could now go home. It was close to three in the morning, and Phil was so tired that the two short blocks felt like an excursion.

Once home, he dropped himself on the sofa while Kevin prepared drinks. Alfred came into the living room and wanted to get all the details. Their mood was lousy. "This has to stop immediately!" Phil said to the others. Kevin replied that they were hopeful to have at least two of the hooligans; usually these guys acted tough at first but were soon broken and singing like birds. After a nightcap, they decided to catch some sleep. The next day would certainly be full of surprises again.

It felt good cozying up to Kevin in bed; Phil felt love, warmth, and security in his arms. Kevin kissed Phil on the shoulder while their bodies produced a vacuum between them. Phil felt his penis getting harder, and when his lover started lubing his back, he looked forward to the imminent penetration. He slowly pushed in, and Phil felt wonderful, so close, so connected, as if they were one. Kevin moved very slowly, and Phil felt that he was in no rush. Even dead tired, he got excited and offered himself to his lover. It felt so good; he just wanted him to be in him and release all the stored tension. While kissing and biting Phil's shoulders, his breathing became heavier, and Phil soon felt Kevin filling him up. He continued to move in and out, but once his breathing was back to normal, he left his manhood in him, and they both fell asleep.

While Kevin and Phil had this wonderful time, back at the NYPD, Summers was dragging himself up the stairs. He was told by the night receptionist that the two characters were in interrogation rooms one and two. Two detectives familiar with the case started the questioning. Summers went to the observation room between the two, and as he watched through the one-way mirrors, he listened in on the conversations. The guy in number two tried to play tough; he sat there nonchalantly with a dirty smirk on his face. When he was asked why he wanted to run away when he saw the police patrol, he just said that all policemen were racists and wouldn't be fair to him, since he was from Eastern Europe. He slid down in his chair even more, probably thinking that with this gesture of boredom would impress the detective.

The young man in room one seemed more cooperative. He explained that he was just driving the other man to the city as a favor for a friend in Queens. He said that he was asked to give Andrei a lift into town; he would pay him $100 for the evening. When he was asked if he knew Andrei's surname, he responded with no hesitation, "Enescu." Summers transferred this information into the headset of the interrogator in Room 2, who used this information immediately. He told the smartass opposite him that his friend was providing all the information, and it was enough to end the interrogation, lock him up, and go home and have a restful night.

This evoked a reaction from the guy. He straightened up a little but was still not willing to give any further information. The officer got up from his chair and walked toward the door to call an officer to take Andrei in for the night.

In Room 1, the officer said that he could only release Serge earliest the following morning, since the papers would have to be signed by the chief detective, and he would not come in until 9:00. This was, of course, a blunt lie, but they wanted to observe the two guys facing each other. They were put in adjacent cells in the basement. After locking them up securely, the officer closed the outer door and left the two by themselves.

It took only a few minutes before Andrei started to attack Serge in Romanian. Summers, who was waiting for this discourse in the monitoring room, taped the conversation. He called an officer on duty and requested a translator. Of course, there was nobody in the department at this time of night who spoke Romanian, so he let the recording continue all night and awaited translation the next day. Summers knew that he couldn't do much at this point and decided to withdraw into one of the resting rooms for a few hours of sleep.

CHAPTER 19

The evening in Charles's penthouse was uneventful. The three guys had their wonderful steak dinner with fresh vegetables and a good bottle of French red wine. Charles felt great in the company of Connors and Jeffrey. A new friendship grew right there and then. After cleaning up, Rosa brought in coffee for the three men. While saying good night, she looked into Connors's eyes and said, "I will be here tomorrow morning." She then left the room with a smile on her lips.

"What was that all about?" asked Jeffrey, and Connors told him about his early-morning encounter with Rosa and his revealing sleepwear. Jeffrey laughed like a madman.

Connors decided to take a walk around the block, to see if there was anything suspicious outside. He got up and left the room. It was then when Charles finally got the courage to ask Jeffrey if he would spend the night with him; he even suggested paying. Jeffrey accepted the invitation and jokingly said, "It's on the house!" It was past midnight when Connors came back, reporting that everything seemed clear outside, and decided to call it a day.

Back in the bedroom, Charles turned around and held Jeffrey by the shoulders and looked deep into his eyes. Without saying a word, he closed in with his lips until they were in a tender kissing embrace. Jeffrey felt very good and comfortable, and while they were moving slowly toward the bed, he didn't let go for a second. They fell on the mattress and smiled at each other. Charles was more relaxed than before; he affectionately touched Jeffrey more like a lover, and Jeffrey seemed to enjoy the loving touch very much. With no rush, they undressed each other, and when they were both in their shorts, the outcome of the night was obvious. Jeffrey could not wait to go down on Charles; he first lightly caressed the tip of the erect penis with his tongue and soon opened his lips and wrapped them around the shaft. Charles was just lying there, moving his hips up to meet with slow movements Jeffrey's deep throat. When the tongue started to go lower and caress the scrotum, Charles became extremely excited. This inspired Jeffrey to wet his finger and start playing with the anus. His hips began spastically jumping into the air.

"You seem to like this," Jeffrey remarked softly, and Charles could only nod approvingly.

Without stopping, Jeffrey's eyes searched for lube. It seemed that Charles was reading his thoughts, and with his outstretched left arm, he opened a drawer on the side table and handed Jeffrey the bottle. He opened it, applied a little on Charles's back, and then a bigger portion on himself. Seconds later, he was gesturing acceptance for entry, which was immediately granted. At first, he moved very slowly, and every time he brushed by the prostate, Charles screamed with pleasure. This excited Jeffrey, even more and his thrusts became faster and more vigorous. The room was soon filled with moans and groans of pleasure, and while Jeffrey was holding the arms down so Charles could not touch himself, he sensed that Charles started to get close to release. Jeffrey continued and soon brought Charles to a monumental orgasm without touching himself. Jeffrey was very close too, and immediately when Charles contracted his muscles in excitement, he filled him up with his love juice. He let go of the arms and fell on the chest but stayed deep inside him. They were breathing heavily on top of each other when Jeffrey whispered, "I could fall for you."

Charles just looked him in the eyes and smiled. Finally, Jeffrey got up and went to the bathroom, where he started a hot shower. When he came out, Charles was still lying on his bed and whispered, "Thank you." Jeffrey jumped on the mattress and kissed him on the lips. After Charles returned from the shower, the two climbed under the covers and fell asleep in a tight embrace.

The next morning, Bill Connors walked into the kitchen wearing a robe. He greeted Rosa with a big smile, she offered him a cup of coffee. He walked into the living room, where he called the station to report. It was then when Summers gave him all the details about the previous night, the beating of Carlos and the subsequent arrest of the two guys. Summers asked if Rosa could possibly identify the man who gave her the letter. He said he would ask and call back.

Rosa was not sure but was willing to face a lineup and give it a try. Connors called back, and they agreed to be there before noon. When Charles finally entered the room with a cup of coffee and a huge smile on his face, Connors informed him of all the activities and said he would take Rosa to the station for a lineup later this morning.

Charles told him that he needed to go into his office briefly, but he would take Jeffrey with him, if that was okay. Connors thought it a good idea not to leave the place by himself and approved of the company. Then Bill Connors raised his eyes and said with a big smile, "On a different note, do you know that the apartment is not really soundproof?"

At first Charles didn't get the hint, but then it seemed that all the blood was concentrating in his face. "Don't worry, it inspired me, and I had a good time with myself too," he answered, which made both men laugh.

Jeffrey bolted into the room and asked if they had heard all the gruesome details of the night before. Connors gave him the police version and told him that the two guys were still behind bars and would most probably remain there for some time. "Will this ever stop?" Jeffrey asked.

"Yes, but only when we get the very last of these creeps under wraps. They're like a virus. New smartasses always appear when you think you have them all," was all Bill could respond.

At 11:30, Bill and Rosa left the apartment. The station was close by, so he suggested they walk. Across the street, he spotted a loitering bike rider with a black helmet. He asked Rosa to see if this was the same guy, but she said no; the other man was not as tall. The way this guy observed the two, Bill was sure he was another courier, but since Rosa was in his company, the guy wouldn't have the guts to hand her instructions. He took his phone and called the station to see if they had a squad car nearby to check him out, and seconds later he received a confirmation. They rounded the corner, and Bill stopped. He asked Rosa to bear with him for a short while, and he watched as the police car stopped just behind the guy and the officers came up to him. He waited until he saw them asking him for ID, and then they continued their walk to the station.

When they climbed the stairs, Connors noticed with satisfaction that the guy from across the street was brought in handcuffed. "Another one," he said to Rosa, who was more than confused. They walked into Summers' office. He looked sleep-deprived but professional. He briefly explained the procedure to Rosa and guaranteed that everything would be anonymous.

She followed the two detectives back to the ground floor, where she was led into a dark room. Over a microphone, Summers said, "Ready," and a door opened. The light came on, and seven dark-clad guys with helmets walked in. At first they all looked more or less alike, and Rosa thought it was a bad sequence out of a science-fiction movie.

"Please concentrate. Try to recall the situation," Summers said in a warm and reassuring voice.

Rosa said she could not recognize the face, but she remembered that the guy had a yellow emblem on his jacket, like the one standing near number three. Summers beamed with satisfaction, thanked Rosa for her time, and gave orders for the guys to step out. Number three was Andrei Enescu, the guy they picked up the night before in front of Lenox Hill Hospital.

CHAPTER 20

P hil was unaware of what was going on, and he could not rid his concern for Carlos. Just after twelve he left for the hospital and went directly to the emergency room, where another nurse and doctor were on duty. They asked if he was related to the patient, which he had to deny. When Phil told them he was his best friend and the one who brought him here the night before, they checked in the papers.

"Are you Phil Sherwin?" asked the nurse. He said yes. "Okay, he's awake, and if he is back from the MRI, he should be in Room 305. You can go there if you want."

Phil walked swiftly through the long corridors until he stood in front of 305. His heart was beating fast, and suddenly he was afraid to open the door, not knowing what to expect on the other side. Phil was relieved when he saw a completely bandaged Carlos lying calmly in his bed. He walked up to him and ever so lightly touched his hand. Carlos tried to move his head, but the restraints didn't allow him to do so.

"How are you?" was the first stupid thing that came over Phil's lips. Carlos moved his eyelids and tried to talk, but Phil couldn't understand anything from his mumbling. He felt his hand closing in on his and Phil took this as a sign of gladness. He didn't want to stress him and decided to move a chair next to the bed and just hold his hand to give him comfort. Phil must have been there for nearly an hour before the door opened and a tall, good-looking female doctor walked in, came over, and introduced herself. "Hi, I'm Dr. Ann Kirk." She looked at Phil expectantly and then asked, "And you are?"

"Oh, I'm sorry; I'm Phil, a friend of Carlos. I was the one who brought him to emergency last night." This seemed sufficient for her.

Then she checked his pulse, looked at his eyes, and said "Carlos, if you are in pain, please close your eyes. If you are okay, please keep them open." They both looked at him, and when he closed his eyes, she wrote something on the note board. "I'll take care of it immediately," she said and left the room. A few moments later, she came back and injected a liquid into the plastic tube attached to Carlos's arm. "That should help and make you sleep some more."

She then looked at Phil, making a sign to follow her outside. In the corridor, she told him that Carlos was very lucky; he had internal bleeding, but they could not find any problems with his organs. She said that he would most probably be here for a few days until they were sure that he was on his way to recovery. Then she looked again at her notes on the clipboard and asked if Phil would let her know where they could contact his mother. He promised to find out; Phil knew where Carlos lived and thought that somewhere in his apartment he would find the answer. She thanked him, and Phil asked where his clothes were, to see if he could find a key to his place.

Phil inquired if he could come back later to see Carlos, and the doctor told him that was no problem. He would probably not be very receptive, but this was mainly because of the painkillers. Before he left, she said, "It is so wonderful to have good friends that care."

Phil was shocked to hear that and could only respond, "Guess this is what friends are for. And I owe him a lot."

Back home, Phil told Kevin that he wanted to go to Carlos's apartment to find his mother's address, but Kevin asked him to wait. He wanted to call in and make sure it was not a crime scene, but they learned that so far, the police were not interested in the place, since it was not connected to the assault.

At the police station, the interrogation of the new captive went quite well. After searching him, they found another anonymous note specifying the date, time, and place of the first payment of $10,000. In an instruction letter, Charles was ordered to deliver this note to Good Times, Inc. and make sure they would comply with the requests. With this evidence, the detective had a firm case of blackmail in hand. The next step was to find out who the initiators were. It was obvious that all three guys held at the station were only handlers, and the police were hopeful to get more information on the higher-ranking goons of the organization. By playing them with the limited knowledge they had, Summers was adding piece by piece to the puzzle.

At the end of the day of questioning, they were brought back to their cells, tired and fragile. Summers was sure that they would soon start to sing, but he felt he had to cook them a little more, and the charming surroundings of the precinct and the prospect that they would soon be transferred to Riker was certainly spinning in their heads. They all knew that once they were taken there, things would be much more serious. Summers was sure that they would land there sooner or later, but he wanted to get more out of them, if possible a confession that they were involved in Oscar's killing and the assault on Carlos.

Meanwhile, Kevin and Phil went through Carlos's meticulous apartment. "This is a nice place," Kevin noted.

They found a few photos scattered around, some of Carlos and his mother and possibly younger siblings. While Phil was gathering more paper, Kevin went to the phone and flipped through the speed dial list. There was a New Jersey number under "M," which they suspected could stand for *Mom*. He didn't want to make the call until he dialed the department and asked for the name associated with this number. He learned that it was an unlisted number, but they would investigate and let him know. Phil asked Kevin why he didn't just try the number, but he responded that if his assumption was correct, he didn't want to explain to Carlos's mother what had happened.

They continued for another hour, searching for leads, but found nothing except detailed listings of his incoming money and a list of regular payments he made to a small bank in Allentown, New Jersey. Phil guessed this was another lead to his mother. He got a kick out of playing detective, and whenever he found something he thought important or mysterious, he called Kevin over to look at it. At the end of their search, they left the apartment in Washington Heights and returned to the Upper East Side.

Kevin took numerous photos of documents that would hopefully prove helpful. They first took the subway and then a bus cross town and down Fifth Avenue. When they got back to the apartment, Kevin received the confirmation from the department that the number was for a Clementina Sabartes in Allentown, New Jersey. They were contemplating if they should call but decided first going over to Lenox Hill and check on Carlos, hoping that they could give good—or at least more accurate—news to his mother.

The business was suffering; Phil was more interested in helping the police break the case than satisfying a few men in need. He was nice to the callers and invented excuses why they couldn't provide services. Phil also didn't want to put anybody in danger. He explained the situation to all of the escorts, and they seemed cool with his decision. House and hotel calls to well-known regulars continued, but they all agreed that for the time being, they would not host clients at their place, for everybody's security.

Kevin and Phil walked over to the hospital, and when they entered the emergency room, Dr. Kirk came out of the office and greeted them with a wide smile. "He is doing much better. We were able to stabilize him, and he is receptive. You can go to his room. He'll be happy to see you," she said.

Phil felt tremendous relief. He took Kevin by the hand, and they rushed through the corridors to Carlos's room. When they opened the door, they got a huge shock. He was lying in his bed, with most of the bandages removed, and completely bruised.

He must have seen their faces, because he said in a very soft voice, "Nothing to worry about. It just looks bad, but it's only bruises. They will heal in no time."

They were smiling, and Kevin jokingly complimented him on the rather exotic coloring. Carlos lifted his sheet and showed them his body, which was in all shades of blue, green, and red. Phil asked if he could call his mother and told him that they took the liberty of going to his apartment to find her number. He was shocked at first, because he must have realized how bad it was, but he gave them his consent, asking to play it down, he didn't want her to see him this way; he knew if they sounded too alarming, she would jump on a bus and come here.

They promised him that they would convince her that everything was under control and that he would call her soon. They also told him about the three suspects the NYPD held. Kevin asked if Carlos could remember anything, and after a short pause, Carlos said that they were all hidden behind bike helmets; however, one of the guys had a yellow sign or emblem stitched to his jacket. Other than that, he could not recognize anything; he was just trying to cover his face from all the kicking and beating.

Kevin had a smile on his face and said, "The housekeeper has identified one of the suspects by the same emblem." He took his cell phone and called Summers at the station to give him the information. They stayed for a few more minutes. Phil promised that he would look in on him again later today, and then they left for home.

CHAPTER 21

At the police station, Summers summoned Andrei Enescu into an interrogation room. He wanted to confront him with the new ammunition. Not only did he have Rosa's statement but Carlos's too. Both recognized the yellow emblem on his jacket. He was quite sure that he was one of the rougher ones in the group and most probably also involved in the killing of Oscar. Unfortunately, they had no witnesses there, but Summers felt comfortable, with his long experience, to trick this smartass into a statement. If not, the assault on Carlos would already be enough to keep him locked up and ship him to Riker.

As part of the game, he kept Andrei waiting in the barren room for a little longer than necessary. He knew that would build insecurity and anticipation. Summers was not surprised upon entering the room to see Andrei nonchalantly hanging in his chair with an arrogant smirk on his face. Summers knew this was the perfect gesture of trying to hide fear. He moved slowly to the table while another officer positioned himself near the door. The detective placed the growing file on the table and after a few long moments flipped the folder open and exposed a pile of gruesome photographs of Carlos. He just left them sitting there, as he watched Andrei who tried to make them out upside down.

"You want to see them?" the detective asked rather passively.

Andrei just raised his shoulders as if to say, *who cares? But if you show them, I will look at them.* Summers turned the file around and started to spread out all the pictures on the wooden table. While doing so, he kept his eyes on Andrei, who showed little reaction.

152

"Gruesome?" was all the detective remarked.

Andrei responded, "Shit happens!"

After a short pause, Summers remarked, "As a matter of fact, we have a witness who said that you were part of this gathering."

This stiffened Andrei's back. Fully aware of what could happen, he said, "No way. I was never there!"

"You were never where?" Summers countered.

"There. I don't know where that is!"

Summers calmly piled the photos back together and then looked his adversary in the eyes. "Okay, sorry I tried to trick you, but I guess you're too clever," he said with a smile. Andrei, reassured of his position, smiled back, feeling like the winner of round one. After a few silent seconds, Summers caught the yellow emblem on the jacket and innocently asked what it stood for. Andrei was flattered and told him that this was a souvenir from Romania, where he was part of a boy group, possibly meaning a street gang. Without further questioning, he told the detective that it was a high honor to receive this emblem.

Summers asked only short questions, and Andrei, proud of his accomplishments, told him that only a very few ever received this, making it sound like a medal of honor. When Summers asked if he knew of any others with this qualification and the emblem who lived around here, Andrei just laughed and shook his head. Summers felt success coming up but didn't show any excitement.

"You would never give anybody else permission to wear your jacket?" he asked, sure of the response.

"No way. This is more than just an emblem. This is culture!" Andrei exclaimed.

Summers stood up and spread the photos again. "Well, Andrei, the person here, beaten to a pulp, is on his way to recovery, and he has identified your 'medal of honor,' as has another person."

It now dawned on Andrei that he had been tricked, and for the first time, worry crossed his face. "I am not saying anything more. You want to hang me for this stupid emblem? This will never happen."

Summers grinned and remarked how fast a sign of accomplishment and pride can become stupid. He packed up all his papers, went to the door, and just before leaving the room, turned around and said, "Enjoy tonight, since tomorrow you will be brought to Riker. The food there must be bad and the company not very pleasant to newcomers."

A second officer came in, and the two brought Andrei back to the cell.

CHAPTER 22

At home, Phil got a call from Jeffrey, who asked if we would like to join him and Charles for dinner later. He asked Kevin, who thought this would be a nice distraction. They accepted, but before, Phil still had some work to do. Even when he tried to keep a low profile, there were always clients requesting company, which was good.

The hectic day called for a nice, hot shower, which as usual was followed by a very sexy drying period. Phil and Kevin knew that they didn't have too much time but felt some real quality time together was well deserved. When Kevin walked out of the bathroom, hair still dripping, Phil couldn't stop lusting after his magnificent body. Before he stood in front of him he was already showing excitement. Kevin licked his lips and soon proceeded to the main course. The young detective was a master at pleasing. He knew all the critical places, and sometimes Phil felt he was touching them all at the same time.

Phil could only run his fingers through Kevin's wet hair while he engulfed the shaft as if he'd been starving for a very long time. He sensed that Phil's tolerance was low and soon left the front for the back. He was maneuvering his tongue masterfully, and after the intense treatment, there was nothing Phil would deny him; Kevin was well aware of this. He didn't have to ask; he knew when Phil raised and moved his hips that he was ready to welcome him. What followed was a very intense few minutes. This was not lovemaking, just a hot romp of pre-dinner sex. Phil reached climax sooner than he wanted to, but it didn't seem to bother him. When Kevin withdrew, he only had to move up and down a few times until he gushed all over Phil's chest and shot as far as his lips—a welcome first course. Once they regained their composure, they cleaned off all the evidence got dressed and were ready to leave.

When they came out of the room, Alfred was in the kitchen, preparing some food. They told him they were going out for dinner, and he offered to cover the phone.

On their way they passed by the hospital to check on Carlos, whose condition had improved further. He agreed that they could contact his mother the following day. When Phil and Kevin arrived at the tall condo-building where Charles lived, the doorman announced their arrival. They were taken up to the penthouse by an elevator man, who made sure they were really expected. "Wow," was all Phil could utter when he entered the place. It was probably the most sophisticated and beautiful place he had ever seen.

When they got to the living room, Bill Connors was sitting there with his beer, and Jeffrey came up and greeted them he was in a great mood. Charles took our cocktail orders, but Phil was not yet ready to join the others on the couch. He had to take in all the décor. A small Rothko painting was surrounded by a number of delicate drawings and watercolors by artists like de Kooning, Kline, Motherwell, Johns, and Still. It was not just the works of art but also the arrangement. All over the large living room treasures were placed—a gallery of sculptures from many centuries, including a wood piece of St. Sebastian, possibly from the sixteenth century as well as works by Calder, Smith, and Rodin.

Charles came up to Phil and gave him a tour with explanations of a few works. "You'll see more later. Come and join us now," he said. He was a really nice guy, and now that he was more himself again, Phil saw that he was also very handsome. Once he joined the others, he observed that there was tremendous chemistry between Jeffrey and Charles. They were always searching each other's eyes and exchanging smiles. It was a nice group of people, and Connors was very involved, talking shop with Kevin. He optimistically said that he felt they were getting very close to the inner circle of the organization. One of the guys was spilling information, and they were pretty certain that the guy with the emblem was the roughest of the three caught. "His days are numbered. He will be moved to Riker tomorrow," he said.

"What ever happened to the car that was surveying the apartment?" Kevin asked.

"Well, it was never moved, but the tapes must have been taken out by the two students. Since it was illegally parked, it was towed," Bill responded.

Jeffrey got up for a refill, and when he returned, he sat next to me and whispered in my ear, "I think I'm in love!" Phil looked at Charles, who produced a monumental smile. He was very happy for them but realized that he might lose one of his best guys.

A door opened, and Rosa came in to announce that dinner was ready. Charles took the lead with his arm over Jeffrey's shoulder, and they entered a formal dining room, again decorated in the best of taste. Beside the huge glass table, beautifully set, there was a very large Ocean Park by Diebenkorn and a Motherwell black-and-white painting. Above the table, instead of a chandelier, was a wide mobile by Calder. The entire room was lit by indirect light, which produced a very cozy effect. Charles could see Phil's wide-open eyes and remarked that he was happy that somebody appreciated his and his wife's taste.

We sat down, and Charles poured some wine as Rosa walked in with the first course, which was a beautiful salad. This was followed by a huge pot roast with vegetables and potatoes. It was delicious, and I could see how happy Charles was with a group of men he could share his feelings with. Bill Connors adapted really well and seemed not to mind his assignment; on the contrary, he seemed very interested and asked questions about Good Times, Inc.

They all agreed that even if the reason for them to be here together was anything but uplifting, especially thinking of Oscar and Carlos, without it they would never have met. Rosa peered in from time to time, proud of how they cleaned their plates. When she inquired about dessert, they all decided that this would be too much, but coffee would be great. Back to the living room, coffee was soon served. Charles asked if Phil would be interested in seeing some more art, and he nodded enthusiastically.

Charles took Phil back to his study, where he showed him a late Picasso still life facing his desk and a large male Roman torso on a metal pedestal. There were also a number of smaller works, mainly portraits of family. Next to it was a room that would probably be a nursery, but kids were not in the plan, so it was used as a TV parlor with very comfortable fauteuils and a couple of Andy Warhol's. His bedroom had more established works, two great Egon Schieles, one a nearly nude, tormented-looking woman, the other a nude self-portrait. There was also a sizable late Matisse cutout work facing the bed. Then there was another guest room next to his, where Bill stayed for the moment.

Through a narrow corridor were Rosa's quarters. Charles then turned around, looked Phil in the eyes, and said that he was very happy to have connected with Jeffrey. He hoped that this would not pose a problem for G.T., but honestly, he always had a crush on him, and when Jeffrey offered the other day to keep him company, everything seemed to fall into place. Phil told him that he was very happy for them, and that Jeffrey was already hinting something to him.

They joined the others back in the living room; Phil felt like he was in a trance and just grabbed his coffee and fantasized about having art like this just for him.

When they returned home, Alfred greeted them and said that Jeremy had called from Florida. He just wanted to know how everything was, and he would probably come up and visit for a couple of days. He wanted to know if he could stay here; if not, he would go to a hotel, but he would love to see them.

CHAPTER 23

At the police station, the three Romanians in the holding cells had major arguments. Andrei was still trying to play tough, while Serge—who seemed to be the most intelligent among them—appeared ready to cooperate. This was the impression the translator got from their taped conversations. Andrei told the others that they had him on the beating and angrily said, "I should have finished this fucking homo."

The others were both shocked, but Andrei appeared more convinced than ever that a dead witness is the best witness. Then it slipped out that "the other freak" would not talk, which was immediately interpreted to mean Oscar.

"I think we're on a roll. Continue to listen in carefully," Summers demanded, hoping finally to return home for a peaceful night. He was aware that recordings would not hold in court, but with the knowledge he would be able to lead them into statements.

Andrei appeared very scared of the prospect of being transferred to Riker the next day. Serge, on the other hand, was much calmer; he said that he would talk, because Emilian had promised him the American dream and not the American jail when he recruited him. "I have never done anything bad," he said, "just taken people with my bike to places and waited for them, to bring them home."

On the video intercom, it was obvious that he was distressed to be in here. "I just wanted to go to university, become a doctor and help. I never wanted to be a criminal, and now that I am here, I will probably never have my dream come true."

The translator felt sorry for the guy; he knew that most probably he would be deported. Stefan, the last to join the group, was somewhere in between the two. He was certainly not as fierce as Andrei but not as innocent as Serge either. He just said that if he ever gets out of here in one piece, he would flee from Emilian and start a new life far away. The talk became slower, as they tried to get some sleep.

Jeffrey stayed with Charles while Bill watched a repeat episode of *Law and Order.* In his imagination, he could see the current case as perfect material for an episode. It had everything to make it a hit: murder, assault, and lots of sexy talk. He even thought he could get involved in it. He hoped that he would meet a nice girl soon and have a lasting and intimate relationship. While all this went through his head, a longing made him start touching himself. Under the covers, he rubbed delicately on his rapidly growing shaft. He moistened his finger and circled it over the head of his penis, which made his lust for intimacy grow even stronger. He took his other hand and started to massage his scrotum and sometimes let a finger wander as far as his anus. All this and the thought of closeness to another person drove him into an erotic fantasy. He enjoyed this very much and tried to slow down every time he felt his climax approaching. He kicked the blanket off and got rid of the T-shirt. Then he went to the bathroom and picked up a bottle of lotion to lube his genitals.

Back on the bed, he ignored the TV and was very happy just playing with himself. Several times he thought he reached the point of no return but was always successful in stalling it a little longer, until he was so excited that with a couple of loud screams, he gushed out multiple shots of wonderful white sperm. The noise was heard next door, and Charles got up, put on a robe, and knocked on his guest's door.

"Everything okay in there?" he called.

Very surprised, Bill answered, "Oh yes. Guess I had a wet dream. It was wonderful."

Both guys laughed on either side of the closed door, and Charles returned to his room.

The next morning, Jeffrey and Charles were sitting over coffee in the living room when Bill walked in. They wished each other good morning, and Bill helped himself to a cup. Then he said that he was expected at the station, and that his time at the penthouse was probably coming to an end. Charles was sorry to hear that; he enjoyed Bill's company, and with every passing day, Bill seemed to adjust more and more to this lifestyle.

Bill added that he hoped that he could stay another day or so; he liked the assignment and felt he'd gained a lot of new experiences and was much more open today. Charles suggested that he would give Bill a farewell present, if he wanted to get more experience. Bill raised his brows and waited for more. Charles suggested that he could pay for an evening at Good Times, Inc., if he was open to this. At first, Bill shook his head but then said, "Let me think about this. First I have to face my boss in an hour and get the updates."

When Bill Connors arrived at the station, he was asked to join Summers on the second floor, where he was questioning Stefan. Next to the interrogation room, behind the one-sided mirror, Bill followed the masterful questioning of Summers. Stefan made good on what he told his two companions the night before. He answered all the questions asked, explained that he was a cousin of Emilian but came to the United States as the hope of the family to study medicine. Emilian was a shady character, but the other night, he asked Stefan for a favor, and he didn't think too much of it. He was asked to give a letter to a woman who lived in the building and then return. He thought for the hundred dollars he was promised for this errand, he could do this. He needed the money for rent and never thought it would turn out this way. When he was asked where Emilian lived, he couldn't say, but he told them he always met him at the office in Astoria. Summers made a note and then asked if he could give the exact address. Stefan said he had it written down in his notebook, which was in the bag they confiscated.

Summers pushed a call button and asked the officer who appeared to fetch Stefan's bag from the evidence lockup. Stefan said that his family believed Emilian was a well-to-do businessman in import and export and then added that even back in the homeland, he was always the black sheep of the family. When he was asked if he knew Andrei and Serge before, he said no; he met them for the first time here at the station.

The policeman came in with a canvas shoulder bag and set it on the table. Summers asked Stefan to take his notebook out and give him the address. He flipped through the pages and then gave him an address of a place near Astoria Park and a cellular number. Outside, Bill wrote the information down and immediately requested information on the phone number. As he feared, it turned out to be a disposable prepaid. Then he inquired about the address. It was a warehouse that was rented out short term, usually without any lease or guarantee, and all in cash. They thought it was unlikely they would find anything there; nevertheless, they didn't want to leave any stone unturned.

Over the microphone and headset attached to Summers, Bill asked if he should go there, and Summers nodded through the mirror. Bill and an assigned detective left the building with a squad car following them. Once they crossed the bridge into Queens, the drive to their destination only took them a few minutes. As expected, there was no response at the door. When Bill walked around the building, he ran into a laborer. He asked if the man knew where the tenants from unit 105 were, but he just shrugged and said that they had cleaned out the night before and that he was only responsible to keep the place tidy. Then he said he put all the garbage they left in the container.

Bill thanked him, and when he turned the corner, he saw a truck approaching the containers. He ran there, holding up his badge, and declared the containers evidence in a murder case. The driver and his coworker made some indistinguishable remarks but seemed happy to do one less job and get an early lunch break.

Bill called the laborer over and asked him what came out of unit 105. He could only guess, mainly waste from bins, papers, etc. Bill hated to dig in garbage, but at this point, he and his partner had little choice and started to unfold every little scrap of paper they found in the containers.

"Shit, this is going to take us forever. Call in and ask for assistance," Bill told his partner, who was more than happy to turn this tedious work over to somebody else. While Bill stayed with the containers, his partner went to the car, where he got tape to close off the crime scene. They continued on their search until a new crew of specialists arrived.

Once a four-man crew got there, Connors gave them instructions and was soon in his car with his partner, driving back to Manhattan. He was remembering the fun times of the past few days, protecting Charles. He felt sorry that it might come to an end soon but remembered it as a special perk of his job. In addition to the interesting times at the penthouse, he could not get rid of the idea of accepting the gift at Good Times, Inc. that Charles offered him this morning. He was intrigued, but it also made him nervous that he would even consider such a move.

He told his partner that he met some really nice guys, and that he was sorry it would soon be over. "I could get used to this lifestyle," he said.

Back at the station, they ran into a smiling Detective Summers. Stefan was giving them information that proved to be valuable, and a penetration into the core of the organization was imminent. A group of policemen and detectives were on their way to Brooklyn, where they hoped to find Emilian. Stefan remembered that his mother was staying with an aunt when she first came to the United States, and Emilian appeared to live there, though he was hardly ever around. He gave a detailed description of his cousin. "We are looking for a thirty-four-year-old tall and well-built man with dark-brown hair. He has numerous tattoos; one extends onto his neck."

Bill inquired about his next step, and his boss told him that according to Stefan, this guy was ready to kill at any time, without fear or reason, and ordered him back to his duties at Charles's place. First he said to call and make sure Charles would not leave the apartment until he was back there to accompany and protect him. Bill seemed happy at this assignment, and after calling Charles to tell him that he would be back soon and he should wait for him, he took his jacket and was on his way.

It was a sunny, beautiful day, and the few blocks would be a nice stroll. When he turned the corner on Park Avenue to Charles's building, he scanned all the parked cars but could not see anything irregular. The doorman was already informed, and the elevator man took him up to the penthouse. Charles greeted him at the door and said that he was ready to leave for the office; he was expected to sign a few papers.

Without any further delay, the two men left the apartment and went downstairs. They decided to walk the short distance, which gave Bill the opportunity to update Charles. He told him about the three guys they were holding and how one of them was most probably responsible for Oscar's murder. He also told him about the alleged boss, Emilian, who must be aware that they were closing in on him. This person was described as brutal and unpredictable, Summers prolonged his protection assignment.

"Do you mind?" Charles asked.

Bill shook his head and confirmed that he very much enjoyed being with Charles and the other guys. "I have experienced so much the past few days. I learned a lot, and I believe I have broadened my horizons."

Charles seemed very pleased and just said that whenever he was ready to take it a step further, his offer at Good Times, Inc. was standing. This brought an insecure smile to Bill's lips, and he responded, "I have been thinking about this much more than I should."

They arrived at the office building on Third Avenue. Charles went straight to the elevator, and Bill followed him. When they reached the twenty-eighth floor, a very nice young woman greeted them. Charles continued down a long corridor until he reached his corner office. He motioned to Bill to take a seat on a sofa while he sat down behind his desk. "You want coffee?" he asked and then pushed the intercom and asked for two coffees and the papers he was meant to sign. Seconds later, a young man knocked and walked in.

"Hello, Craig," Charles greeted his assistant, who walked over to the desk with a large leather binder.

"Good afternoon, boss," he responded. "Everything okay? We haven't seen you in a couple of days."

Charles nodded and introduced Craig to Detective Connors. This seemed to worry the assistant a little, but Charles assured him that everything was okay, just a little complicated at the moment; he was not under investigation, but Bill was actually here for his protection.

Seemingly relieved, Craig said that Charles's wife had called and arranged to return in five days, if this was okay with him.

Charles looked at Bill, who said, "I guess by then everything should be solved."

Another intern walked in with the coffee. She set one cup on the desk, walked over to Bill, and set the other cup with some cream and sugar on the table in front of him and left the room again.

Craig went through the papers with Charles, indicating where he was meant to sign, while Bill got up and started looking at the many photographs displayed in the office. They recorded a full, rich life: Charles on a yacht with other men, Charles with important people on the golf course, and Charles in the company of a very attractive woman somewhere in a Caribbean paradise.

Craig, who seemed very efficient, was soon done. He took the binder and asked if there was anything else; otherwise he would get back to work. Charles just said that he could call him always at home, but he would probably not come to the office for another couple of days. Craig offered to have the pending contracts brought over to the apartment later, if that was more convenient. Charles said that would be great, and he could stay for a drink if he had nothing better to do. Craig smiled in acceptance and left the office.

With the closing of the door, Bill's phone buzzed. It was Summers, who inquired about his whereabouts. Bill told him that they were at the office but about to leave.

"Stay there until I call you. We believe Emilian has found out that we're after him and might be losing it. We believe he's in Manhattan, and at this point, it would be dangerous for you to wander the streets." Bill gave the address where they were and was promised a car to pick them up and bring them back. He was also informed that plainclothes policemen were surveying the building where Charles lived.

Charles was listening uncomfortably to the conversation when his phone rang. "Hi, Jeffrey, how are you?" he asked casually, but he felt that there was something wrong.

Jeffrey's voice was low and hard to understand. "I think I'm being followed. There was a dark Chevy cruising on Seventy-Eighth and Lexington while I was walking to the subway. Then I saw one of the guys jumping out and entering the same subway car. When I looked up, he threw me a nasty smile."

"Wait. Bill is here. I want him to hear this. I'm turning the speaker on." Charles pushed the button and said to continue.

Jeffrey then said that when he reached the Sixty-Eighth Street station, there were lots of students on the platform, and he could take advantage of the crowd and escape the train, but he was not sure if the other guy was still behind him. "I am now somewhere in Hunter College, in a bathroom, hiding."

Bill walked over to the desk and asked into the speaker if he was able to get a good look at the guy, and Jeffrey said that he was hard to miss. He was tattooed all over, wearing a white T-shirt, with his arms exposed. "He looks like a real rough character."

Bill said that he should go to the bookshop on the corner of Sixty-Seventh Street and Lexington, hoping there would be many other people there, and wait for him. He could sense the fear in Jeffrey, and with a few calming words said that he should not hang up his phone but stay in contact while walking to his destination.

There was a knock on the door, and Craig announced that the car was waiting downstairs. Bill told Jeffrey that they would be there within minutes. Then he wrote down Jeffrey's number and told him to hang up; he would call him back immediately from his cell phone. While they took the elevator down, Bill entered the number into his phone, and when they reached the lobby, he pushed *call*. Jeffrey was on before the first ring ended. Bill could hear that he was breathing heavily, and then he said that he was on his way.

"Are there other students around?"

"Yes," was all Jeffrey said.

"Good. Go to the bookshop now; we're on our way."

Bill and Charles climbed into the waiting car and gave the driver the new destination. It took them only a few minutes until they stopped on the corner of Lexington and Sixty-Seventh Street, next to the precinct. Charles remained in the car, and Bill ran across the sidewalk, into the store. He looked around and then said into his phone, "I'm here; where are you?"

In the back, he saw a scared Jeffrey peek over some shelves. He came running to Bill, who closed his phone, took Jeffrey by the arm, and pushed him into the car. Outside on the sidewalk were a few students, not noticing much happening, until a couple of shots were heard. Nobody was hurt, but a scene of hysteria ensued.

"Go to the house!" Bill screamed at the driver, who took off at high speed toward Park Avenue. Bill leaned back and smiled at Jeffrey, signaling that everything was okay and then called Summers and reported the incident. He said Summers should send men to Hunter College to investigate the shots and make sure nobody was hurt. Then he added, "May I make a suggestion? I believe we should put some cover on Good Times, Inc. This guy is on a vendetta and will not stop at anything." Summers agreed and immediately called Kevin to give him an update and ordered not to leave the place until further notice.

The three of them reached home, but before leaving the car, Bill made sure the coast was clear. He couldn't see anything suspicious, so he opened the door and was the first to leave the sedan. He then made sure the other two got into the building.

The moment Jeffrey entered the safety of the penthouse, he exclaimed, still in shock, "I need a drink fast!"

Charles felt the anxiety in Jeffrey and in front of Bill took him in his arms and tried to offer all the reassuring comfort he could give. With a tumbler filled with ice and scotch, he finally asked "Who is this freak?"

Bill gave him the short version and concluded that Emilian must realize that he was on a one-way street and was just out to do as much harm as possible until they caught him. The description Jeffrey gave of him was pretty accurate with Stefan's.

When Rosa came in, Charles told her that they would not be going out for dinner; he was sure she could create a delicious dinner from what was in the house. Nobody was to leave the safety of the apartment until further notice.

CHAPTER 24

Four cops rushed out of the station to the corner at Hunter College. The officers started to question the student witnesses. Most of them could say nothing more than that they heard two shots in quick succession, but all of them were sure that it must have come from across the street. One of the witnesses thought he saw a guy in a white T-shirt with lots of tattoos running east, shortly after the commotion, and he saw a dark sedan speed toward Park Avenue. Other than that, there was nothing of importance.

One of the officers went to the place where the student thought the shots originated, and found a couple of shells. He picked them up with a pencil and placed them into a plastic bag. Not much could be done there; they were sure that the shooter was long gone, and miraculously, nobody was hurt. They reported back to the station.

A few blocks away, a furious Emilian was nervously walking north. He was blinded with anger and constantly said to himself in a low voice, "I am going to kill you all, you fucking bastards." He bumped into other pedestrians, but in his rage he didn't acknowledge it. The further he got, the more his rage grew, and at this point, all rational thought left his body. A man talking to himself, furious against the entire world and bumping into other people seems quite common on the streets of Manhattan, so the other pedestrians paid little attention to him.

At Good Times, Inc., Alfred, Kevin, and Phil were sitting silently around the table. They felt helpless and hated the idea that they were not allowed to leave the apartment. Alfred had plans to go out, but

Kevin told him that for his own sake, he should cancel them. Phil didn't mind being home with Kevin, even if the circumstances didn't inspire him of his favorite distractions. He tried to read a book but couldn't concentrate. He also felt guilty that he couldn't go to see Carlos at the hospital, but fortunately he was able to call him and was very relieved when he heard his voice sounding stronger.

Carlos told him that his mother was visiting and that he felt much better. He seemed a little sad that they had reduced his painkillers; with a weak laugh, he said that it was a very pleasant experience. Phil was happy he could joke again and offered that if his mother wanted to stay here, she was welcome. Carlos thanked him for the offer but said that they had put a bed up for her, and she was happy to be there with him.

While Phil was on the phone, Kevin went to the kitchen to inspect the refrigerator for some possible dinner. It looked bleak, and he announced that they might have to settle for a liquid dinner, but getting drunk was not really an option at this time. They became very inventive, and with a package of pasta and ketchup and a few other ingredients, they created a survival dinner. The appetite was not big, and they all agreed that this recipe would never make it into any cookbook. Most of it ended up in the trash, but at least they knew the basic needs were satisfied.

It was different at the penthouse. Rosa had stocked up on everything and had no problems; she created a three-course dinner as usual.

NY1 reported on a shooting on Lexington Avenue earlier this afternoon, but at this point, they could not name a source or a reason. They interviewed a few students, who mainly said that they were scared but knew little more. Even though the police knew that Emilian had other things in mind than watching TV, they were very selective with the information. At the station, they were all optimistic that this nightmare was coming to an end.

All involved were glued to the TV, but it seemed they knew far more than what was reported. Bill, Jeffrey, and Charles relaxed in the living room with a cocktail; Bill started to get more comfortable with the gay lifestyle. It was obvious that his curiosity grew stronger every day, and he started asking questions more frequently. Charles and Jeffrey openly offered answers, which impressed him; they felt very comfortable with the subject. Charles now felt that he had to be a little inquisitive and bluntly asked Bill if he had ever had sex with another man. Bill blushed crimson and said, "Not really."

Charles and Jeffrey laughed, and with a wide grin, Charles said, "Not really? What does that mean? Did you or didn't you?"

With a cough of embarrassment, Bill said that as a teenager, he was fooling around with his best friend, but it was innocent. They jerked off together, and he once tasted his friend's sperm but didn't like it too much. He sometimes let his eyes wander in the shower at the gym, and he got a little excited watching other well-built guys, but other than that, no.

For Charles, this became a fun game, and he wanted to tease Bill a little further, but the intercom rang and the doorman announced Craig. Bill took his gun and went to the door; only when he saw the assistant leaving the elevator by himself did he open the door. Craig walked in with his briefcase, and Bill said that his boss was in the living room. He looked astonished to see Jeffrey there. Charles sensed the tension and introduced Craig to his new lover.

"Thanks, but I've met Craig before. We were quite close, may I say." He laughed, leaving Craig standing there a little uncomfortable, to say the least.

"I guess you need a drink," Charles suggested.

Craig was still trying to recover. Charles walked over to the bar and asked, "What shall it be?"

Craig was still speechless, so Jeffrey jumped in and said, "Gin and tonic." This broke the ice, and they all started to laugh.

The assistant finally joined the party, and after a few sips, he started to loosen up a little. While Jeffrey and Craig spoke of old times, the other two listened, very interested. Rosa appeared in the doorway and asked if she should set for one more. Charles looked at Craig and asked if he would join them for dinner. Craig checked his watch and said, "I might as well. It's too late for my classes now anyway."

Before Rosa left the room, Craig said that he took classes at the Swedish Institute for Massage, but they started already, and it would be awkward to be so late. Charles was a little astonished, but Craig immediately said that this was only a hobby. He would never leave his $80,000 job to become a masseur, but he always loved to be massaged, so he wanted to learn how to do massage.

While he was talking, Rosa announced that dinner was ready, and the four men went into the next room.

Charles poured some red wine from a decanter, and Rosa served dinner. The conversation was lively, but Bill seemed very interested in the massage thing, and continued trying to bring up the subject again. He asked Craig if he had some experience already and what kind of massages he was doing. Craig diplomatically answered that he was practicing on friends, and most of them seemed very happy and relaxed afterward. Bill was digging for more details, but Craig was a little uncomfortable at the boss's table and tried to avoid the more intimate details.

Charles followed the conversation with certain sarcasm and finally asked Craig if he would be willing to give Bill a massage after dinner. Craig blushed a little and thought he was getting off by saying that he didn't have a table and no oils. "This would be the least of the problems. We have all that here, and you could set up in Bill's room, but of course only if you want."

Craig looked at Bill, saw his pleading eyes, and finally gave in. Bill seemed very chipper now, possibly a little nervous, since he'd never had a massage from another man, much less a gay man.

Dinner was delicious, and coffee was served in the living room. While Jeffrey offered brandy, Charles went back into the storage room, got the foldable massage table out, and set it up in Bill's room. He put fresh towels in there and got some bio-tone massage oil and cream. Everything was neatly placed and a couple of candles lit on the side table to enhance the atmosphere. Then he joined the others with a wide grin on his face and said, "Whenever you are ready, the place is ready."

Now there was no way back out. Bill got nervous and said that he would like to take a shower first, and Craig, less nervous, said that this would be an absolute must. But he promised that he would shower too beforehand, since he was at the office the entire day. After Bill finished his coffee and brandy, he got up and said, *"Que sera sera, whatever will be will be"* and with a laugh, left the other guys for his shower.

He came back a few minutes later, dressed in a robe, and said that he was more or less ready. Craig said he would need a few minutes and asked where he could freshen up. Bill showed him his room and the bathroom and went back to join the others. When they were sure that Craig was out, Charles asked what he expected, Bill couldn't give him a specific answer, because he didn't know.

"Well, if you want more to happen, you might have to take the initiative. Touch him too; give him a sign that he's free to touch you wherever you want, and so on, but I'm sure you're a big boy, and you'll find out yourself."

Craig appeared in the door in shorts and a T-shirt. "Mr. Detective, are you ready?"

Bill got up and said, "As ready as I'll ever be," and followed Craig into his room. When he asked what was next, Craig told him to get on the table. When he dropped his robe, Craig dropped his jaw but hoped it was not too obvious. Bill lay on his stomach, and Craig covered his butt with a towel. At first Craig, was shy about starting the massage, but once he kneaded on the shoulders and felt how Bill enjoyed his touch, he became more aggressive. He was trying to go by the book and act very professional, until he came to the lower back. He folded the towel to the left and started to knead the right butt cheek; it was nice and firm but a little hairy. Craig got really involved; he then took all his courage and brushed lightly with a finger through the crack, which resulted in a moan of pleasure from Bill. He softly asked, "Is this okay?" and a confirming groan made him remove the towel altogether. He now had full liberty to work on this beautiful butt, and from time to time, he accidentally went through the center and down to the scrotum. Bill enjoyed this, and suddenly Craig felt Bill's hand searching for his shorts. He seemed to want to touch his penis, which Craig didn't mind at all, but he tried to continue without showing too much reaction. It was difficult to concentrate, because he also felt that Bill was sporting an erection, which didn't help matters.

The masseur had to concentrate not to get aroused as he started to work on the thighs. On his upward strokes, he couldn't resist not giving a slight tease to the scrotum and then down to the lower legs and feet. He picked up the towel he'd discarded earlier and asked Bill to turn onto his back. He was holding the towel to cover his midsection. The towel was tenting big time, and when Craig asked in a soft voice how he was doing, Bill only mumbled that this was the closest he had been to heaven in his life.

Craig was happy and expertly started on the head. He massaged the full head of hair and then the face very gently. When he touched the lips, Bill parted them and carefully licked Craig's finger. While doing this, the towel moved up and down ever so slightly. It was very sensual, and the air was charged with eroticism. It became harder and harder to remain professional. The well-built chest was a sheer pleasure to work on, and the very sensitive nipples made Bill's hand search for Craig's shorts again. He got very excited and started holding on to Craig, who enjoyed this manly grab.

He couldn't avoid getting hard, but at this point, he didn't resist anymore. He continued on to the stomach and decided to remove the towel completely. Bill didn't seem to mind, and his full erection seemed thankful to be freed from the unnecessary cloth. Craig whispered that this was not according to the rules of the Swedish Institute, but he liked it. He now took the courage to hold Bill's huge shaft in his hand and with a little extra oil started to move his hand slowly up and down. Bill got very excited, and a tiny drop of pre-sperm oozed out. Craig didn't want to waste it and cleaned it off with the tip of his tongue. Then he parted his lips and engulfed the large head of Bill's penis and slowly worked himself down the shaft. This got Bill so excited that with a fast movement, he tore the shorts off of Craig and grabbed hold of his fully erect penis.

He was moaning and groaning while Craig played with his tongue. He licked the scrotum and then went back to the shaft, which was now dripping huge quantities of translucent pre-sperm. The masseur knew how to please, and Bill could not have had a better introduction to man-to-man sex. The detective felt a little helpless; he didn't know what to do but hold on to Craig. He moved his hand slightly. Craig didn't mind; he loved to please, and it has been one of his biggest fantasies to please a straight man. In his devious mind, he decided to take it a step further and lubed his index finger with oil and slowly inserted it into Bill. At first, he was shocked and seemed to resist, but he soon allowed access, and when Craig touched the prostate, Bill released a loud cry of lust.

Craig now knew that he had him at the point where he would soon be shooting a huge load. While he was massaging Bill's prostate, he didn't let go of his penis. His mouth was opening more, and he was hoping that he would be rewarded with a huge load of sperm. He was; Bill couldn't control himself any longer and gushed eight streams of delicious sperm deep into Craig's mouth. He gulped it down.

Emptied completely, Bill was now lying exhausted and breathing heavily on the massage table, covering his eyes with his hands. He uttered, "This was the most intense orgasm I ever experienced."

Craig, a little sorry that it was over, slowly released Bill from his mouth and responded, "And I have never had a load like that going down my throat."

Bill was surprised and couldn't believe that he swallowed it all. "You like this?" he asked.

Craig nodded and said, "Love it."

Bill was lying there with a big, happy smile and completely surprised himself with the next question. "Would you let me suck you?"

Craig now wore the astonished face. He slowly moved his semi-hard penis closer to Bill's mouth. Bill got up from the table and asked him to get comfortable. While Craig settled on the table, Bill assured him that this was the first time he is doing this, but he had the strong urge to experience it. At first he was hesitant and only played with the head of Craig's penis, but when he felt that his movements were well received, he became bolder and started to go down completely. When he felt that Craig was close to shooting, he took the rock-hard shaft in his hand and massaged it to a beautiful orgasm. Now it was Craig's turn to be happy.

The two decided that they had to clean up before they joined Charles and Jeffrey again, so they took turns in the shower and got dressed. On the way out, Bill grabbed Craig by the shoulders, looked him deep in the eyes, and said, "Thank you that was fantastic." He then drew him closer and kissed him on the lips.

A very startled Craig opened his mouth and let Bill play with his tongue. When they parted, they both seemed surprised and a little uncomfortable at what had just happened, as they went to the living room.

Charles and Jeffrey sat on the sofa, but when they heard the door open, both turned around and looked at the newcomers with questioning eyes. The pair was beaming in such a way that any further question seemed superfluous. Craig asked if he could help himself to a drink, and Charles said he could. Then he asked Bill if he could get him something too, and Bill gladly accepted a beer.

CHAPTER 25

Emilian knew that the impulsive actions of his vendetta were irrational. After his unsuccessful attempt to eliminate Jeffrey in front of Hunter College, he walked furiously north. After a few blocks, he regained his composure and started to think of a temporary escape scenario. He was sure that by now his description must have hit most police cars and they were out looking for him. He remembered a friend in the Bronx, where he could probably stay for some time until he had a new plan. He hailed a cab and gave directions near where he intended to go. He didn't want to give a proper final destination, since he was sure that they would soon extend the search to all possible escapes, taxis included.

When he crossed Madison Avenue Bridge into the Bronx, he started feeling safer and soon asked the driver to stop near Yankee Stadium. He paid his fare and disappeared around the corner. He knew that it was a good distance to his friend's place but didn't want to leave a lead. He walked into a discount store and bought a black sweatshirt to cover his tattooed arms—a sure giveaway. He never gave a thought to what was happening to the three guys locked up; he blamed them for all the problems and thought it was good that they were out of the way. They were useless in his eyes. He was also convinced that his no-good cousin would sing like a bird to save his own skin.

He was still certain that he could get away with everything, and with some time to regroup, he could start again. After the raid in Frankfurt and simultaneously in New York, with the imprisonment of his father, Gregory Amoff, he thought of himself as the big guy. He was fully aware that at this point in his career, he could not compete with the international organization, but he was content to have his little local empire, convinced that in due time, he would deal in a bigger league. All this went through his head as he finally reached his friend Victor's place. It was in a very questionable neighborhood, where the police tried to avoid any major confrontations. *Great place to hide out for a few days.*

After a strong knocking that overpowered the loud music, Victor opened the door. When he saw Emilian standing there, he just turned around, and Emilian followed him. There was a nearly empty bottle of vodka on the table, the reason for Victor's passiveness. He dropped himself heavy on the beaten-up sofa and motioned to Emilian to help himself to the bottle. He refused; he wanted to keep a clear head. Emilian turned down the music and asked if he could crash here for a few days.

Victor didn't seem very pleased, since he suspected that his friend was in trouble—of which he had plenty already. But then he immediately saw an opportunity and said if Emilian had money to pay the rent, he could stay, because Victor was hours away from being evicted. Emilian was more than willing to pay the $450 for a safe haven and accepted the deal. He grabbed a bundle of bills out of his pocket and said, "Deal." Victor thought Emilian was a gift from heaven. He grabbed the bills and took another big gulp out of the bottle. He told Emilian that the nasty landlord would be here any moment for the money, and if he was running, he should hide in the other room while the man was here.

Just a few minutes later, a very loud and unpleasant knock was heard, and Emilian went into the bedroom while Victor settled his debt. When the coast was clear, he walked into the room where Emilian was hiding and asked if he had another twenty bucks; he wanted to get some more liquor and pizza, as he had no food in the house. Hungry himself, Emilian produced another bill and ordered his toppings. Victor disappeared with the money and left Emilian there to recover from the hectic day's events.

CHAPTER 26

At the Upper East Side police station, Summers was happy with his achievements of the day. He was able to get a lot of information on Emilian, and with his long experience, he concluded that the villain was probably pretty lonely at this moment, left on the sinking ship by himself. However, Summers didn't take this lightly; he knew he had to get his hands on Emilian soon, because by shooting into the innocent crowed earlier today, he proved that he was unpredictable.

Summers was also aware that it would not take Emilian long to recruit new soldiers for his cause. If he promised them sufficient money, there would be many illegal aliens who would take the opportunity to work for him. But first and foremost, he wanted to be sure that all of the perspective targets were safe. He first called Kevin and received a satisfactory report; then he called Bill and there too it seemed he had nothing to worry about. Andrei was transferred earlier to Riker, while Stefan and Serge remained in the holding cells at the precinct. Summers was optimistic that he could get more out of them, but once they were in the system, immediate access to them would be more difficult. He was also sure that the two were not really all that involved in the doings, especially Stefan, for whom he developed a liking. The boy was intelligent and had a real goal in life, and he was only made to believe that he was the courier for some information.

At Good Times, Inc. the day was over, and the guys enjoyed sitting in front of the TV, watching a funny movie. At the penthouse, Craig said that he had to leave, and he put the signed papers back in his briefcase. When he got up, he saw how Bill was looking at him, and when he walked toward the door, he heard a clear, "Thank you again." He turned around and just smiled and said, "Anytime."

When he was gone, Charles couldn't resist any longer and was pressing him for details. At first, Bill was very correct and told him that Craig had magic hands, and he felt like he was in heaven, but this was not enough for Charles; he wanted details. After some contemplation, Bill thought, *what the heck,* and he told them that he experienced the orgasm of his life, that Craig found triggers in and on his body he never thought were there. He needed another stiff sip from his beer before he confessed with his eyes cast down that after everything was over, he had sucked Craig off. It seemed difficult for him; he raised his eyes and looked straight at Charles, saying that he very much enjoyed it, and it kind of made him afraid.

"So that's it; I had a good time with another man, and I liked it," he repeated.

Jeffrey and Charles were sitting there, trying not to laugh too hard, afraid that this would make Bill even more uncomfortable. Instead Charles raised his tumbler and said "And the world has one virgin less."

It got late, and Jeffrey said he needed some sleep; he got up and left the other two behind.

Bill wanted to talk, and he felt at ease with Charles. He asked if it was always like this. When Craig had put his finger in him, he was thinking he would hit the ceiling. It felt so incredible when he massaged the prostate; he never expected this. And when he finally emptied into Craig's warm mouth, it was much more sensual than fucking a woman. "Do you think I'm gay?"

Charles knew that this would come up, and he had prepared his answer ahead of time. "First, do you have regularly sex with women?" he asked, and Bill confessed that lately he had not. He used to be in a relationship, but his girlfriend had a problem with his job, and so they called it quits over two years ago. The past two years didn't seem very exciting in his private life; he'd had some casual encounters, but it was never more than a one-night stand. In order to give Bill a satisfactory answer to his question, Charles asked him if, after tonight, he would sleep with another man.

This got Bill thinking, and finally he said yes, if the other man would be as nice as Craig. He then also confessed that the past few days, in the company of Charles and Jeffrey, he felt really good. He enjoyed the company of other men, not in the usual macho way, but in this civilized way. The two men got up, and on the way to the bedroom, Bill thanked Charles for all the nice things he was experiencing the past few days. Just before closing the door, he asked if the offer of a meeting at Good Times, Inc. was still an option. Charles responded that he would never go back on a promise.

In the Bronx, Emilian started to compete with Victor on the consumption of cheap vodka. He had a lot to catch up with but was quite successful in getting drunk fast. The pizza set some ground in his stomach, but the running and the hectic nature of the day gave him little resistance. He was mumbling incoherently about his doings and that the police were after him. They had three guys in custody and must have cooked them so much that they were probably talking to save their own skins. Then he said that he was rarely taking part, only once when they had to pose an example with this little asshole gay guy. They were a little rough on the fairy, and the asshole died. But usually he was only giving orders, and had done nothing.

Victor understood a fraction of what his friend was telling him and soon was fast asleep. Emilian made it to the dirty mattresses in the next room, threw himself onto it, and passed out too. The next day, when he woke up, he had to get his bearings. At first he couldn't even remember where he was; only when he walked into the next room and saw Victor lying on the floor did he remember. He searched for a bathroom, opening every door until he finally found a filthy place with a toilet and a sink. He couldn't believe his eyes, but he was in desperate need of relieving himself.

Cockroaches were crawling all over the walls and even on a toothbrush next to the sink. If he didn't have such a headache, he would probably have been revolted, but he just sat there and watched the little bugs chasing each other. As he went into the living room, he remembered that while searching for the bathroom, he opened a closet with some cans in it. He went back there and found some Nescafe.

Next came the quest for a hotplate, which was unplugged and sitting in a corner. He found an old pan, put some water in it, and made himself a cup of strong coffee. It tasted awful, but he blamed it on his condition rather than on the coffee.

He sat down on the broken sofa and only now started to realize the severity of the situation he was in. He couldn't really leave this dump until things calmed down outside. Nevertheless, he was making plans how to recruit new guys to complete the work. He was still banking on regular blackmail income but was really pissed that money would not flow as fast and easy as anticipated.

While all this crossed his mind, Victor started to show first signs of life. He slowly opened his eyes, but the daylight was hurting him, and he covered them with his hands. He had a bursting headache and asked if there was any coffee left. Emilian got up, took a dirty mug, put some of the rather disgusting coffee in it, and handed it to him. He took a small sip, and his senses registered that this was a perfectly awful concoction, but he was too weak to complain. It took them both some time until they were ready to talk sensibly. Then Victor admitted that he only got part of last night's conversation and wanted Emilian to repeat it.

He offered the short version, telling him that the police were after him big time, and he was in hiding until things calmed. He also told him of his plan to create a blackmail business, and that he'd had a good start, but unfortunately his handlers were stupid, and now he was forced to look for replacements. Victor, always out for a buck, became interested and more alert. He even took a second cup of coffee, knowing that nothing could worsen the state of his stomach. The two started to get excited by the new prospects, and both saw dollars falling on them. Victor admitted that he had to get out of this dump, but he had no idea how. With that new enterprise, they would probably soon be living in a posh place with all the chicks they wanted.

Emilian had not planned to be away from his place for so long and therefore only pocketed the cash he thought he needed. Between paying for the rent and food, he was running low, but he also knew that he couldn't go close to his place. Even if he never told anybody his address, he was sure the police were able to find his crib. Always anticipating that something like this could happen, he had deposited some cash with a friend, and he hoped that the police weren't aware of it. He didn't trust Victor, but at this point, he knew he depended on his help. He was brainstorming but always came to the conclusion that he had to put his confidence in Victor. He knew if he had been in Victor's position, he would run with the cash, and probably to be safe even denounce him to the police. This would solve two problems: money and the awareness that Emilian would not be free and going after him for a very long time, if ever.

Emilian hated the idea of opening up to anybody; he was far too egotistical to share money and possibly lucrative information. Then he remembered that in movies, people changed their looks so they wouldn't be recognized, and it went through his head that this might be the better solution. He handed Victor another twenty and said that he should go to the drugstore and buy a razor, scissors, and blond hair coloring.

Victor didn't want to ask too many questions and just said, "If you throw in another ten, I can get something to eat too." The bundle got thinner, but Emilian agreed; he knew they had to stay indoors most of the day, and some food would be necessary. Victor got up and left with the thirty dollars.

At the police station, Summers was again drilling Serge for information. He asked the same questions over and over but got nowhere and finally believed that he had to change to a different approach. He started asking if Serge knew where Emilian hung out—bars, clubs, or friends—but Serge wasn't part of Emilian's intimate circle and only knew of a handful of harmless creatures. When Summers asked how long he was working for the clan, Serge said that he was running errands for Gregory Amoff, and when Amoff got caught, Serge continued working for his son Emilian.

"What kind of errands?"

Serge contemplated briefly and then said, "All kinds, from picking up dry cleaning to delivering messages and packages."

This created some major curiosity in Summers, and he went deeper on the deliveries. He asked if there were addresses he had to go to regularly or more frequently, but Serge couldn't really think of one that was suspicious. The detective felt that Serge was not trying to protect Emilian at this point, so he had to take another route of questioning. "Which was the most frequent place you had to make deliveries, no matter what?" he asked. Serge thought hard and then said that it must have been to Emilian's uncle. He had to bring him envelopes, big ones sometimes with just a few papers in them. Emilian had said that his uncle was a lawyer who specialized in immigration, and these were applications for Romanians who wanted to get into the United States.

Summers asked where this uncle was living, and Serge responded that he didn't know; he always went to the office on Queens Boulevard. There was a very nice secretary named Miranda who took the envelopes. He never saw the uncle, but Miranda was always expecting him. Serge remembered the address, more or less, but added that the office was above a Dunkin Donuts. Summers asked if he could remember Miranda's last name, but he couldn't. At least he had a new lead, even if at this point he was unsure how it would help. Everything was to find Emilian's inner circle. They dispatched a car to the given address for observation.

In the Bronx, Victor returned from his shopping trip, and Emilian got to work immediately. First he took the scissors and started to cut his hair in the filthy bathroom, but he soon discovered that he needed assistance and called Victor for help. After he had his new punk hairdo, he started with the coloring. He didn't really care about the result; he just wanted to be unrecognizable. He was sorry to shave off his moustache but knew there was no way around it if the result had to be drastic.

After the ordeal, he stood in front of the mirror, seemingly happy with the outcome. He hardly recognized himself and thought that he looked much younger. He asked Victor for a sweatshirt, preferably with a hood, and then got ready for his quest.

At first, he had to make a phone call, but he was afraid to use his cell or even turn it on. He started to walk around, looking for an operational phone booth. This was more difficult than anticipated. All the public phones on the street corners were damaged; they were either missing the receivers or simply smashed up to a pulp. He had to walk more than five blocks, until he found a small hotel with a payphone in the lobby. He went in and dialed Miranda's number at the office.

The phone rang twice, and she answered with her Hispanic accent. "Hey, it's me," he said.

Miranda immediately recognized his voice. "Hey, darling, where are you?" she responded cheerfully, but he cut her short and said that he needed money and would come to collect it. She told him that she was not keeping it at the office and would have to go to her place. He looked at his cheap fake Rolex and said that he would be at her place around five, and she should not be surprised if he looked a little different.

Outside on Queens Boulevard, Detective Sullivan called in and reported that Ms. Miranda was at the office and that they took pictures of her. So far, there was nobody else there. He asked for further instructions. Summers was not really sure, but he had a hunch that they should continue the observation, and anyone who entered the place should be photographed.

The young detective got ready for a perfectly boring day with a large coffee from the store below the office. Back in the car, he continued to concentrate on the door across the street, but with the exception of the mailman's arrival around noon, nothing happened. At half past four, Miranda came out, closed the door with her key, and started walking down Queens Boulevard. Summers received the update and Sullivan reported that he was following her at a safe distance. She walked into a store and soon came out with some groceries. It was difficult to follow her in the car, and when he saw a space he parked, grabbed the camera-phone, and followed her on foot. The young detective was told that when he reached the destination, he had to call and ask for reinforcement.

Miranda started to walk a little faster, as if she had to be somewhere soon, he had no problem following, and since the sidewalk was rather busy with pedestrians, extra hiding was not even required. She turned the corner a couple of times until she entered a residential area. In between some large housing complexes was a small recreational area with a playground. Miranda went straight to the swings, where a young man appeared to be waiting for her. When he saw her, he got up and took his hood down to show her his appearance; perfect opportunity for a quick picture. They embraced and kissed, and then they talked for a few seconds and in a tight embrace left for one of the many entrances and disappeared in the darkness of the hall.

The detective immediately reported the status and gave the address. He was asked to transmit the picture with the couple to the office via his smart phone. He observed that the guy didn't have any similarity to the description he was given but obliged the request. Meanwhile, Summers had Serge and Stefan ordered into an interrogation room. He was waiting behind his computer for the transmission, which seemed to take forever. Once it got there, he made a print out of the picture, which was taken from a distance with the subjects too far from the photographer. He called one of the tech guys in the department and requested to zoom in on the subjects and then print it; in addition, he requested a few random close-ups of differed sections of the couple.

With the printouts in a folder, Summers entered the interrogation room where Serge and Stefan were sitting in silence. They seemed more relaxed than when they were first brought here; they felt that if they cooperated, they might get another chance. Summers spread the pictures on the table, and Serge recognized Miranda immediately but not her companion. Summers reminded them that he might have changed his looks, but still the photos were not clear enough. Stefan said that Emilian looked older, but then Summers detected a change in Serge's eyes, as if he saw something. Summers looked at him questioningly, awaiting something.

After several long seconds, he finally said, "What, is there something?"

Serge hesitantly said, "Here, you see the person is wearing probably a large gold watch. Emilian was always flashing his large Rolex; this looks like it."

Summers called the tech guy and asked if he could get this shot blown up even more without losing too much of its quality. The tech was not very hopeful but promised to do his best. Summers' cell started to vibrate; he looked at the display, and when he saw that it was Sullivan in Queens, he answered the call.

"The male suspect is leaving the building. Do I follow him?"

Summers answered without having to think about it. "Yes, absolutely, follow wherever he goes, but also try to see if he is wearing a flashy gold Rolex on his left arm and has a tattoo reaching up to the hairline on his neck."

The detective told him that the suspect had a hood on, but he could certainly look for the wristwatch. Summers instructed that he had to call in whenever possible and give updates and his location, and then he hung up.

The technician came back in and said that it was not good enough quality to enlarge any further; it was just a blur. He showed Summers the disappointing result. The chief detective looked at the two guys and said, "Thank you, that's it for now." He got up and left the room. When he returned to his desk, he got another call. "Have not yet seen a watch, but I am going into the subway, taking the E train direction Manhattan."

He ended the call and went down to the platform, always staying close to the suspect. The evening crowd going into the city was perfect cover; the platform was busy, but not rush-hour packed. Sullivan sat across from Emilian, separated only by a group of excited youngsters who were going to a concert in the city. He could see that once they passed the East River, Emilian was getting ready to leave. At the Lexington Avenue stop, he left the car, looking for directions to the number six train. Sullivan checked if he had a signal on his phone to report to Summers, but he was still too far underground, and no bars showed on his cell.

He followed Emilian at a safe distance, always keeping his eyes on the cell phone. A couple of bars moved, and Sullivan quickly pushed redial, reaching Summers with a bad connection. "I seem to be heading north with the six train" he was able to say before the connection was cut again.

Summers got the message but was at a loss; he could not station men at every single subway stop with such short notice. The six train was going deep into the Bronx. Sullivan hoped that the suspect had not noticed him and continued his quest as commanded. He hated the uncertainty and was not really comfortable venturing all by himself into completely unknown territory.

Summers was contemplating what he could do; he strongly suspected that the train would take Sullivan into the Bronx. He called the precincts of Southview, Pelham, and Webster to alert them. The chiefs in charge all promised to wait for his call and would keep a reserve ready until further notice.

Even though the six line was running through the posh Upper East Side, it was probably the worst and oldest equipment in the entire New York subway system. The cars were outdated and the ride very loud. After what seemed an eternity, Emilian made a move toward the door. Sullivan slowly rose from his uncomfortable seat and waited at another door. The car was nearly empty by now, as they got close to the end of the line. When the train stopped, Sullivan left the car facing a large sign that read Middletown Road. He followed Emilian to the street and at the same time pressed the redial to inform Summers of his whereabouts.

The chief checked on the map and called his colleague at Pelham Precinct, which was the closest of the three he alerted earlier. Chuck, a rough-sounding individual, promised to be there soon and requested Sullivan's phone number. Seconds later, the young detective received a call, and Chuck briefly told him about the plan, but he needed to know at all times exactly where he was.

Sullivan told him that they were walking north, and he was at a safe distance. "He just disappeared into a shady hotel." He went closer to see a name but could only see the first three letters, PEL; the rest was missing. Chuck knew the place and said he would have a man there in two minutes.

Inside the Pelham Park Hotel, Emilian went to the payphone and called Miranda as promised, to tell her that he was back in the Bronx. Miranda suggested that he should not return to Victor, but rather take a room at the hotel, but Emilian was afraid that they would ask for ID, and he didn't want to take the risk. She agreed and told him to be in touch whenever possible.

The door of the hotel moved again and a blond Emilian walked out. For the first time, he felt safe enough to take the hood off. Sullivan could see a policeman coming around the corner and signaled to him toward Emilian. The policeman, a heavyset black guy, immediately understood and passed by the young detective, following the suspect. A few steps back was Sullivan, who saw the cop communicating with his boss. Sullivan called Summers, who was already on his way to the Bronx, and gave him the latest news.

Emilian turned the corner, and the cop crossed the street, as if not involved in the chase. He wanted to tell Summers that he was by himself again, when he saw a younger patrolman continuing where the heavy guy left off. "Guess they know what they're doing," he reported to Summers.

Five blocks south, Emilian disappeared into a small building and was out of sight. Sullivan crossed the street and placed himself at the next corner, waiting for further instructions. The second policeman must have informed his precinct of the location, and only moments later, three squad cars stopped around the corner. Out of the first came a gigantic officer who approached Sullivan. "I'm Chuck. Which door is it?"

Sullivan pointed to the second down, and Chuck called in a request for a tenants list, well aware that this would probably be useless, since around here most were illegal aliens, but he had to follow the code.

Upstairs, Emilian entered Victor's apartment. His host was still sitting on the sofa and somehow managed to get a new bottle of vodka. "Okay, everything went well. I got the cash, and now we can relax for a few days." Slowly Victor lifted his head and invited Emilian to celebrate with him. While he passed the bottle, Emilian said that Miranda thought he looked cute with his new hairstyle. They both chuckled, unaware of what was going on just outside the building. They made dinner plans, and Emilian felt safe enough to suggest spoiling themselves at the chicken place down the street. Victor was very excited. A real meal was not in his plans, but he was certainly looking forward.

On the street, the policemen were waiting for instructions from their superiors, who were still contemplating the best approach. They were afraid if they created too much commotion in the building, the guys could escape. It was already dark, and Summers was getting anxious to put an end to this. He saw the door open on the surveyed building and the two guys walking out. He could see that they had celebrated; they appeared to be under the influence of alcohol. "I'll follow, and we wait until the time is right," Summers instructed.

They walked down the street away from where the police was hiding. Summers, and a few yards further back, Sullivan followed Emilian and Victor, who entered the rather disgusting Chicken BBQ. They sat down at the counter and ordered. Summers walked in and sat close by, placing himself strategically between the pair and the entrance to the greasy place. He wanted to look casual, but food in here was a no-go, so he just ordered a Coke. The two guys spoke rapidly in Romanian, but it was easy to figure out that they felt safe and were excited. They were both given a huge portion of grilled chicken with potatoes and immediately started digging in. Summers was trying to look for either the watch or the tattoo but could spot neither from his location. He signaled that he would go to the bathroom, and the men outside should be watching.

He got up and tried to look down on Emilian's neck, but the hood was covering too far up. He walked to the restroom and stayed there for a couple of minutes. When he returned, he saw the wristwatch, exactly as Serge described it, a gaudy, fake Rolex. This was sufficient evidence at this point, and he signaled Sullivan to come in. The two detectives flanked the suspects and pulled their badges out as Summers said, "NYPD, you're under arrest."

Victor and Emilian were surprised, but before they could ask why, Summers and Sullivan cuffed them and read their Miranda rights. Summers paid their tab, and the four left the place. Outside, they were greeted by a number of policemen, who swiftly accompanied them to the waiting cars. Chuck offered to put the suspects in his holding cell overnight, but Summers wanted them down at his precinct. The heavy Pelham chief seemed relieved by the decision; now he could at least go home and have a quite night. He ordered two of his men to bring them to the Upper East Side or just follow Detective Summers.

Thirty minutes later, they all parked in front of the 67th Street station. The two uniformed men brought them to the basement cells, and when they were locked up safely, they returned to the Bronx.

Summers went to his office and called Kevin and Bill, telling them that he thought he got Emilian, and he would appreciate if they could meet at the station ASAP. Both were thrilled, and Kevin told Phil that he might be out very late, and he shouldn't wait. Bill, on the other hand, was not that thrilled. If it was Emilian, he'd have no reason to come back, but Charles offered him a key to the penthouse and just said, *"Mi casa es tu casa."* Bill happily accepted and left for his duties. Meanwhile, Summers and Sullivan finally ordered some food while waiting for the others to arrive.

CHAPTER 27

Bill got there first, and when he entered Summers' office, the two detectives were just biting into their burgers. "Oh, enjoy your meal!" Bill said sarcastically.

Summers raised his head and said, "I don't even want to know what your three-course dinner consisted of."

Bill took the nearest chair, sat down, and said, "For sure not burgers."

A few minutes later, Kevin arrived. Summers informed the two briefly of what would happen in the few hours ahead and said that Sullivan was the one who should get the most credit for Emilian's capture.

Once they finished their sodas, Summers pushed the intercom button on his phone and ordered the two suspects brought to separate interrogation rooms. Then he asked Sullivan and Kevin to go down and bring the two others up for identification purposes, keeping them in the back room.

"Okay, let's take these guys down!"

Summers got up and walked with Connors to the second floor, where they put their ear buds in. Summers went into Room 1, where Emilian hung in his chair like a real smartass, while Connors went to face Victor next door. Summers knew Emilian would play hardball, but once he had his confirmation from Stefan or Serge, he would make this fast, and if Emilian would not cooperate, he would have him shipped one way to Riker, with a final destination of Sing Sing.

At first, the chief detective tried to be nice, asking for his name and address. Then he asked Emilian if he knew why he was here, but of course Emilian was playing the innocent one and had no idea what this charade was all about. Summers heard over his earpiece that he should ask Emilian to take his sweatshirt off, which he couldn't do, because he was still cuffed. Summers asked the uniformed policeman standing guard at the door to please help the prisoner take off his sweatshirt. "Why? It is not that warm in here," Emilian protested, but his opinion was not respected, and the officer removed the shirt. Behind the mirror, Serge and Stefan nodded, and both identified him as Emilian Amoff, son of Gregory Amoff.

Summers said, "If you're cold, we can help you to put your sweatshirt back on."

Kevin and Sullivan brought the two guys back to the holding cells and then joined Summers and Connors.

When Kevin entered the room, Summers looked up with a wide and satisfied grin. Then he got up, walked slowly around the table, and in clear voice said, "I, Detective Summers, charge you, Emilian Amoff, with murder, blackmail, and assault." Emilian wanted to jump up in protest, but Summers was faster and pushed him back into the chair. Then he turned to Kevin and with a very satisfied face said that he believed they were done for the night, and someone should bring the accused back to his cell. Kevin and the uniformed policeman accompanied Emilian to his very temporary home. Summers was eager to get him into a safer facility the following day.

In Room 2, Connors was not as successful, or perhaps Victor was really not involved in any wrongdoing. Victor confessed to a few petty crimes, like shoplifting for food or clothes, but he had no ties to the clan. When asked how Emilian ended up at his place, he said that they were friends in Brooklyn, but when his parents died, he moved away, and since then, he was trying to survive. He said that he wanted to move far from the Romanians, because if you didn't kill, you were killed; there was no alternative. When Stefan and Serge confirmed that they had never seen this person before, Connors started to believe him. Connors told Victor that he was probably just at the wrong place at the wrong time, and they would hold him until the following morning, but then he would most probably be released and free to go, but he had to be available for possible further questioning.

Left by himself, with Kevin gone to the precinct and Alfred on an outcall, Phil decided to call Jeffrey, who was at Charles's place. He was restless and wanted to celebrate the regained freedom. Jeffrey asked if I wanted to come over for a drink; Phil immediately accepted, grabbed a jacket, and was on his way. When he arrived, the two were already in a celebratory mood; a bottle of expensive champagne was in the ice bucket. They all hugged, and Phil joined the round. They were all excited that this nightmare seemed to be over, and they all could move freely again.

Charles then said that he still had to fulfill a promise, and the three started to plan a "freedom dinner" for the next evening. Charles asked if Phil could get the best three or four guys from Good Times, Inc. for the evening. He even offered to pay, but Phil said this wasn't necessary. He then explained that he promised Bill a good time with a guy, and he wanted him to make his selection. Jeffrey laughed and called Charles a devil, but loved the idea. Phil decided on Jack, Alfred, John, and of course, Carlos, who would not be working, but he was released from the hospital and could at least enjoy a good meal. Then there would also be Bill, Kevin, which brought the group to nine; Charles said he would ask Rosa to prepare for ten, just in case Summers wanted to join. It was unlikely, but with this guy, one never knew. When Phil told them that Kevin said that the young detective who found Emilian was very cute, Charles just laughed and said that they should not try to corrupt the entire NYPD at this point and concentrate on Bill.

Phil promised to call all the guys the next morning, and they would be here for drinks at seven. Then Jeffrey told him that Charles had offered to renovate the nice apartment in Chelsea and make it their love nest. He was happy for the two, even if this meant he lost one of his most trusted escorts. Phil made him promise that even if he would not be working anymore, they would stay friends and in close touch.

After a second bottle of champagne, Phil decided to go back and sleep the alcohol off. When he arrived home, Kevin was already there waiting. Phil told him about tomorrow evening's plan, and he seemed to be looking forward to it, but he agreed that Charles was playing a devious game with Bill. It was very late and they were both exhausted, and were soon asleep in a tight embrace.

The next morning, life seemed normal again. Kevin left for work, and I was able to catch up on various things—the most important being to get all the guys to accept for dinner later this evening. Jack said that he had plans but was certainly trying to change them; he didn't want to miss out on the party.

Sullivan had to pick up his car on Queens Boulevard, where he'd left it the day before, and at the same time he needed to take Miranda into the precinct for questioning. Kevin was assigned to be his partner. The two detectives took the number six train and changed over to the E at Fifty-First/Fifty-Third Street Station. They only knew each other by sight, but Kevin was quite famous at the Sixty-Seventh Street precinct for his undercover work in Germany, and Sullivan was eager to get all the details. Then he told Kevin about his odyssey the previous day with the arrests of Emilian and Victor.

When they reached the car, they got in and drove to the lawyer's office, where Miranda sat behind her desk. They buzzed, walked up the stairs, and when they were in front of her, showed their badges. She appeared shocked. They requested her to accompany them for questioning. She first said that she couldn't leave the office, but the detectives insisted, and the three left for Manhattan. "My boss will kill me when he finds out that I'm not at work, so let me give him a call at least," she requested. She took out her cell and dialed the number, briefly explained that she was taken for questioning, and would not be at the office. Her boss seemed unhappy but had little choice but to accept the situation.

Miranda got nervous. She expected that it had to do with Emilian, but assured them that she had no knowledge of his activities.

Summers and Connors were drilling Emilian, who denied all accusations, but they didn't expect him to break easily. They had sufficient ammunition from Stefan and Serge, who were cooperating in the hopes of getting out soon. When Connors spread out a number of pictures of Carlos, bruised and beaten up, in front of Emilian, Summers was trying to read his reaction, but the only thing he got was a smirk and some incomprehensible mumbling. Emilian was unaware that a translator was behind the mirror who understood what he was saying.

He communicated over the ear bud with Summers, "He just mumbled that this freak should have died like the other moron before."

Summers smiled and looked Emilian in the eyes while putting a picture of Oscar in front of him and said, "Like this moron?"

Emilian lost it "What the fuck are you talking about?" Summers repeated what the translator told him, making the accused believe that he understood his Romanian mumbling. Emilian was trapped; he sank into the chair while Connors stood up and said, "You murdered Oscar, attempted to murder Carlos Fuentes, and tried to blackmail Good Times, Inc." Then he signaled the uniformed policeman at the door to bring Emilian back to the cell and prepare for his transfer to Riker until he was presented to the DA.

Summers and Connors were very happy about the day, and while leaving the interrogation room, Connors told his boss that Charles was giving a thank-you dinner this evening, and he wanted to invite him too. Summers, very surprised by the gesture, accepted. Connors said that drinks would be at seven, and since they were all off for the evening, they could enjoy some booze.

Next door, Sullivan and Kevin were questioning Miranda but soon discovered that Emilian was only using her. She admitted that they had great sex together, and Emilian always brought her cash to keep safe for him, but other than that, she was not involved. Summers, happy with the result, let her and Victor go, while Serge and Stefan had to be patient for some more time. But when they were told about Emilian's accidental statement, they prayed for a quick release.

CHAPTER 28

A
t the penthouse, Rosa was very busy with the preparations for the evening. She set a beautiful table, opened several bottles of wine, and stocked the liquor cabinet. She was cooking up a storm, hoping it would be appreciated. While Charles took a shower to get ready, Jeffrey sneaked into the room, and when he heard the water running he ripped his clothes off and rushed into the bathroom, where he surprised his lover. They started kissing madly, but aware that the guests would arrive soon, they knew they had little time to enjoy, and Jeffrey went down on his knees and started satisfying Charles with a very deep and love-filled blowjob. Charles more than appreciated the attention and faster than anticipated shot his full load into the mouth of Jeffrey, who kept it and rose for a strong kiss. Once they separated their lips, they beamed into each other's eyes, finished their shower, and got ready for the guests.

Kevin and Phil arrived just before seven and were greeted by Jeffrey; Charles was in the kitchen with Rosa, overseeing her preparation. Jeffrey played host and seduced them with a glass of fantastic champagne. There were little homemade petit fours on silver trays, and Phil couldn't resist helping himself to one. They were just saying how happy they were that the nightmare was over when Bill and Jack entered the room. They met in the elevator coming up, and were already becoming friends.

Within another fifteen minutes, all the guests except Summers were there. He arrived fifteen minutes later, and when he walked into the room, they were all smiling. For the first time, he wore a different, more casual suit and no wrinkled trench coat. He looked quite snappy. At first he was a little shocked, seeing the room filled with only men, but after the second glass of champagne, he started to get adjusted to the situation and loosened up to the level of being human. They all had only one subject at first: the end of their horrible time.

Summers took Phil aside and said that he was grateful for their cooperation, and he made sure that thanks to the help, they would not have any further problems with Good Times, Inc. This meant they could continue the business with a certain protection. Phil was happy and thanked him. He saw Charles take Bill onto the terrace and hand him an envelope, and Phil could see Bill thank him for it. Charles asked him to read it and then give him the answer at the end of the evening. Bill took the card out which read:

> Gift Certificate
> Bill Connors receives a full treatment at
> Good Times, Inc. with the company of his choice.
> The people suggested are: Jack, Alfred, John.
> We thank you for your help.
> Charles and Jeffrey

Bill blushed, reading the lines. He looked up and said, "I will give the others a chance, but I think I am set."

Charles held his arm and said, "Great choice."

They came back in to join the others. During dinner, the conversation became very friendly. Rosa outdid herself, and Summers turned into a fun storyteller. Bill was seated next to Jack, and halfway into dinner, he looked over to Charles, smiled, and received definite approval from the host.

END

CPSIA information can be obtained at www.ICGtesting.com
Printed in the USA
LVOW08*2059130813

347741LV00001BA/38/P